BLACK SECONDS

Karin Fossum began her writing career in 1974. She has won numerous awards, including the Glass Key Award for the best Nordic crime novel, an honour shared with Henning Mankell and Jo Nesbo, and the *Los Angeles Times* Book Prize for *Calling Out For You*, which was also shortlisted for the Crime Writers' Association Gold Dagger Award.

Charlotte Barslund translates Scandinavian novels and plays. Her recent work includes *Broken* by Karin Fossum, *Machine* by Peter Adolphsen and *We, The Drowned* by Carsten Jensen.

ALSO BY KARIN FOSSUM

The Inspector Sejer series

Don't Look Back
He Who Fears the Wolf
When the Devil Holds the Candle
Calling Out For You
Black Seconds
The Water's Edge
Bad Intentions
The Caller
In the Darkness

Standalone crime fiction

Broken

KARIN FOSSUM

Black Seconds

TRANSLATED FROM THE NORWEGIAN BY
Charlotte Barslund

VINTAGE BOOKS
London

Published by Vintage 2013

English translation copyright ....

Karin Fossum .... the Copyright, Designs and Patents Act 1988 to be identified as the author of the work

First published with the title ....
J. W. Cappelens Forlag. AS ....

First published in Great Britain in 2007 by
Harvill Secker

Vintage
Random House, 20 Vauxhall Bridge Road,
London SW1V 2SA

www.vintage-books.co.uk

Addresses for companies within The Random House Group Limited
can be found at: www.randomhouse.co.uk/offices.htm

The Random House Group Limited Reg. No. 954009

A CIP catalogue record for this book
is available from the British Library

ISBN 9780099565529

The Random House Group Limited supports the Forest Stewardship
Council® (FSC®), the leading international forest-certification organisation.
Our books carrying the FSC label are printed on FSC®-certified paper.
FSC is the only forest-certification scheme supported by the leading
environmental organisations, including Greenpeace. Our paper
procurement policy can be found at:
www.randomhouse.co.uk/environment

MIX
Paper from
responsible sources
FSC® C016897

Printed and bound by Clays Ltd, St Ives plc

TO ØYSTEIN, MY YOUNGER BROTHER

Chapter 1

The days went by so slowly.

Ida Joner held up her hands and counted her fingers. Her birthday was on the tenth of September. And it was only the first today. There were so many things she wanted. Most of all she wanted a pet of her own. Something warm and cuddly, which would belong only to her. Ida had a sweet face with large brown eyes. Her body was slender and trim, her hair thick and curly. She was bright and happy. She was just too good to be true. Her mother often thought so, especially whenever Ida left the house and she would watch her daughter's back disappear around the corner. Too good to last.

Ida jumped up on her bicycle, her brand-new Nakamura bicycle. She was going out. The living room was a mess: she had been lying on the sofa playing with her plastic figures and several other toys, and it was chaos when she left. At first her absence would create a great void. After a while a strange mood would creep in through the walls and fill the house with a sense of unease. Her mother hated it. But she could not keep her daughter locked up for ever, like some caged bird. She waved to Ida and put on a brave face. Lost herself in domestic chores. The humming of the Hoover would drown out the strange feeling in the room. When her body began to grow hot and sweaty, or started to ache from beating the rugs, it would numb the faint stabbing sensation in her chest which was always triggered by Ida going out.

She glanced out of the window. The bicycle turned left. Ida was going into town. Everything was fine; she was wearing her bicycle helmet. A hard shell that protected her head. Helga thought of it as a type of life insurance. In her pocket she had her zebra-striped purse, which contained thirty kroner about to be spent on the latest issue of *Wendy*. She usually spent the rest of her money on Bugg chewing gum. The ride down to Laila's Kiosk would take her fifteen minutes. Her mother did the mental arithmetic. Ida would be back home again by 6.40 p.m. Then she factored in the possibility of Ida meeting someone and spending ten minutes chatting. While she waited, she started to tidy up. Picked up toys and figures from the sofa. Helga knew that her daughter would hear her words of warning wherever she went. She had planted her own voice of authority firmly in the girl's head and knew that from there it sent out clear and constant instructions. She felt ashamed at this, the kind of shame that overcomes you after an assault, but she did not dare do otherwise. Because it was this very voice that would one day save Ida from danger.

2

Ida was a well-brought-up girl who would never cross her mother or forget to keep a promise. But now the wall clock in Helga Joner's house was approaching 7 p.m. and Ida had still not come home. Helga experienced the first prickling of fear. And later that sinking feeling in the pit of her stomach that made her stand by the window from which she would see Ida appear on her yellow bicycle any second now. The red helmet would gleam in the sun. She would hear the crunch of the tyres on the pebbled drive. Perhaps even the ringing of the bell: hi, I'm home! Followed by a thud on the wall from the handlebars. But Ida did not come.

Helga Joner floated away from everything that was safe and familiar. The floor vanished beneath her feet. Her normally heavy body became weightless; she hovered like a ghost around the rooms. Then with a thump to her chest she came back down. Stopped abruptly and looked around. Why did this feel so familiar? Because she had already, for many years now, been rehearsing this moment in her mind. Because she had always known that this beautiful child was not hers to keep. It was the very realisation that she had known this day would come that terrified her. The knowledge that she could predict the future and that she had known this would happen right from the beginning made her head spin. That's why I'm always so scared, Helga thought. I've been terrified every day for nearly ten years, and for good reason. Now it's finally happened. My worst nightmare. Huge, black, and tearing my heart to pieces.

It was 7.15 p.m. when she forced herself to snap out of her apathy and find the number for Laila's Kiosk in the phone book. She tried to keep her voice calm. The telephone rang many times before someone answered. Her phoning and thus revealing her fear made her even more convinced that Ida would turn up any minute now. The ultimate proof that she was an overprotective mother. But Ida was nowhere to be seen, and a woman answered. Helga laughed apologetically because she could hear from the other woman's voice that she was mature and might have children of her own. She would understand.

'My daughter went out on her bicycle to get a copy of *Wendy*. From your shop. I told her she was to come straight back home and she ought to be here by now, but she isn't. So I'm just calling to check that she did come to your shop and bought what she wanted,' said Helga Joner. She looked out of the window as if to shield herself against the reply.

'No,' the voice answered. 'There was no girl here, not that I remember.'

Helga was silent. This was the wrong answer. Ida had to have been there. Why would the woman say no? She demanded another reply. 'She's short with dark hair,' she went on stubbornly, 'nine years old. She is wearing a blue tracksuit and a red helmet. Her bicycle's yellow.' The bit about the bicycle was left hanging in the air. After all, Ida would not have taken it with her inside the kiosk.

4

Laila Heggen, the owner of the kiosk, felt anxious and scared of replying. She heard the budding panic in the voice of Ida's mother and did not want to release it in all its horror. So she went through the last few hours in her mind. But even though she wanted to, she could find no little girl there. 'Well, so many kids come here,' she said. 'All day long. But at that time it's usually quiet. Most people eat between five and seven. Then it gets busy again up until ten. That's when I close.' She could think of nothing more to say. Besides, she had two burgers under the grill; they were beginning to burn, and a customer was waiting.

Helga struggled to find the right words. She could not hang up, did not want to sever the link with Ida that this woman embodied. After all, the kiosk was where Ida had been going. Once more she stared out into the road. The cars were few and far between. The afternoon rush was over.

'When she turns up,' she tried, 'please tell her I'm waiting.'

Silence once again. The woman in the kiosk wanted to help, but did not know how to. How awful, she thought, having to say no. When she needed a yes.

Helga Joner hung up. A new era had begun. A creeping, unpleasant shift that brought about a change in the light, in the temperature, in the land-scape outside. Trees and bushes stood lined up like militant soldiers. Suddenly she noticed how the sky, which had not released rain for weeks, had filled

5

with dark, dense clouds. When had that happened? Her heart was pounding hard and it hurt; she could hear the clock on the wall ticking mechanically. She had always thought of seconds as tiny metallic dots; now they turned into heavy black drops and she felt them fall one by one. She looked at her hands; they were chapped and wrinkled. No longer the hands of a young woman. She had become a mother late in life and had just turned forty-nine. Suddenly her fear turned into anger and she reached for the telephone once more. There was so much she could do: Ida had friends and family in the area. Helga had a sister, Ruth, and her sister had a twelve-year-old daughter, Marion, and an eighteen-year-old son, Tomme, Ida's cousins. Ida's father, who lived on his own, had two brothers in town, Ida's uncles, both of whom were married and had four children in total. They were family. Ida could be with any of them. But they would have called. Helga hesitated. Friends first, she thought. Therese. Or Kjersti, perhaps. Ida also spent time with Richard, a twelve-year-old boy from the neighbourhood, who had a horse. She found the contact sheet for her daughter's classmates stuck on the fridge, it listed everyone's name and number. She started at the top with Kjersti.

'No, sorry, Ida's not here.' The other woman's concern, her anxiety and sympathy, which concluded with the reassuring words, 'She'll turn up, you know what kids are like,' tormented and haunted her.

'Yes,' Helga lied. But she did not know. Ida was never late. No one was home at Therese's. She spoke to Richard's father, who told her his son had gone down to the stable. So she waited while he went to look for him. The clock on the wall mocked her, its constant ticking: she hated it. Richard's father came back. His son was alone in the stable. Helga hung up and rested for a while. Her eyes were drawn to the window as if it were a powerful magnet. She called her sister and crumbled a little when she heard her voice. Could not stand upright any longer, her body was beginning to fail her, paralysis was setting in.

'Get in your car straight away,' Ruth said. 'Get yourself over here and together we'll drive round and look for her. We'll find her, you'll see!'

'I know we will,' Helga said. 'But Ida doesn't have a key. What if she comes back while we're out looking for her?'

'Leave the door open. It'll be fine, don't you worry. She's probably been distracted by something. A fire or a car crash. And she's lost track of time.'

Helga tore open the door to the garage. Her sister's voice had calmed her down. A fire, she thought. Of course. Ida is staring at the flames, her cheeks are flushed, the firemen are exciting and appealing in their black uniforms and yellow helmets, she is rooted to the spot, she is bewitched by the sirens and the screaming and crackling of the flames. If there really was a fire, I too would be standing there mesmerised by the shimmering heat. And besides, everything around here is like a tinder-box, it hasn't rained for ages. Or a car crash. She fumbled with her keys while she conjured up the scene. Images of twisted metal, ambulances, resuscitation efforts and spattered blood rushed through her mind. No wonder Ida had lost track of time!

Distracted, she drove to her sister's house in Madseberget. It took four minutes. She scanned the verges the whole time; Ida was likely to appear without warning, cycling on the right-hand side of the road as she should, carefree, safe and sound. But she did not see her. Still, taking action felt better. Helga had to change gears, steer and brake; her body was occupied. If fate wanted to hurt her, she would fight back. Fight this looming monster tooth and nail.

Ruth was home alone. Her son Tom Erik, whom everyone called Tomme, had just passed his driving test. He had scrimped and scraped together enough money to buy an old Opel.

'He practically lives in it,' Ruth sighed. 'I hope to God he takes care when he drives. Marion has gone to the library. They close at eight, so she'll be home soon, but she'll be fine on her own. Sverre is away on business. That man's never here, I tell you.' She had her back to Helga and was struggling to put on her coat as she spoke the last sentence. Her smile was in place when she turned around.

'Come on, Helga, let's go.'

Ruth was a slimmer and taller version of her sister.

Five years younger and of a more cheerful disposition. They were very close and it had always been Ruth who had looked out for Helga. Even when she was five, she had been looking out for ten-year-old Helga. Helga was chunky, slow and shy. Ruth was lively, confident and capable. Always knew what to do. Now she took charge of her older sister once again. She managed to suppress her own fears by comforting Helga. She reversed the Volvo out of the garage and Helga got in. First they went to Laila's Kiosk and spoke briefly to the owner. They had a look around outside. They were searching for clues that Ida had been there, even though Laila Heggen said she had not. Then they went into the centre of Glassverket. They wandered round the square scanning the passing faces and bodies, but no sign of Ida. Just to be sure, they went past the school where Ida was a Year Five pupil, but the playground lay deserted. Three times during the trip Helga borrowed Ruth's mobile phone to call her home number. Perhaps Ida was waiting in the living room. But there was no reply. The nightmare was growing; it was lying in wait somewhere, quivering, gathering strength. Soon it would rise and crash over them like a wave. It would drown out everything. Helga could feel it in her body: a war was being fought inside her; her circulation, her heartbeat, her breathing, everything was violently disturbed.

'Perhaps she's had a puncture,' Ruth said, 'and had to ask someone to help her. Perhaps someone is trying to mend her bike right now.'

Helga nodded fiercely. She had not considered this possibility. She felt incredibly relieved. There were so many explanations, so many possibilities, and hardly any of them scary; she had just been unable to see them. She sat rigidly in her seat next to her sister, hoping that Ida's bicycle really had had a bad puncture. This would explain everything. Then she was gripped by panic, terrified by this very image. A little girl with brown eyes might make a driver stop. Under the pretext of wanting to help her! Pretending! Once again her heart ached. Besides, if Ida had had a puncture, they would have spotted her; after all, they were on the very route Ida would have taken. There were no short cuts.

Helga stared right ahead. She didn't want to turn her head to the left because that way lay the river, swift and dark. She wanted to proceed as quickly as possible to the moment when everything would be all right again.

They drove back to the house. There was nothing else they could do. The only sound was the humming of the engine in Ruth's Volvo. She had turned off the radio. It was inappropriate to listen to music when Ida was missing. There was still a bit of traffic. Then they spotted a strange vehicle. They saw it from a distance; at first it looked unfamiliar. The vehicle was part motorcycle, part small truck. It had three wheels, motorcycle handlebars, and behind the seat was a drop-sided body, the size of a small trailer. Both the motorcycle and the truck body were painted green. The driver was going very slowly, but they could tell from his bearing that he had sensed the car, that he knew they were approaching. He pulled over to the right to let them pass. His eyes were fixed on the road.

'That's Emil Johannes,' Ruth said. 'He's always out and about. Why don't we ask him?'

'He doesn't talk,' Helga objected.

'That's just a rumour,' Ruth said. 'I'm sure he can talk. When he wants to.'

'Why do you think that?' Helga said doubtfully.

'Because that's what people around here say. That he just doesn't want to.'

Helga could not imagine why someone would want to stop talking of their own free will. She had never heard anything like it. The man on the large three-wheeler was in his fifties. He was wearing an old-fashioned leather cap with earflaps, and a jacket. It was not zipped up. It flapped behind him in the wind. As he became aware of the car pulling up alongside him, he started to wobble. He gave them a hostile look, but Ruth refused to be put off. She waved her arms at him and gestured that he should stop. He did so reluctantly. But he did not look at them. He just waited, still staring right ahead, his hands clasping the handlebars tightly, the flaps of his cap hanging like dog ears down his cheeks. Ruth lowered the car window.

'We're looking for a girl!' she called out.

The man pulled a face. He did not understand why she was shouting like that. There was nothing wrong with his hearing.

11

'A dark-haired girl, she's nine. She rides a yellow bike. You're always on the road. Have you seen her?'

The man stared down at the tarmac. His face was partly hidden by his cap. Helga Joner stared at the trailer. It was covered by a black tarpaulin. She thought she could see something lying underneath. Her thoughts went off in all directions. There was room for both a girl and a bicycle underneath that tarpaulin. Did he look guilty? Then again, she knew that he always wore this remote expression. Sometimes she would see him in the local shop. He lived in a world of his own.

The thought that Ida might be lying under the black tarpaulin struck her as absurd. I'm really starting to lose it, she thought.

'Have you seen her?' Ruth repeated. She had a firm voice, Helga thought. So commanding. It made people sit up and take notice.

Finally he returned her gaze, but only for a moment. His eyes were round and grey. Had he blinked quickly? Helga bit her lip. But that was the way he was; she knew he didn't want to talk to people or look at them. It meant nothing. His voice sounded somewhat gruff as he replied.

'No,' he said.

Ruth held his gaze. The grey eyes flickered away once more. He put the three-wheeler into gear and revved the engine. The accelerator was on the right handlebar. He liked revving the engine. Ruth indicated left and drove past him. But she kept

12

looking at him in the mirror. 'Hah!' she snorted. 'Everyone says he can't talk. What rubbish!'

A heavy silence fell on the car. Helga thought, she'll be back now. Laila from the kiosk doesn't remember it, but Ida was there. She's lying on the sofa reading *Wendy* and chewing gum; her cheeks are bulging with gum. There are sweet wrappers everywhere. The pink gum makes her breath smell sweet.

But the living room was deserted. Helga broke down completely. Everything inside her crumpled.

'Oh my God,' she sobbed. 'It's really true now. Do you hear me, Ruth? Something terrible has happened!' Her sobs culminated in a scream.

Ruth went over to the telephone.

Ida Joner was reported missing at 8.35 p.m. The female caller introduced herself as Ruth Emilie Rix. She took great care to appear businesslike, afraid that the police would not take her call seriously otherwise. At the same time there was an undercurrent of desperation in her voice. Jacob Skarre made notes on a pad while the woman talked, and he experienced many contradictory feelings. Ida Joner, a nine-year-old girl from Glassverket, had been missing for two hours. Clearly something had happened. However, it did not necessarily follow that it was bad news. Most of the time, in fact, it was not bad news at all, but a minor upset. At first it would cause pain and fear, only to culminate in the most soothing comfort of all: a mother's embrace. The thought of it made him smile; he had seen it so many times. Yet the thought of what might have happened made him shudder.

It was 9 p.m. when the patrol car pulled up in front of Mrs Joner's house. She lived at Glassblåserveien 8, eleven kilometres from town and sufficiently remote for it to be considered a rural area, with scattered farms and fields and a range of new housing developments. Glassverket had its own village centre, with a school, a few shops and a petrol station. Mrs Joner's house was in a residential area. It was attractive and painted red. A hedge of white dogwood with thin bristling branches formed a spectacular, spiky border around the property. The lawn had yellow patches from the drought.

Helga was standing by the window. The sight of the white police car made her feel faint. She had gone too far, she had tempted fate. It was like admitting that something terrible had happened. They should not have called the police. If they had not called, Ida would have come back of her own accord. Helga could no longer keep on top of her own thoughts; she longed desperately for someone to take over, take control and make all the decisions. Two police officers were walking up the drive, and Helga stared at the older of them, a very tall grey-haired man in his fifties. He moved quietly and thoughtfully, as if nothing in the world could unsettle him. Helga thought, he's exactly what I need. He'll fix this, because that's his job; he's done this before. Shaking his hand felt unreal. This isn't really happening, she thought; please let me wake up from this terrible nightmare. But she did not wake up.

Helga was stout and thickset, with coarse dark hair brushed away from her face. Her skin was pale, her brows strong and thick. Inspector Sejer looked at her calmly.

'Are you on your own?' he asked.

'My sister will be here shortly. She was the one who called you. She just had to go tell her own family.'

Her voice was panicky. She looked at the two men, at Jacob Skarre with his blond curls and Konrad Sejer with his steel-grey hair. She looked at them with the pleading expression of a beggar. Then she disappeared into the house. Stood by the window with her arms folded across her chest. Sitting down was out of the question; she had to remain standing, had to be able to see the road, the yellow bicycle when it finally turned up. Because it would turn up now, the very moment she had set this huge machine in motion. She started talking. Desperate to fill the void with words, to keep the images at bay, hideous images that kept appearing in her mind.

'I'm on my own with her. We had her late,' she stuttered. 'I'm nearly fifty. Her dad moved out eight years ago. He knows nothing. I'm reluctant to call him. I'm sure there's an explanation and I don't want to worry him for no reason.'

'So you don't consider it possible that she might be with her father?' Sejer said.

15

'No,' she said firmly. 'Anders would have called. He's a good dad.'

'So you get on well as far as Ida is concerned?'

'Oh, absolutely!'

'Then I think you should call him,' Sejer said.

He said this because he was a father himself and he did not want Ida's father kept in the dark. Helga walked reluctantly towards the telephone. The living room fell quiet as she punched in the number.

'There's no reply,' she reported and hung up.

'Leave a message,' Sejer said, 'if he has an answerphone.'

She nodded and rang back. Her voice acquired an embarrassed quality because she had an audience.

'Anders,' they heard, 'it's Helga. I've been waiting for Ida; she should have been home ages ago. I was just wondering if she was with you.'

She paused and then stuttered: 'Call me, please! The police are here.' She turned to Sejer. 'He travels a lot. He could be anywhere.'

'We need a good description of her,' Sejer said. 'And a photo, which I'm sure you have.'

Helga sensed how strong he was. It was strange to think that he must have sat like this before. In other living rooms with other mothers. Most of all she wanted to fall into his arms and cling to him, but she did not dare. So she gritted her teeth.

Sejer rang the station and ordered two patrol cars to drive down the highway towards Glassverket. A nine-year-old girl riding a yellow bicycle, Helga heard him say. And she thought how nice it was to hear him talk about her daughter in this way; he made it sound like they were just looking for a missing vehicle. Later, a cacophony of voices and car engines followed, nightmarish images flickering in front of her eyes. Ringing telephones, snappy orders and strange faces. They wanted to see Ida's room. Helga didn't like that because it reminded her of something. Something she had seen on TV, in crime dramas. Young girls' rooms, howling with emptiness. Quietly she walked upstairs and opened the door. Sejer and Skarre stayed in the doorway, taken aback by the large room and the chaos inside it. Animals, in all shapes and sizes. In all sorts of materials. Glass and stone, clay and wood, plastic and fabric. Horses and dogs. Birds and mice, fish and snakes. They hung suspended from the ceiling on fine wires, they took up the whole of the pale wooden bed, they were piled up on top of bookshelves and lined up on the windowsill. Sejer noticed that every book on the bookshelves was about animals. There were animal pictures and posters on the walls. The curtains were green and had seahorses printed on them.

'Now you see what she's into,' Helga said. She stood in the open doorway, shuddering. It was as if she was seeing this for the very first time, the excess of it all. How many animals were in there? Hundreds?

Sejer nodded. Skarre was lost for words. The room was extraordinarily messy and contained too many things. They went back downstairs. Helga

17

Joner took down a photo from the living room wall. Sejer held it up. The moment he stared into her brown eyes, Ida imprinted herself on his brain. Most kids are cute, he thought, but this girl is adorable. She was sweet and enchanting. Like a child in a fairy tale. She made him think of Little Red Riding Hood, Snow White and Cinderella. Large dark eyes. Rosy red cheeks. Slender as a reed. He looked at Helga Joner.

'You went out looking for her? You and your sister?'

'We drove around for nearly an hour,' Helga said. 'There was only a little traffic, not many people to ask. I've called most of her friends, I've called Laila's Kiosk. She hasn't been there and I don't understand that. What do I do now?' She looked at him with red eyes.

'You shouldn't be on your own,' he said. 'Stay calm and wait for your sister. We'll round up all the officers we have and start looking for her.'

'Do you remember Mary Pickford?' Sejer asked.

They were back in the car. He watched Helga's house disappear in the mirror. Her sister Ruth had come back. Jacob Skarre gave him a blank look. He was far too young to remember any of the silent movie stars.

'Ida looks like her,' Sejer said.

Skarre asked no more questions. He was desperate for a cigarette, but smoking was not allowed in the patrol car. Instead he rummaged round in his

18

pockets for some sweets and dug out a packet of fruit gums.

'She wouldn't get into a strange car,' he said pensively.

'All mothers say that,' Sejer said. 'It depends who does the asking. Adults are much smarter than kids, that's the bottom line.'

His answer made Skarre uneasy. He wanted to believe that children were intuitive and sensed danger much sooner than adults. Like dogs. That they could smell it. Though, come to think of it, dogs were not very smart. His train of thought was starting to depress him. The fruit gum was softening in his mouth so he began chewing it. 'But they'll get into a car if it's someone they know,' he said out loud. 'And it often is someone they know.'

'You're talking as if we're already dealing with a crime,' Sejer said. 'Surely that's a bit premature.'

'I know,' Skarre conceded. 'I'm just trying to prepare myself.'

Sejer watched him covertly. Skarre was young and ambitious. Keen and eager. His talent was well hidden behind his large sky-blue eyes, and his curls added to his harmless appearance. No one ever felt intimidated by Skarre. People relaxed and chatted freely to him, which was precisely what he wanted them to do. Sejer drove the patrol car through the landscape at the permitted speed. All the time he was in contact with the search parties. They had nothing to report.

The speedometer showed a steady sixty kilometres per hour, and eighty when they reached the highway.

Their eyes scanned the fields automatically, but they saw nothing. No little dark-haired girl, no yellow bicycle. Sejer could visualise her face. The tiny mouth and the big curls. Then a far more terrifying image appeared in his mind's eye. No, a voice inside him called out. It's not like that. Not this time. This girl is coming home. They come home all the time, I have seen it before. And why on earth do I love this job so much?

Helga inhaled deeply and exhaled irregularly. Ruth grabbed her sister's shoulders while talking to her in a loud and exaggerated voice. 'You need to breathe, Helga. Breathe!'

Several frenzied inhalations followed, but nothing came out and the thickset body on the sofa struggled to regain control.

'What if Ida were to come in now and see you like this!' Ruth shouted in desperation; she could think of nothing else to say. 'Do you hear me?' She started shaking her sister. Finally Helga managed to breathe normally. Then she collapsed and became strangely lethargic.

'Now you have to rest,' Ruth pleaded. 'I need to phone home. Then you must eat. Or at least drink something.'

Helga shook her head. She could hear her sister's voice coming distantly from the other end of the room. A low murmur that made no sense to her. Shortly afterwards she came to.

'I told Marion to go to bed and lock the door,' Ruth said.

The moment she said that, she felt an intense fear. Marion was alone in the house. Then she realised how inappropriate and needless her anxiety was, but now every word had suddenly become laden, every comment potentially explosive. She disappeared back into the kitchen. Helga heard the clinking of glass. A drawer was pulled out and she thought, Ruth is slicing bread. Having to eat now. I can't manage that. She stared towards the window, her eyes aching. When the telephone rang she was so startled that she let out a sharp scream. Ruth rushed in.

'Shall I get it?'

'No!'

Helga snatched up the receiver and shouted her own name into the telephone. Then she crumbled. 'No, she hasn't turned up,' she cried. 'It's almost eleven thirty and she left at six. I can't take it any more!'

On the other end, Ida Joner's father fell completely silent.

'And the police?' he said anxiously. 'Where are they?'

'They've all left, but they're out looking. They have asked the Home Guard and some other volunteers to join in the search, but they haven't called me yet. They won't find her, I know they won't!'

Ruth waited in the doorway. The gravity of the situation dawned on them both simultaneously. It was dark outside, almost midnight. Ida was out there somewhere, unable to make her way home. Helga could not speak. Eating was out of the question. She did not want to move or go anywhere. Just wait, the two of them together, hugging each other while their fear sent a rush of blood to the head.

CHAPTER 2

'What is it about kids and sweets?' Sejer said. 'Why do they crave them all the time? Do all children suffer from low blood sugar?'

Skarre perched on the edge of the desk. 'Ida went to buy a magazine,' he objected.

'And sweets with the rest of her money,' Sejer said. 'Bugg. What on earth is that?'

'Chewing gum,' Skarre explained.

A couple of hours means nothing, Sejer thought, staring at his wristwatch. After all we are talking about a child who is nearly ten. She could speak up for herself and ask questions. However, it was 1 a.m. now. Outside, it was a black September night, and Ida had been missing from her home for seven hours. He became aware of a low murmur. For a while he sat still, listening to it. The sound increased. Rain, he thought. An early autumn rainstorm. It pelted the windows of the police station, washing dust and dirt from the panes in broad streams. He had wished for rain. Everything was so dry. But now it was bad timing. His body ached with a mixture of restlessness and tension. He should not be sitting here shuffling paper; he should be outside in the darkness looking for Ida. Then he remembered her bicycle. Chrome yellow and brand new. That too was still missing.

'She might have fallen off her bike,' Skarre said. 'Perhaps she's lying unconscious in a ditch somewhere. It's been known to happen. Or she might have met someone who talked her into going for a bike ride. Someone irresponsible, but essentially harmless. Like Raymond. Do you remember Raymond?'

Sejer nodded. 'He keeps rabbits. He could use them to entice a little girl.'

'And Ida is animal mad,' Skarre argued. 'However, it's also possible that she's run away from home because of some row her mother doesn't want to tell us about. Perhaps she's asleep in a shed somewhere. Hell-bent on making her mother pay for something or other.'

'They hadn't been arguing,' Sejer objected.

'Perhaps her father was involved,' Skarre went on. 'They are, sometimes. A teacher or another adult she knows might have picked her up. For reasons we don't understand yet. Perhaps they've given her a hot meal and a bed for the night. People do all sorts of things. We imagine the worst because we've been in this job for too long.'

Skarre undid the top button of his shirt. The semi-darkness and silence in Sejer's office were poignant.

'We have a case,' he concluded.

'Granted.' Sejer nodded. 'Though there's not

much we can do for the time being. We just have to sit here and wait. Until she turns up in some form or other.'

Skarre leapt down from the desk and went over to the window.

'Has Sara gone?' he asked with his back to Sejer. The tarmac on the car park outside the police station gleamed black and oily in the rain.

'Yes. This morning. She'll be gone four months,' Sejer said.

Skarre nodded. 'Research?'

'She intends to find out why some people grow less than others,' Sejer smiled.

'In which case,' Skarre chuckled, 'you being two metres tall is no use to her.'

Sejer shook his head. 'One theory is that some people refuse to grow,' he said. 'That they simply refuse to grow up.'

'You're kidding?' Skarre turned from the window and looked at his boss open-mouthed.

'No, no. I'm not. Often the explanation is much more straightforward than we'd like to believe. According to Sara, anyway.'

Skarre stared despondently out of the window. 'I hate the rain,' he said.

The shrill sound of the doorbell cut through the house without warning. Helga stared wildly at her sister; her eyes had a metallic sheen of terror. It was very late. An insane mixture of fear and hope surged through her body.

25

'I'll get it!' Ruth said, rushing out. She trembled as she pushed the door handle down. Outside, standing on the doorstep, was Ida's father.

'Anders,' she said, and could barely hide her disappointment. She stared at him and took a step back.

'Have they found her?' he asked.

'No. We're still waiting.'

'I'm staying here tonight,' Anders Joner said firmly. 'I can sleep on the sofa.'

He sounded very determined. Ruth moved to let him in. Helga heard his voice and braced herself. She felt so many things. Relief and anger at the same time. He walked across the floor. A thin, lean man whose head was practically bald. She recognised his old grey coat and a jumper she had knitted him a long time ago. It was hard to look at his face. She could not bear to see the desperation in his eyes; she could barely contain her own.

'You go to bed, Helga,' he said. 'I'll wait by the phone. Have you managed to eat something?'

He took off his coat and placed it over the back of a chair. He made himself at home. But then again, for several years this house had been his home.

Ruth was standing in a corner. She felt that leaving them was like running away. 'Well, I'll be off then,' she said, averting her eyes. 'But promise me you'll call if anything happens, Anders.'

She suddenly became very busy. Patted Helga on the back, tore her coat off the peg in the hall and rushed outside. Drove back to her house in

Madseberget as fast as she could. Thoughts racing through her mind.

The rain was fierce, the wipers swept angrily across the windscreen. Her own cowardice made her feel wretched. When Anders had appeared on the doorstep and she felt she could go home, her sense of relief had been overwhelming. The whole evening she had been consumed by a terrifying, overpowering horror. But she had not allowed herself to give in to it. She had to be stronger than Helga. Now that Anders was keeping her sister company, her feelings surfaced once more and they took her breath away. She would escape it now, that awful moment. Escape the inevitable telephone call, the dreaded words: 'We've found her.' Now it would be Anders who would have to deal with it. I'm a coward, she thought, wiping away her tears.

She parked in the double garage and noticed that Tomme, her son, was still not back. She let herself in and ran up the stairs to the first floor. Her daughter, Marion, was asleep in her bed. She stood for a while, watching her daughter's chubby cheeks. They were warm and rosy. Later she sat by the living room window, waiting for her son. It dawned on her that her sister had sat in the same way for hours waiting for Ida. Tomme was later than usual. She felt a fraction of Helga's fear, but calmed herself down by remembering that he was an adult. Imagine sitting like this, she thought, and they never turn up. It was inconceivable. What if Marion vanished like that? What if the sound of tyres from her son's Opel never materialised? She tried to imagine hours of waiting. Imagined that the familiar sound of tyres never came. That sooner or later she would be waiting for another sound, the sound of the telephone. She rang his mobile, but it was switched off. When he finally turned up, it surprised her that he did not pop in to say hi, but went straight up to his room. He must have seen the light in the window and realised that she was awake. She sat there for a few minutes, deliberating. Dreaded what she had to tell him. Then she went upstairs. Positioned herself in the doorway to his room. He had turned on his computer. Sat facing away from her, his shoulders hunched. His entire body exuded frustration.

'What is it?' she said quickly. 'You're terribly late.'

He cleared his throat. Thumped the table with his fist. 'I bashed the bloody car,' he said sullenly.

Ruth pondered his answer. She thought of everything that had happened and watched his narrow, angry back. Suddenly she felt incensed. Her fear and her rage started to pour out of her and there was nothing she could do to stop them.

'So,' she said, 'you've bashed the car, have you? Well, your dad and I aren't going to pay to have it fixed, so you'll just have to drive it as it is, or you can save up and pay for it yourself!' She was almost gasping for breath. Her son became wary, but he did not turn around.

'I know that,' he said in a monotone voice.

28

A labyrinth appeared on the screen. A cat prowled around inside it. Her son followed it with his eyes and turned up the volume. A mouse was scuttling around in the heart of the labyrinth.

'It's just so fucking annoying,' he exploded.

'I really can't be bothered to talk about that right now,' Ruth yelled. 'Something dreadful has happened. Ida's gone missing!'

Her son was startled, but he continued to stare at the screen. A low sound emanated from the speakers.

'Missing?' he said, shocked, and began to turn around slowly.

'Your cousin Ida,' she said. 'She left home at six to get something from the kiosk. I've been with Helga the whole evening. They haven't found her or her bicycle.'

'They?'

'The police!'

'So where have they been looking?' he asked, looking at her wide-eyed.

'Where have they been looking? Everywhere, of course. She never even got to the kiosk.'

Ruth had to lean against the wall. Yet again she realised just how serious the situation was. Her son was still fiddling with the keyboard, moving the prowling cat into a blind alley. The mouse stayed put, waiting for its next move.

'So that dent of yours is not worth worrying about,' she said in a fraught voice. 'It's just some damage to an old car, which can be fixed. I hope you understand how unimportant it is.'

29

He nodded slowly. She could hear his breathing; it was laboured.

'So what happened, then?' she said with sudden sympathy. 'Were you hurt?'

He shook his head. Ruth felt sorry for him. A dented car represented a defeat. He was young and thought he knew it all, and the dent had undermined his pride in the worst possible way. She did understand, but was not prepared to offer him anything more than basic sympathy. She wanted him to grow up.

'I hit a crash barrier,' he said.

'I see,' she said. 'Where?'

'By the bridge. In the centre of town.'

'Were you with Bjørn?'

'No. Not then.'

'Do you want me to go out to the garage and have a look?' she asked.

'There's no need,' he said in a tired voice. 'I've talked to Willy. He'll help me repair it. I haven't got any money, but he says he can wait.'

'Willy?' Ruth frowned. 'Are you still friends with him? I thought you were going over to Bjørn's?'

'I was,' Tomme said. 'But Willy knows about cars. That's why I drove over to his place. Willy has the tools and a garage, Bjørn doesn't have anything like that.'

He started moving the cat again. Why won't he look at me? Ruth wondered. An awful thought struck her.

'Tomme,' she said breathlessly, 'you haven't been drinking, have you?'

30

He spun around in his chair and gave her an irate look. 'Are you out of your mind? Of course I don't drive when I've been drinking. Are you saying I drink and drive?'

He was so genuinely outraged that she felt ashamed. His face was white as chalk. His longish hair was unkempt, and in the midst of everything that was going on, Ruth noticed that it could do with a wash.

She lingered in the doorway for a while. She could not calm herself down, she did not feel tired; all the time she was listening out for the telephone in case it should ring. She sensed how shocked she would be if it actually did ring. She imagined the moment when she would lift up the receiver and wait. Standing at the edge of the void. She would either fall into it or be pulled back from the edge and into the comforting reassurance of a happy ending. Because this had to have a happy ending. She could not imagine the alternative, not here, in this peaceful place, not for Ida.

'I'm going over to Helga's early tomorrow morning,' she said. 'You've got to give Marion breakfast and help her get ready. I want you to walk her to the school bus. And don't just walk her there,' she added. 'I want you to wait until she's found her seat. Do you hear me? I need to be with Helga in case anything happens. Uncle Anders is there at the moment,' she said quietly.

She sighed forlornly and told her son to go to bed. Left him and went outside. It was a spur-of-the

31

moment decision. She opened the door to the double garage. She was surprised to see that her son had covered the Opel with a tarpaulin. He never usually did. I suppose he can't bear to look at it, she thought. She turned on the garage light. Lifted up the tarpaulin. On the right-hand side she found what she was looking for. A dent, a broken front light and some damage to the paintwork. It was scarred by long grey and white scratches. She shook her head and replaced the tarpaulin. Went back outside. Stood there pondering. Felt the rain on her neck, raw and cold. She glanced quickly up at the window to her son's bedroom, which overlooked the drive. There she saw his pale face partly hidden by the curtain.

CHAPTER 3

Helga woke with a jolt. She sat up in bed. For a brief second everything was as normal. She was Helga waking up to a new day.

Then she remembered. Reality hit her and forced her back down on the mattress. At the same time she heard the slamming of a car door and subdued, murmuring voices. Someone was coming to the house. She lay very still as if lying on a bed of needles, listening. They were moving very quietly, she could hear that. No hasty steps, no eager voices. She remained curled up in her bed. She was going to lie like this until Ida came home again. She would not move, eat or drink. If she stayed there long enough, the miracle would happen. And if it never happened she would let the mattress swallow her up. Lose herself in its stuffing. People could sleep on top of her, they could come and go as they pleased; she would not notice them. She would never feel anything ever again.

She heard Anders' voice. Feet dragging across the floor. The front door being closed ever so gently. If the worst had happened, Anders would be standing in the doorway looking at her. He would not have to say a single word, just stare at her with a silent cry. His eyes, his wide brown eyes, which Ida had inherited, would darken. And she would stand up and scream. Scream so the windows would shatter, so everyone would hear her and the world would cease rotating on its axis. People in the street would stop and listen. They would feel a tremor beneath their feet and know that the end was coming. But the seconds passed and he did not appear. The muted voices in the living room continued. So they haven't found her, dead or alive, Helga thought. Hope is such a fragile thing. She clawed at the duvet to get hold of it and clutch it.

Anders Joner showed Sejer and Skarre into the living room.

'Helga's asleep,' he said. He fumbled in his shirt pocket for his glasses. His glasses were greasy. The state of his clothes indicated that he had slept on the sofa. If indeed he had slept at all.

'What do we do now?' he asked nervously. 'You haven't found her bicycle either?'

'No,' Sejer said.

Jacob Skarre listened attentively, his blue eyes deep in concentration. While Sejer spoke, he studied Joner carefully. From time to time he made a quick note.

'What does that mean?' Joner said.

'We don't know,' Sejer answered.

Joner rubbed his scalp. It was almost bare. His eyes were wide like Ida's and his mouth tiny. He appeared to be somewhat younger than Helga, neat and slender, bordering on the feminine.

'But what do you think?'

Sejer took his time before he answered. 'We don't think anything,' he said simply. 'We just keep looking.'

They continued to watch one another. Sejer's role was to confirm to Ida's father how grave the situation was. That was what he needed, that was why he kept pressing him in this way.

'I'm concerned,' Sejer said. 'I can't deny it.' His voice was steady as a rock. Sometimes he despaired at his own composure, but it was essential. He had to support Joner.

Ida's father nodded. He had got what he wanted. 'But what's going on right now?' he said, his voice taking on a sudden dull tone. 'What are you doing to find her?'

'We've mapped out the route that Ida was cycling,' Sejer said. 'And we're looking for anyone who was in the area at the same time. We're asking them to contact us, and people have started to call. We speak to anyone who might have seen anything of interest, and everything is recorded. That applies to cars, bicycles and pedestrians. We're looking for this one vital clue which will give us a breakthrough.'

'What kind of breakthrough?' Joner stammered. He lowered his voice so that Helga would not be able to hear him. 'When a kid goes missing like that,' he continued, 'you obviously fear that someone has taken her. To use her. You know what for.

And later got rid of her, so she can't tell. That's what I'm scared of!' he whispered. 'And I just can't imagine what else it could be.' He buried his face in his hands. 'How many people have called? Has anyone called at all?'

'Unfortunately we have had very few calls,' Sejer admitted. 'The roads were quiet when Ida went out. And we're talking about a stretch of several kilometres. However, these things take time. So far, we know that Ida was spotted at Solberg Farm. Another, less reliable sighting came from Madseberget.'

Suddenly Joner leapt up from his chair. 'For God's sake. I can't take it any more.'

Sejer tried to rein in Joner's panic by remaining calm himself. Joner slumped back into his chair.

'Helga says that Ida would never ignore the rules she's been taught,' Sejer said. 'The rules all kids need to know about strangers and not getting into cars with them. What do you think?'

Joner considered this. 'Ida's very trusting,' he said. 'She is curious and sweet. And she thinks the best of everyone. If she met someone who was nice to her, if he promised her something, well, I couldn't say for certain.' He was restless as he spoke. He kept taking off his glasses and putting them back on, unable to keep his hands still.

For a while Sejer thought about the paedophiles he had met during his time in the force. They were often nice to children to begin with, kind, inviting and friendly. They knew how to groom them, and they had the ability to spot the most trusting children quickly. A bizarre skill, Sejer thought.

'So she could have gone with someone of her own accord?' he said out loud.

'I suppose so,' Joner said helplessly. 'Anything's possible. I can't answer yes or no to a question like that.'

Sejer knew that Joner was right.

Skarre spoke up. 'Is she interested in boys?' he asked cautiously.

Joner shook his head. 'She's only nine. But then again, she could be starting to take an interest in them. Even though I personally think it's a bit early.'

'How about a diary? Does she keep one?'

'You'll have to ask Helga later,' he said. 'I don't want to wake her now.'

'You and Helga,' Sejer said delicately, 'you get on well?'

Joner nodded. 'Yes, very much so!'

'She called you last night, but didn't manage to get hold of you. Where did you spend the evening?'

Joner blinked nervously. 'At work. I often switch off my mobile so I won't get disturbed.'

'You work shifts?' Sejer asked him.

'No. But I no longer have a family. I mean, not like I used to. So I spend most of my time working. I'm at the office a lot. From time to time I even sleep there,' he said.

'What do you do?'

'I'm in advertising. I work with text and layout.

37

The agency is called Heartbreak,' he added. 'In case you need to know.'

Skarre noted down the name and address of the agency. Joner started talking about his work. It was a welcome distraction from this terrible situation and it seemed to cheer him up. His face took on a boyish expression. He radiated the instant appeal people acquire when they love their work and are given a chance to talk about it.

'Helga's on incapacity benefit,' he said. 'Because of her migraines. So I support both her and Ida.' His face darkened because his daughter was once more at the forefront of his mind. 'Ida is very forward,' he said suddenly.

'Forward?' Sejer said. 'In what way?'

'Pushy. Eager. She's not afraid of anything. She has a great deal of self-confidence,' he said, 'and she thinks very highly of herself. It would never occur to her that she might meet someone who would want to hurt her. She's no experience of that.' Joner placed his glasses on the table. Finally he managed to leave them alone. 'Isn't there anything I can do?'

'We'll round up all the volunteers we can find and organise a search party,' Sejer said. 'It's no problem finding people for something like that. Everyone in the area knows that Ida's gone missing. It will be led by professionals and the volunteers will be told precisely how and where to look.'

'What about the river?' Joner said apprehensively. He did not like to say it out loud.

'Of course we need to think about dragging it,'

38

Sejer said. 'However, in the first instance we need to carry out a search of the immediate area, and our people will visit every single house along the road to Laila's Kiosk as well.'

'I want to join in the search,' Joner said.

'We'll let you know later about a meeting place,' Sejer said. 'We'll probably use the school playground. Please look after Helga until then.'

Joner saw them out. He stayed standing on the steps watching them. Gripped the railings and leant forward. His eyes sought the horizon; Ida was out there. 'She's been gone seventeen hours,' he groaned. 'It's too late and you know it!'

He buried his head in his hands and stood there shaking. Sejer went back up to him. He grabbed Joner's arm and squeezed it hard. There was nothing else he could do. Then he returned to the car. It felt like he was turning his back on a drowning man.

A large group of volunteers had gathered in the playground of Glassverket school. A whole night had passed and the seriousness of the situation was clear to see from every face. It was still raining, but more softly now. The search party was made up of volunteers from the Red Cross, the Home Guard, teachers and pupils from the school, people from the sports club and a range of other organisations. Plus a few people who happened to have heard the police request for volunteers. They had simply left their homes and gone out in the rain in order to help. There were many young people; however, the significant majority were men and older boys. Some smaller kids had turned up but were sent home again. Emil Johannes had noticed the large gathering of people, and he parked his green three-wheeler behind the bicycle shed, where he could observe them from a safe distance. No one thought of asking if he wanted to join in. Not that he wanted to anyway. He watched the dogs on leashes that a few people had brought along. If one of the dogs were to tear itself loose, he would start his three-wheeler as quickly as possible and drive off. He did not like dogs.

The search party examined maps and listened to instructions from the police about how to move around the terrain. How closely together they needed to walk, how to use their eyes. The importance of concentrating one hundred per cent at all times. Not too much talking. One group was sent up towards the waterfall, another group ordered down to search along the banks of the river. Some were sent out across the fields, others into the woods and others again up to the ridge behind Glassverket.

Jacob Skarre gave them their final instructions. 'Remember, Ida's tiny,' he said. 'She doesn't take up much room.'

They nodded earnestly. Skarre looked at them pensively. He knew a fair bit about what they were thinking. Volunteers had multiple and often contradictory motives. Some had turned up out of desperation, because they were fathers themselves and could not bear to sit idly in front of the television. Some had come looking for excitement, each one hoping that he would be the one to find Ida. They fantasised about finding her dead, about being the centre of attention; they fantasised about being the one who would find her safe and well, who would call out the good news and have everyone looking at them. Perhaps lift her up and carry her in their arms. They were also scared, as very few of them had ever seen a dead body and the vast majority were secretly convinced that Ida was dead. These lurid private thoughts troubled them, so they stood there kicking the tarmac. A few carried rucksacks containing flasks. Each and every one of them was eagle-eyed, or they thought so at any rate. Nevertheless, Skarre reminded them of countless searches in the past where people had walked right past the missing person several times. Anders Joner was there. As he had not lived in Glassverket for the last eight years, few people knew him and he was grateful for the anonymity it gave him. His brothers, Tore and Kristian, were there too, as was Helga's nephew, Tomme.

Everyone felt a huge sense of relief when they finally started to walk. One hundred and fifty people dissolved into smaller groups and shuffled out of the school playground. There was a low murmuring of voices. This was a bizarre experience for most of them. Staring into the ground all the time, seeing every straw, every root and twig, every

41

irregularity in the tarmac, the litter along the verges, there was so much to see. The group which had been ordered to search along the riverbanks kept looking furtively into the rapidly flowing water. They lifted up bushes and other shrubs with low-hanging branches. They searched holes and caves. And they did find things. A rusty old pram. A decaying wellington boot. There were mainly empty beer bottles along the riverbank. From time to time they would stop for a short break. One of the groups came across a small shed. It was tilting dangerously. It looked like it might collapse at any moment. A good hiding place, they thought as they stood facing the simple building. Not very far from the road, or the house where Ida lived either. Instinctively they sniffed the air. A man crouched down and crept through the opening, which consisted of a narrow gap in the dilapidated planks. He asked for a torch and was handed one. The beam flickered across the dark space. His heart was beating so fast he could feel it in his temples. The rest of the group waited. Not a sound came from the inside of the shed during these long, tense seconds. Then the man's feet emerged again as he crept backwards out of the tight opening.

'Nothing but old rubbish,' he reported.

'You did lift stuff up, didn't you?' someone asked. 'She could be lying under something. Underneath planks and things like that.'

'She wasn't there,' the man replied, and rubbed his face wearily.

'They did say it was very easy to overlook something. Why don't we double-check?' The other man was not going to let it go.

The man who had crawled inside the damp darkness to look for the body of a dead girl and had not found her gave him a hostile look.

'Are you saying I didn't look properly?' he said.

'No, no. Don't get me wrong. I just want to be sure. We don't want to be the group that walked right past her, do we? We want to do this the right way.'

The first man nodded in agreement. The other man crept through the opening and carefully shone the torch around. He was hoping so desperately that he would find her. Fancy hoping like this, it struck him, as he knelt on the musty ground, feeling the cold seep through the knees of his trousers. Hoping that she would be lying there. Because if she was lying in there, she would have to be dead. But we don't want her to be dead. We're just being realistic. We are helping. He backed out.

'Nothing,' he said. 'Thank God.'

He exhaled deeply. The group moved on.

CHAPTER 4

Willy Oterhals had not been out looking for Ida. He was sitting on the floor of his garage with a book in his lap. The chill from the concrete floor crept through the seat of his trousers. Tomme was sitting on a workbench by the wall watching Willy. His clothes were damp after several hours of being outside in the drizzling rain. The search had yielded no results. Now he was looking at the Opel. From the bench where he was sitting he could not see the damaged wing. He could make himself believe that it had never happened, that it was all a bad dream.

'Up the ridge, was it?' Willy said without looking up at him.

Tomme thought about it for a while. 'It was horrible,' he said. 'Just walking around searching like that. Loads of people had turned up. They're looking everywhere. Including wells and rivers.'

'Will they be searching tomorrow?' Willy asked.

'They're saying they'll go on like this for days.'

He looked across to his older friend. Willy was quite skinny, he thought. He had a lean face with a protruding chin, and bony shoulders. His knees

44

were sharp underneath the nylon boiler suit. Now he was rubbing some dirt off his cheek with his finger, while trying to decipher the text and the illustrations in the book about car repairs. The book was old and dog-eared. The pages were stained with oil. Some of them were torn and someone had tried to mend them with sticky tape. He studied the illustration of a front wing, the right-hand one, as on Tomme's Opel.

'First we need to sand it,' Willy said decisively. 'We need two types of sandpaper, smooth and coarse.' He peered down at the book. 'Number 180 and number 360. The wing needs sanding down first with dry paper and then with wet. We'll need a sanding block and some filler. Rust remover. A degreasing agent. You listening to me, Tomme?'

Tomme nodded. But the truth was that he was far, far away.

Willy read on. 'We need to sand around the dent. It says here: "Start in the middle of the damaged area and work your way outwards in circular movements." Find something to write on. You'll have to go out and buy the stuff we need. Once we've got the wing off.'

'I don't mind doing the shopping,' Tomme said. 'But I'm skint.'

Willy looked up at him. 'I'll lend you the money. You won't be going to school for ever, will you? Sooner or later you'll start earning.' Once more he looked down at the book. 'We'll also need some more tools. I'll see if I can borrow them.'

He put the book aside, climbed back to his feet and went over to the car. Bent over the wing, hands on his hips. He inspected the damage with a seasoned look, his shoulders hunched like two sails billowing in the wind, keen to get started. 'Right, Tomme. Let's get going.'

Tomme heard the crackling of the nylon boiler suit and a groaning, creaking sound coming from the metal. From time to time he heard Willy panting and gasping. An old Opel Ascona that has been in one piece for fifteen years does not give up without a fight.

'I know a bloke down at Shell,' Willy panted. 'Bastian. He'll lend me what I need.'

Willy has so many contacts, Tomme thought.

'Christ, Willy,' he said, relieved. 'If you can fix this, I'll owe you big time.'

'Won't you just,' Willy smiled. His eyes lit up. 'And now it's about time that you cheered up. It'll be all right. I promise you.'

He continued to twist and bend the metal. A vein bulged on his neck. 'Ah, sod it, I need to get underneath it.' He slid under the car. His long white fingers appeared below the wheel arch.

'I don't understand it,' Tomme said. 'I just don't understand it. How it happened.' He was so upset at what had occurred. The colour rose in his face.

'Take it easy,' Willy reassured him. 'Like I said, it'll be all right.' Then he remembered something. 'What did your mum say?'

Tomme groaned. 'The usual. That they wouldn't

pay for it. That they don't like me coming here. But you know, they're mostly worried about this other thing.'

'Yeah, course. I'm seen as the kind of lowlife a nice boy like you shouldn't mix with, I've always known that.' Willy laughed scornfully. 'But you're an adult now, for God's sake. It's for you to decide who you want to hang out with, isn't it?'

'Exactly, and that's what I told my mum,' Tomme lied. 'Hey, listen.' A thought had just occurred to him. 'Do you think we should check the brakes?'

'Oh, give it a rest!' Willy told him. 'The brakes are fine. Now give me a hand. We need to get this wing off. The bastard's stuck. Hold this for me!'

Tomme leapt down from the bench. He was trying to pull himself together. He was relieved that Willy would be able to fix his car. He liked the idea of himself as Willy's gofer. But there were times when he felt stifled by his older, more resourceful friend. Once Tomme had finally passed his driving test – after failing his first attempt, needless to say, and putting up with being ridiculed about this in every way imaginable – he felt they had achieved a kind of equality at last. He could drive himself. On top of that, it had been Willy who had trawled the local papers in search of a used car costing the 20,000 kroner that Tomme had managed to save up. His confirmation alone had brought in 15,000.

'An Opel is a safe bet,' Willy had said confidently. 'Reliable engines, especially in the older models. You can't worry about the colour. Don't even go there. If you find an Opel in good condition, buy it, even if it's bright orange.'

But they had found a black one. Even the paintwork was fine. Tomme was over the moon. He could not wait a minute longer. He just had to get driving.

'What about the police?' Willy said tentatively. 'I suppose they're all over the place because of your cousin.'

'Yes.'

'Have they talked to you?'

'Jesus, no.' Tomme was shocked. He slackened his grip for a second and Willy's finger got crushed.

'Concentrate, you idiot! You've got to lift it up while I'm using the screwdriver!'

Tomme held on. His knuckles were white.

'When it's something like a missing girl and stuff,' Willy panted underneath the car, 'the cops just go crazy. Perhaps they've even checked out her dad. Have they?'

'Dunno,' Tomme mumbled.

'But they'll want to know about her family,' Willy said. 'Perhaps they'll talk to you as well.'

Tomme nodded. He felt like a robot as he listened to the flow of words coming from Willy. It made him feel calm and nervous at the same time.

'You being her cousin, well, that's incriminating in itself,' Willy said. Finally he got up. The wing was loose. 'Especially if they never find her. If they never find out the truth. Something like that brands people for generations. You know a girl was murdered out here forty years ago, don't you?'

Tomme shook his head.

'Well, she was. A guy raped and killed a fifteen-year-old girl. Both their families still live here. And you can tell just by looking at them.'

'Tell what?' Tomme asked. He was growing more and more nervous.

'That it's all they ever think about. And they know everyone knows who they are. That's why they can never look anyone in the eye. That kind of stuff.' He wiped a bead of snot from his upper lip. 'The mother of the guy who killed her is close to seventy now. And you can still tell who she is from miles away.'

'Well I can't,' Tomme snapped. 'I've no idea who she is.' He wanted his friend to shut up. Hated all this talk of death and destruction. The only thing he cared about was the car. Making it whole again. Shiny and new, with unmarked paintwork, like it was before.

She knows she is pretty, Sejer thought sadly. He was holding a photo of Ida in his hand. In his mind he could hear them all, an endless chorus of aunts and uncles, neighbours and friends. What a gorgeous child. He remembered his own aunts, who used to tickle his chin as if he were a puppy or some other dumb creature. And so I was, he realised. A shy, skinny boy with legs that were too long. He kept looking at the photo. For years Ida had seen her own beauty mirrored in the eyes of others. This had made her a confident girl, a girl who was accustomed to being admired, and possibly envied, too. Used to getting her own way with both her friends and her parents, though Helga came across as firm and strict, so Ida had also been given rules. She had never broken them. Who could have made her ignore her mother's warnings? What had he done to lure her away? Or had she simply been grabbed and bundled into a car?

Adorable and precocious, he thought. It was a bad combination. It made her a target. Staring into those brown eyes it was impossible not to melt. He tried to connect these three things. Warm feelings for an enchanting child, followed by physical arousal, and finally destruction. He understood the first one. He even managed to imagine fleeting moments of desire. The purity, the fragility that children embodied. So smooth, uncorrupted and tender; they smelled so good, they trembled and quivered. And purely by being an adult, you had the strength to take what you wanted. But to beat and squeeze the life out of a tiny child was beyond comprehension. The frenzied struggle as life slowly ebbed away in your hands was unimaginable. He rubbed his tired eyes, repelled by his thought experiment. He decided to ring Sara's hotel in New York. She was not in.

It was late in the evening. The town lay smouldering like a dying fire between blue-black ridges. He could go home and pour himself a glass of whisky. He would probably be able to fall asleep quite easily. The fact that he could lie down and

50

sleep while Ida was lost in the darkness, while Helga waited for her with stinging eyes, disturbed him deeply. He would rather be outside. Walk the streets with all his senses alert. Be outside because Ida was. The search parties still had nothing to report.

He was startled by a knock on the door. Jacob Skarre popped his head round.

'You still here?' Sejer asked. 'What are you doing at this hour?'

'Same as you, I suppose. Hanging around.'

Skarre took a look around his boss's office. Beneath Sejer's desk lamp was a salt-dough figure. It was meant to be a police officer wearing a blue uniform and had been made by Sejer's grandchild. Skarre lifted up the figure and inspected it.

'It's starting to go mouldy,' he said. 'Did you know?'

Sejer pretended not to hear him. It would never even cross his mind to throw the figure away. True, it did look a little worse for wear, but it certainly did not smell.

'Can I smoke out of the window?' Skarre asked.

He waited patiently for a reply, holding a Prince cigarette in his hand. He got a brief affirmative nod from Sejer and sat down on the windowsill. He struggled with the heavy window for a few moments.

'Like she's vanished into thin air,' he stated, blowing smoke out into the September night. 'They haven't found so much as a hair slide.'

'She had nothing to lose,' Sejer said. 'No wrist-watch, no jewellery. But I'm pleased about one thing.'

'Really?' Skarre said glumly.

'We haven't found any bloodstained clothing. Or a child's shoe abandoned on the road, or a bicycle dumped in a ditch. I like the fact that we haven't found anything.'

'Why?' Skarre said, surprised.

'I don't know,' Sejer admitted.

'That only goes to show that he is thorough,' Skarre said. 'It doesn't make me feel better at all.' He inhaled the cigarette smoke deeply. 'Waiting like this is pure torture.'

'It certainly is for Anders and Helga Joner,' Sejer said drily.

Skarre fell silent. Was it a rebuke? He kept blowing smoke out of the open window, but some of it still drifted back into the darkened office. Finally he held the glowing cigarette butt under the tap in the sink.

'Time to call it a day?'

Sejer nodded and grabbed his jacket from the back of his chair.

'What did you think about the press coverage?' Skarre asked him later. They were standing in the car park outside the police station. Both of them jingling their car keys.

'Journalists are all right,' Sejer said. 'When you read what they've actually written. What I really object to is the way some editors lay everything out. They use photos and drawings to speculate and insinuate.'

Skarre remembered the pictures from the day's papers. The photos of Ida, the type of bicycle she had, a yellow Nakamura, the type of tracksuit she had been wearing. And the wording: 'This is where Ida was going.' Dotted lines. A close-up of Laila's Kiosk.

'They treat it like it's a soap opera,' Sejer said. 'I hope it's a short one.'

They nodded briefly to each other and went their separate ways. Once he got home, Sejer went into the kitchen and found a bag of dog food. His dog, Kollberg, who had been lying on the floor waiting for his master, stirred gingerly. However, the sound of the dry feed rattling in his metal bowl made him stand up. He trudged wearily into the kitchen. The dog, a Leonberger, was so old he defied all statistics. He looked up at Sejer with dark, impenetrable eyes. Sejer found it hard to look back at him. He knew the dog was suffering, that he ought to be spared further pain. Soon, he thought. But not today. I'll wait till Sara comes back home. He cut himself a slice of bread and put some salami on top. Then he found a tube of mayonnaise in the fridge. He stood for a while weighing up the pros and cons. He considered mayonnaise an extravagance. He unscrewed the cap and was struck by the absurdity of his situation. Here he was squeezing mayonnaise on his sandwich in the shape of an 8 before sitting down to eat it. While Helga Joner could barely breathe.

Sejer woke up at 6 a.m. The dog lay on the floor next to his bed. He registered his master's light movements on the mattress and raised his head. A second later the alarm gave off three short beeps.

53

Sejer leaned over the edge of the bed and patted Kollberg on the head. The dog's skull was clearly outlined underneath his fur; he felt the bumps of it against his palm. Then he thought of Ida. She snapped into place in his mind. He stretched out his long body in the bed and tried to peer out from behind the curtains, searching for daylight. It was no good; he had to get up to have a look. He stared out at the damp morning mist, which lay like a lid across the town. For breakfast he ate two pieces of crispbread with cheese and red pepper. Coaxed Kollberg down the stairs and walked round the block once. Let him back into the living room. It was 7.15 when he opened the door to his office with fresh newspapers tucked under his arm. 'Ida still missing' was the headline.

The first meeting of the day was about dividing up tasks. Not that there was much to divide up in the Ida Joner case. In the first instance it was a question of checking out anyone with a record. People who had finished serving their sentences, people who might have been out on leave during the relevant period, and those previously charged but never convicted. The blunt truth was that they were all waiting for someone to stumble across Ida's mutilated body so they could start the investigation properly. Her photo was pinned up on the board in the meeting room. Her smile sent a jolt of pain through them every time they passed it, and in the midst of it all a slender hope still existed that Ida would suddenly stroll casually into her mother's house with the most incredible story to tell.

When the telephone rang, and it did so frequently, everyone spun around and stared intently at whoever had answered it, feeling certain that they would be able to gauge from his reaction if it was news about Ida. The duty officer had the same hopes whenever he answered the telephone. They knew that it would happen eventually.

A new search was initiated. They were still trying to decide if they should drag the river. The problem was where to start.

Sejer drove out to Helga's house. He could see her face at the window; most likely she had heard the car. He got out slowly, very slowly on purpose so as not to raise her hopes.

'I've almost given up,' she said weakly.

'I know that it's difficult,' he said. 'But we're still looking.'

'I've always known that Ida was too good to be true.'

'Too good to be true?' Sejer said carefully.

Helga's lower lip quivered. 'She was. Now I don't know what she is any more.'

She went into the living room without saying another word. Then she walked over to the window. 'Most of the time I stand here. Or I sit in her room. I don't do anything. I'm frightened that I'll forget about her,' she said anxiously. 'Frightened that she might slip away from my thoughts, frightened that I'll start to think or do something which doesn't include her.'

'No one expects you to be able to do anything now,' Sejer said.

He sat down on the sofa without being asked. He saw that her hair was unwashed and that she was wearing the same clothes as when he had first met her. Or perhaps she had changed back into them.

'I'd like to speak with your sister,' Sejer said.

'Ruth? She lives a few minutes away from here, at Madseberget. She'll be here later.'

'You get on well?' he asked.

'Yes,' she smiled. 'We always have done.'

'And Ida's father. Anders. He has two brothers who also live close by. Ida's uncles?'

She nodded. 'Tore and Kristian Joner. They're both married with children of their own. They live by the racecourse.'

'Do you see them often?' he wanted to know.

She shook her head. 'No, I don't. Funny really. But I know that they were out looking yesterday. Both of them.'

'Have either of them been in touch with you?'

'They daren't,' she said quietly. 'They're afraid, I suppose. I don't know what they're thinking. Don't want to, either. The pictures in my own head are bad enough.' She shuddered as if some awful image had appeared at that very moment.

'But Ida knows her cousins?'

'Of course. She knows Marion and Tomme best of all. Ruth and Sverre's kids. She goes to see them often. She is fond of her aunt Ruth. She's the only aunt she's close to.'

'And your brother-in-law?' he asked. 'What does he do?'

56

'Sverre works in the oil industry and travels a lot. He's hardly ever home. Anders travels a lot too. They moan about all those nights they have to spend in hotels and how boring it is. Though I think that's actually the way they want it. Gets them off the hook when it comes to doing the day-to-day stuff.'

Sejer had no comment to make. 'Is Ida fond of her uncle Sverre?' he said quietly.

Helga was silent for a while, and slowly the significance of the question dawned on her. Then she nodded firmly. 'Yes, Sverre and Ruth are Ida's closest family, apart from Anders and me. She's been going there her whole life and she feels at home there. They're decent people.'

This was said with authority. Sejer looked around the room. There were several photos on the walls of Ida, taken a few years apart. In one of the photos she was holding a cat.

'She's very interested in animals,' he said. 'Her room is full of them. That cat there, you don't have it any more?'

An eerie calm fell upon the room. Sejer was completely unprepared for the reaction provoked by his question. Helga buckled by the window and buried her face in her hands. Then she howled out into the room in a voice that cut right through him.

'The cat belonged to Marion! It was knocked down and killed. But Ida has never had a pet of her own. Not even a mouse! I told her no. Always no! Because I didn't want one, and now I can't begin to understand how I could have been so selfish. So she's never had a kitten or a puppy or any of those other pets she wanted so desperately, none of the animals she begged and begged me to get her, but I didn't want the hassle with pets, hairs and shit everywhere and so on! But if only she'll come home again, she can have all the animals she wants! I promise you, I promise!'

Total silence. Helga's face was red. She started to sob loudly. 'I'm at my wits' end,' she cried. 'I'm so desperate I decided I would go buy a puppy. Because then Ida would be sure to come home again. She'd hear the puppy whimper wherever she was and rush straight home. That was my logic. What an idiot.'

'Well,' Sejer said. 'You're allowed to buy a puppy.'

She shook her head. 'I think so many strange thoughts,' she admitted. 'Utterly impossible thoughts.' She wiped her wet cheeks with the sleeve of her jumper.

'I understand,' Sejer said softly. 'You're in a place you've never been before.'

Her eyes widened. 'Oh no! I've been here many times. This is what I've always feared. I've been preparing for this. This is what having children is like!'

'Okay,' he said, 'so you're in a place you visited in your mind. Is it different from what you imagined?'

'It's much, much worse,' she sobbed.

*

Ruth Rix had walked her daughter Marion to the school bus. Now she was watching her son Tomme as he raised the milk carton to his mouth. Then she let him have it.

'Tom Erik! I don't like you doing that and you know it.'

He put the carton down and tried to leave the kitchen.

'You need to eat something,' she ordered him.

'Not hungry,' he mumbled.

She heard him out in the hallway. He was tying the laces on his trainers. 'Don't you have study leave today?' she called out. She followed him, he was not going to get away that easily.

'Yeah?' he said, looking up at her.

'Then I'll expect you to study,' she said, thinking that this was his last, crucial year at sixth-form college.

'Just going over to Willy's first. We're mending the car.'

She digested this and looked at him. His face was still turned away from her. 'You're making a big deal out of this dent,' she said hesitantly. 'It's only a car, for God's sake.'

He did not answer; instead, he tightened his laces. Hard, she noticed.

'Bjørn called, he was asking after you,' she remembered. 'He's a nice boy, I think. You're still friends with him, aren't you?'

'Yes, of course,' Tomme said. 'But he doesn't know about cars. And neither does Helge.'

'No, no. But Willy is so much older than you. Surely it would better for you to be with friends of your own age?'

'I am,' he argued. 'But I need help with the car. Willy has a garage. And tools.' He said this without getting up. He even tied his laces into a double knot. His fingers were trembling. Ruth noticed this and felt troubled. A sudden sensation that this tender eighteen-year-old boy was someone she hardly knew. It was distressing. When he finally got up he continued to face away from her. He was fumbling among the hangers, looking for his coat.

'Tomme,' she said, this time more affectionately. 'I know it's a pain about the car. But Ida's gone missing. She might even be dead. I can't bear it that you get so upset about a dent in the car. It upsets me because it's wrong!'

Her outburst made him feel ill at ease. He wanted to get out of the door, but she grabbed his arm and forced him to turn around. She was astonished to see a tear in his eye.

'Tomme,' she said, frightened. 'What is it?'

He wiped his cheek quickly. 'Oh, lots of things,' he said. 'This business with Ida. It's not that I'm not thinking about it. They're out looking for her today, but I don't know if I can handle going with them.'

'You thought it was that awful?' Ruth whispered.

Tomme nodded. 'Every time you lift a branch, your heart skips a beat,' he said.

60

Then he was gone. She stood in the hallway listening to him leave. His footsteps were rapid as if he was running. Ruth slumped against the wall. Everything is horrible, she thought. We won't survive this.

CHAPTER 5

Emil Johannes was on the road on his three-wheeler as usual. The weather was milder and the green paintwork gleamed in the September sun. People he passed turned to stare at his vehicle. It was very unusual and odd-looking. On his back he carried an old grey rucksack. The expression on his face was closed and distant, and he was unable to relax. He had a lot on his mind. He kept a steady speed, just below forty. The flaps on his leather cap were down and the strings knotted underneath his chin. The truck body was empty and the black tarpaulin rolled up like a sausage and tied with string. Emil was going shopping. He always shopped at The Joker, because it was a small local shop and he knew where everything was kept. Not that he was incapable of looking until he found what he wanted. But this was easier. It was always the same girl at the checkout. She had got used to the fact that he never spoke and she never embarrassed him. He liked that everything was the same. And it meant that he avoided the traffic in town.

Emil lived at the end of Brenneriveien. Past the

racecourse and up towards the ridge, in a bungalow with a kitchen, a living room and one bedroom. The house had a basement. He did not have a bathroom, but a nice loo with a sink and a mirror. The house was clean and fairly tidy. Not because Emil was tidy, but because his seventy-three-year-old mother turned up every week to clean it. Emil's appearance was a little disturbing and depended on the mood he was in. What people saw was a heavy, broad and slow man who could not speak. A man who would turn away if anyone stared at him, who would walk off immediately if anyone spoke to him. Still, he took an interest in people, especially when he could watch them from a safe distance.

There was a lot of gossip about Emil's speech. Some thought that he was quite simply mute. Others that he had stopped speaking in protest at some dreadful trauma he had been subjected to in his childhood. From time to time the rumours flared up. There was talk of a fire in which his father and a multitude of siblings had perished while Emil and his mother, barefoot in the snow, listened to their terrified screams. The truth was that Emil was an only child. Others claimed that he could talk the hind legs off a donkey if only he wanted to. But that he did not want to. He just wanted to be left in peace. No one ever wondered what thoughts and dreams might exist inside his enormous head. Most people assumed that not much went on in there. They could not have been more wrong. Emil thought of many strange things and every thought was an image. Sometimes they were still; at other times they would roll slowly like a film in his mind, or flash rapidly like lightning. Every time he parked outside The Joker he saw a row of cards spread out in a fan with the joker at the top. Sometimes the joker might wink at him or laugh scornfully. That would startle Emil and make him cross. When he entered the shop and smelled the bread, he visualised his mother's hands kneading dough. No one could knead dough like Emil's mother. It was bashed and thumped, but ultimately her sweaty, plump hands handled it lovingly. When he thought of his mother he recalled her smell and remembered something she had once said or a phrase she was fond of using. Her voice, sharp like a carving knife, the plastic smell of new playing cards, the dough; all this took up so much space. There was so much happening in his brain that there was no room for contact with others. He perceived any approach as an intrusion. He preferred the images. He could handle those.

It was his mother who took care of him, who made sure he had clean clothes and a clean home. Emil accepted that his mother came to his house, but at times she irritated him. She never stopped talking. He could hear her words and he understood them, but he felt that most of them were superfluous. The noise they made rolled towards him like waves and reminded him of the sound of heavy surf. When she started her torrential flow of words he closed up and looked stubborn. Not that this made her stop. She told him off, corrected him, ordered him about and made demands on him, but underneath it all she was very fond of him, and the truth was that she worried about him. She was scared that he might have an argument with someone, scared that he would frighten people with his appearance. He was never going to fit in and she had accepted that. She was also afraid that cruel people might want to harm him or force him into situations he could not control, because she knew the great forces hidden beneath his closed exterior. She had only seen it happen once. She had seen Emil go berserk in an insane and almost frenzied rage. It was a nightmare she managed to suppress most of the time, but it made itself known anyway, sometimes, in her dreams. Then she would wake up, drenched in sweat, terrified at the memory, at herself and her son. She was obsessed by the thought of what might happen if he were to become frightened again. Or if someone attacked him. At times her fear manifested itself as nagging.

'Do you have to go around wearing that stupid old cap?' she would say. 'Surely you could get yourself a new one? It would look so much better. I know you think your three-wheeler is the bee's knees, but you do realise that people stop and stare at you, don't you? Most people make do with two-wheeled motorbikes. It's not like there's anything wrong with your balance, either.'

She put on a martyred expression that was lost on her son. Afterwards she sank down in shame because she had tormented him like this, but she just could not help herself.

Emil parked the three-wheeler outside The Joker and went in. For a while he padded around the shelves on his wide splayed feet. He wore thick boots whether it was summer or winter. They were so worn that he could stick his feet into them without untying the laces. He carried the red shopping basket on one arm; he never did enough shopping to get a trolley. Today he was buying coffee, milk and cream, a granary loaf and some soft cheese. When he got to the checkout he added three newspapers. The checkout assistant noticed the papers. Emil had the local paper delivered and did not normally buy the national ones. However, he had started doing so in the last few days. But then again, so had most people, she thought. Ida Joner's disappearance affected everyone who came there to do their shopping. Everyone had their own views about what had happened, and the shop provided an opportunity to air them. She was keying in the prices when Emil remembered something important. He shuffled back towards the shelves and returned with a bag of monkey nuts. The checkout assistant frowned at the sight of them, she could not imagine why anyone would want to buy peanuts which had not been shelled, roasted and salted. Emil always bought monkey nuts. He was particularly sullen today, she thought. He never spoke to her, but he normally allowed himself plenty of time, as though the business of shopping was an important one, a ritual he enjoyed. This time he paid as fast as he could, his fingers trembling a little as he searched for change in his wallet. He stuffed his shopping into the old rucksack. Then he left without touching his cap as a goodbye. The door slammed behind him. She could see him through the window as he mounted his three-wheeler. How offhand he seemed today, she thought, and immediately wondered how she could think that, given that he had never exchanged a single word with her.

Emil started the engine. Once more he kept a steady pace and headed for the racecourse. As he approached Laila's Kiosk he spotted a police car and a couple of officers. Emil tightened like a coil. Clenched the handlebars and stared deliberately right ahead of him. One of the officers looked up and noticed the strange vehicle. Emil had never had any contact with the police, but he had a profound respect for anyone who wore a uniform. Besides, the condition of his vehicle was such that he really ought to have it serviced, but his only income was his incapacity benefit and he could not afford it. He often thought that sooner or later someone would turn up with a pair of pliers and remove the number plates. Fortunately the police were otherwise engaged. They were looking for this girl, Ida. He knew that and concentrated deeply so as not to distract them. He drove past them still staring rigidly ahead of him, but he sensed that he was being watched. Then he turned right. A few minutes later he took a left and reached Brenneriveien 12, where he lived. He parked and covered the vehicle with the black tarpaulin. His garage was full of junk; there was no longer any room for the three-wheeler.

He entered the house. In the kitchen he stopped and listened. Alert like a cat. He put down his rucksack on the table and took out his shopping. Opened the bag of monkey nuts and emptied a few into the palm of his hand. Softly he went into the living room. The door to the bedroom was ajar. He kicked it shut and stood for a while breathing heavily. The monkey nuts grew moist in his clenched fist. Finally he went over to the window. Emil kept a birdcage where a grey parrot the size of a pigeon sat on a perch. It began singing a pretty low tune to earn the monkey nuts. Emil stuck his fingers through the bars and dropped the nuts into the feeding tray. Immediately the bird ducked, grabbed a nut with its claw and sank its beak into it. A dry, cracking sound was heard as the nut split. At that moment the telephone rang.

It was his mother.

'Well,' she said. 'The thing is that I'm busy tomorrow and the day after, so we'd better do the cleaning today.'

Emil began chewing. But his mouth was empty and he had nothing to chew on.

'I can't stay long,' she went on. 'I've got my sewing circle at Tulla's tonight and I missed the last one, so I really want to go this evening. I'll start the washing machine for you and then you'll have to hang up the clothes yourself. You can manage that, can't you? Just make sure you reshape them before you hang them on the line, otherwise they get crumpled. And we both know you're not very good at ironing. I'm just about to wash my own floors, so I'll be with you in about an hour's time.'

'No,' Emil said, frightened.

He regarded his mother as a cleaning machine, and now she would want access to every corner of his house. He visualised splashing water, foaming soap and his mother's face slowly turning red. He recalled the strong smell of Ajax, the upset when the furniture was moved from its usual place, fresh air coming in from the windows, which she insisted on opening, the nasty draught, the unfamiliar smell of freshly washed bed linen. He imagined—

'You know I have to,' his mother insisted. 'We've talked about this.' Her voice started to quiver.

Emil kept breathing into the handset, did not want to hear what she was about to say.

'Have you had something to eat today?' she went on. She cared about him, she always had. 'You never eat properly. Have you heard about fruit and vegetables? I suspect you only ever eat bread, but your body needs more than that. You ought to buy some vitamins and take them during the autumn and winter, Emil. You can get them at Møller's. I'm sure they would have some at The Joker; if not, they'll order them for you. You just need to make an effort, you should take some responsibility for yourself, you know. It's not as if I'm getting any younger,' she banged on.

69

Emil threw a quick glance at the door to the bedroom. Then he looked at the clock.

'Have you washed yourself today?' she went on. 'God only knows how often you wash your hair. I don't suppose you do it properly either, standing there hunched over the sink. And anyway . . .' she droned on, not expecting an answer, 'do you dress up warm when you go out on the three-wheeler? It's autumn now, you've got to watch you don't catch the flu. If you're sick in bed, you'll be helpless: I can't come over every single day. I'm busy enough as it is. Margot Janson from next door is still confined to her chair by the window since she broke her hip. If it hadn't been for me, God only knows what she would have done. I wonder if anyone will be there for me the day I can't manage on my own. If only you had a wife, you would have some hope of a comfortable old age, but if it's true what people say, that we all get what we deserve, then I must have done something bad in my life that I don't even know about.'

She got ready to conclude her monologue. 'You can start by pulling the furniture away. Hang the rugs over the fence outside, so I can get going faster. I do hope the car will start,' she said anxiously. 'It was making noises yesterday; I wonder if perhaps the battery is run down. Do you have detergents and things like that to hand?'

'No!' Emil said. Once again he visualised his mother. She was like a hurricane now, a tornado. Her tirade blocked out all the thoughts she did not dare think; she swept them out of the way with words.

'I'll bring a bottle of Ajax,' she said. 'One day we'll go through your cupboards. You always forget to stock up on things. How many times have I been to see you and found there was no loo paper? I've lost count. After all, you're a grown man. Anyway, I've got to go now. Just make sure you get started and I'll be with you soon.'

'No!' Emil said. He said it louder this time.

His mother heard the rising intonation in his voice; it was unusual. He always said 'no' and he said it in many different ways, but this was bordering on something else. A kind of desperation. She frowned and pressed her lips together. She did not want any more problems, not a single one.

'Yes!' she said.

Ruth stuck her arms into the sleeves of her coat. On hearing the slam of a car door she stopped. With one hand still in the coat sleeve, she pushed down the handle and opened the door. A very tall man with grey hair was walking across the drive. Ruth recognised him straight away. He stopped at the foot of the steps, bowed, then walked up the steps to her. She finished putting on her coat and held out her hand. He was so tall that she felt like a little girl. She almost wanted to curtsey.

'I've just been to see Helga,' Sejer said.

'I'm on my way there now,' she said quickly.

'Could I have a word?'

'Of course.'

71

She pulled off her coat. Led him into the kitchen. There was an L-shaped bench with cushions.

'Now about Ida,' Ruth said despondently. 'I don't suppose there are that many options left?' She stared at him with frightened eyes. 'Helga is losing hope,' she groaned. 'I don't know what will become of us if the worst has happened. It will be the death of her. She only lives for that child. Ever since Anders moved out.'

Sejer listened while Ruth talked. She spoke rapidly because she was so worried.

'It's not good to be on your own with a child,' she said, bustling around the kitchen but not actually doing anything. 'Children shouldn't become your whole life, it's too much for them to bear. I can't begin to imagine what Helga's going to do the day Ida becomes a teenager and goes out all the time.' She blinked, confused by her own leap of thought.

'Can you tell me why Helga got divorced?' Sejer asked.

Ruth looked at him wide-eyed. 'Why do you want to know about that?' she asked, baffled.

He smiled quickly. 'I don't really know myself. But I ask all sorts of questions.'

He said it so simply, his eyes downcast as if he was genuinely tormented by this. It made her want to help him.

'But surely their divorce has nothing to do with Ida going missing?' She frowned.

Sejer looked at her. 'No, we don't think so either. I'm just being curious. Is it hard to talk about?'

72

She hesitated. 'Well, I don't really know.' She placed her hands on the table, as if she wanted to prove to him that they were clean, metaphorically speaking.

'So,' he said. 'What can you tell me about the break-up between Helga and Anders Joner? You're her sister. You're close, aren't you?'

She nodded without looking at him. 'I don't know the whole story,' she said evasively, 'but I think there was another woman. Anders had a one-night stand and Helga couldn't handle it. She threw him out. Anders is ten years younger than her,' she continued. 'And don't get me wrong. He is a good man, not the kind who sleeps around. But it happened this one time and Helga couldn't deal with it. She's so, well, how shall I put it, so principled. So rigid.'

'Did she give you any details?'

Ruth looked away and ended up staring at the valance above the window. 'She did. But I don't feel it's for me to tell you. It wouldn't help you either.'

He accepted this and nodded. 'Helga says that Ida is very fond of both you and your husband, Sverre?'

Ruth could picture Ida once more, a quick shiny flash of a living, breathing girl, here, in her own kitchen. Then she blinked and the image vanished. 'We're used to her coming here.' She nodded. 'It's so quiet when she's not around. She is the kind of child who attracts a lot of attention. She has several other aunts and uncles, but she never visits them.'

'Is there any particular reason why she doesn't see them?' Sejer asked cautiously.

'That's just how it is, I guess. Anders' brothers have never shown any interest in Helga and Ida. They're busy with their own families. Or perhaps they just don't have anything in common. They live a bit further away than we do.'

'Do you work?' he wanted to know.

'I do a few hours' supply teaching at Glassverket school,' she said. 'When someone's ill and so on. Otherwise I'm at home.'

'Your daughter, Marion, how old is she?'

'Twelve,' Ruth said. 'She's in Year Seven. She spends a lot of time with Ida. This is very difficult for her; I don't know what to tell her. But she reads the papers and watches the news. It's impossible to keep anything from her.'

'You have nothing to keep from her,' he said. 'We don't know what's happened.'

Again she was puzzled by the neutral way in which he expressed himself, since she was convinced that Ida was dead. And not only dead, but killed in some horrific way. The worst one of all, in unimaginable pain and fear.

'How about your son, Tom Erik?' he asked.

When he mentioned her son, she frowned. 'Well, what about him?' she said.

'How is he handling it?'

She shook her head forlornly. 'Badly,' she admitted. 'He never really talks about his feelings. At least Marion and I are trying. Tomme took part in the search yesterday and said it was awful. I must admit that I often think of him as a rather selfish boy.

He cares mostly about himself. The other day he dented his car.' She smiled. 'His reaction was out of all proportion. He's only had it for three weeks,' she added. 'And I stood there listening to him whining about it when there are much more important things going on, so I gave him a piece of my mind,' she concluded. She had talked herself warm; her cheeks were flushed.

'Does he work?' Sejer wanted to know.

'He's just started his last year at sixth-form college. He's not enjoying it and is unlikely to go on to higher education. He just wants a job and a salary, to keep his car and see his friends. He spends a lot a time in front of his computer. Or watching videos. That's all right with me,' she said. 'I'm not particularly ambitious on my kids' behalf. I just want them to be happy.'

'He was involved in an accident,' Sejer said. 'On the first of September? If I understood you correctly?'

'Yes,' she said. 'He drove off early that evening and didn't come home until later that night. He was really upset, poor boy. You know how it is with boys and their cars. But I certainly made it quite clear to him that a dented car is nothing compared to what can happen to people.'

'You said "early that evening". Do you remember when?'

She frowned. 'Just after six. He called out from the hallway. The evening news was just starting and I usually watch it.'

'And where was he going?'

'He spends a great deal of time with a boy called Bjørn. I think that's where he was going,' she said. 'He lives at Frydenlund.'

'I'd like to have a word with your son,' Sejer said. 'He might have seen something along the road. He's at college today?' he continued.

'No,' she said. 'He's spending the day with Willy. Another friend. Or rather they used to be friends. I'm not all that keen on him and I've told Tomme that. However, Willy's good with cars. They're trying to repair the damage.'

Sejer was curious. 'Why aren't you all that keen on him?'

'Willy is four years older,' Ruth said. 'I think he might have nicked a car, or maybe done something even worse. So I'm not happy about it. True, it was a long time ago. But it's so important to Tomme to get the car mended.'

'Sverre, your husband,' Sejer said. 'Helga says he travels a great deal?'

'He's in Stavanger right now,' she said. 'But he'll be here at the weekend. Normally I don't have a problem with him being away, we don't need to spend every single moment together, and the kids are older and can take care of themselves. But right now it's hard. With everything that's happened. We call each other every evening.'

'About Willy,' Sejer said. 'Does he live nearby?'

'Further towards Glassverket. Willy Oterhals. I think he lives on Meieriveien, it's a large yellow house with a big garage. He lives with his mother.'

'You said he was older. Does he have a job?'

'He works at the bowling alley. Or he used to. Sometimes he does shifts at the Shell petrol station next door to it. He has access to tools there, you see. He's not a trained mechanic, but he knows a bit.'

Ruth was surprised at Sejer's interest in her son's friend. She glanced at her watch and exclaimed: 'I've got to get going. Helga is expecting me!'

'I've kept you a long time,' Sejer said. 'I didn't mean to.'

This was followed once again by that brief bow of his. His manner made an impression on her. Everything about him was so calm and assured. Together they left the house. Ruth opened the garage door. Sejer looked at the white Volvo and the empty space next to it. At the far end of the wall stood four tyres, snow tyres most likely, which would soon need to be fitted. Various bits of junk, a few boxes on the shelves. Right by the door lay four worn rubber mats. Opel, he thought. Her son drives an Opel.

Why do I talk so much? Ruth wondered.

CHAPTER 6

Willy Oterhals was sweating. A work lamp dangled from a beam in the roof and the heat from the strong bulb roasted his scalp. He had scraped away a large area of the paintwork with a pocket knife and the grey metal shone through. It was some dent. Retouching the paintwork would be the hardest bit. Willy felt optimistic, but he was in need of a break. He manoeuvred himself up on to the worktop and lit a cigarette. His eyes were deep set, so when he lowered his head they seemed like two black holes in his gaunt face. His gaze wandered along the walls of the garage, took in the shelves with their packets of nails, boxes of screws and nuts, spark plugs, oil and various tools. Up against the rear wall stood an old apothecary's chest with hundreds of tiny drawers. No one apart from Willy knew what the drawers contained. If anyone were to look they would find nothing but small boxes and jars. But one thing was certain. The contents of some of the boxes would fetch a lot of money on the street.

Willy inhaled the smoke and his eyes narrowed

while he thought. Then he heard the sound of car tyres on the gravel. A tall grey-haired man appeared. Willy was ever vigilant and he was immediately on his guard. He managed to feign a look of surprise just as Sejer appeared, towering in the entrance to the garage. Willy saw him as a clearly outlined silhouette. There was something familiar about the feeling Sejer evoked in him, and he quickly tried to work out what it was. For a while the man stood there without saying a word. But he stared at the black Opel with interest, at the tools spread out on the floor and finally at Willy.

'Oterhals?' he said politely.

Willy nodded. A muscle contracted in his stomach. The man standing in the entrance watching him was nearly two metres tall and he was a police officer. Willy was quite sure of it.

'You fix cars?' Sejer asked with interest.

'Not really.' Willy shrugged. 'This is purely cosmetic.'

Sejer walked a few steps closer. He inspected the dent. 'I'm a police officer,' he said. 'Could I speak to Tom Erik Rix, please?' He met Willy's gaze. At the same time he pulled his badge out of his pocket.

'He's not here,' Willy said quickly. He leapt down from the worktop and stood with his arms folded across his chest.

'Do you know where he is?' Sejer asked.

Willy resisted the temptation to look out on to the drive. Tomme had gone to the kiosk. He could be back any second.

'He'll turn up, I guess. But I don't know when. What do you want to talk to Tomme for?' he said.

'I'm sure you've heard about his cousin.'

'Christ, yeah.'

'I just wanted a quick word. Did you take part in the search?' Sejer asked.

'No. But Tomme did.' Willy took a few steps across the floor, his hands deep in his pockets.

'You had an accident?' Sejer continued, changing the subject; he stared at the black Opel.

'That's not my car,' Willy said abruptly. 'I'm a good driver and I don't have accidents. It's Tomme's. He ran into a crash barrier by the bridge in town. Just got his licence.' He sighed and tried out a knowing smile. He had been driving for fours years now and he considered himself to be an excellent driver.

'A newly qualified driver is no laughing matter.' Sejer nodded. 'However, we should be grateful that he only hit the crash barrier. And not something else.'

'Christ, yeah,' Willy repeated. He let the cigarette fall to the floor. A number of thoughts raced through his head. Was this a coincidence? A cop right inside his own garage. Had someone been talking? He felt dizzy and had to lean against the wall. He wanted to wipe the sweat off his brow, but managed to suppress his reflexes at the last minute.

'Lucky for Tomme that you're good with cars,' Sejer said.

Willy nodded. He was starting to panic. Tomme could pull up outside at any moment, driving Willy's Scorpio, with two bottles of Coke and a packet of cigarettes. He did not know where to look. Could not look into Sejer's scrutinising grey eyes, or at the apothecary's chest, or at Tomme's dented Opel. He ended up staring at the floor.

Sejer took one step forward towards the Opel and peered inside. Then he walked around the car. 'A tough car, the old Opel,' he said with authority.

Willy nodded.

'Well, I'll catch Tomme some other time,' Sejer said. Then he looked over his shoulder, towards the rear wall of the garage.

'By the way, that's a nice chest. You keep nuts and bolts in it?'

Willy nodded indifferently, but his heart was beating wildly inside the boiler suit. Now he's going to pull out one of the drawers, he thought; now he'll start rummaging around. He knows who I am. It's all on the computer. All he needs to do is enter my name and everything will be there. They were mostly petty crimes, but Willy was sweating. However, Sejer appeared to be satisfied. He left the garage. A car door slammed. Willy stood still as if glued to the floor, listening to the engine noise coming from the big Volvo. Then it drove off and disappeared out through the gate. He was still standing, trying to get his nerves back under control, when he heard the sound of another car outside. It was his own Scorpio. Tomme walked in with a bag.

'Who was that?' He looked at Willy suspiciously. Willy had to think on his feet. It was a question of keeping Tomme calm.

'Give me some Coke,' he said. 'I'm fucking parched.'

Tomme handed him a bottle and opened one for himself.

'He was from the police,' Willy said slowly.

Tomme paled. 'What?'

Willy looked away from Tomme, a quick glance that finally settled on the floor. 'He was looking for you. Christ, I nearly had a heart attack. He kept staring at the chest.'

'The chest?' Tomme said blankly.

'It contains a bit of everything. If you get my drift,' Willy said.

'But what did he want with me?' Tomme said anxiously.

'For God's sake, you're her cousin. Of course they want to talk to you.' Willy downed half the Coke in one gulp. 'Hey, take it easy. Let's get to work,' he said harshly.

CHAPTER 7

Elsa Marie Mork was born in 1929 and she still had her driving licence. Her eyes were tested every year and she always passed with flying colours. She was eagle-eyed. She did not miss a thing, not a speck of dust, nothing. Her hearing, though, was not good. However, as she rarely listened to anything anyone had to say, she hardly noticed. She placed an assortment of cleaning materials in a box in the boot of her car and headed for her son's house. This son, she thought, who was beyond hope. When she was young she had wanted a daughter, maybe two, and finally a son to complete her family, but that was not how it had turned out. Just one angry, grunting boy. His father had died when Emil Johannes was seven years old. The shock of becoming a mother to a child she did not understand had stopped her from finding a new husband or having any more children. But he was hers. She was not the type to shy away from her duties. She did not want people thinking she was irresponsible. So she went to Emil's house every single week and took care of him. His furniture and his clothes. She created distance between them by talking

83

incessantly while keeping her gaze ten centimetres above his heavy head. He never replied anyway.

Now she was thinking about their telephone conversation. He was upset about something, and as she pulled out on to the highway, a feeling of anxiety crept up on her. Since she detested any feelings resembling sentimentality, her anxiety turned to anger. If Emil had got himself into trouble, she would force him to confess to her whatever it was and then she would clear it up. For more than forty years she had been waiting for something to happen. So she braced herself. She hated tears, despair and grief, everything that turned sensible adults into soppy, pathetic creatures incapable of action. Whenever it happened she lost her confidence. Her heart was encased in a hard shell, but it still beat with compassion on the inside even when her eyes were bone dry. She hoped for nothing in this world, nothing at all, except death. She had friends, but she was not close to them. They were her audience when she needed to have a good moan and she allowed herself to be used for the same in return. Occasionally she would laugh, but mostly at the misfortune of others. She was happy to help others, such as her neighbour, Margot, who had broken her hip, but she always did so with a martyred air. Nevertheless, when she finally went to bed at night, she would lie awake worrying about everyone who could not manage as well as she could. Unable to sleep she would agonise over Margot's hip and the pain it caused her.

Now Emil was troubling her. He had said 'no'. That was all he ever said, but she knew him well enough to suspect that something had happened. Deep down she believed that her son was able to speak, but that he just did not want to. She had never said it out loud to anyone; no one would believe her anyway, and she regarded it as a personal insult that he had chosen silence. She was less concerned with whether or not he was backward. She no longer had the strength to speculate about him. He was Emil Johannes and she was used to him. She reminded herself that in a few years she might very well be dead and Emil would be pottering about the house while everything grew wild around him. In her mind she could see grass and dandelions creeping up between the floorboards in his kitchen. Perhaps the council would allocate him some home help. If anyone dared be around this gruff creature.

She shuddered and realised that they were already in September and all the windows would need a thorough clean before the frost set in. Or she could just add a dash of white spirit to the soapy water. Elsa always had a solution to things like that. She pulled up in front of the house and got out of the car. Opened the boot and lifted out the plastic box. Then she slammed the boot hard and went over to Emil's front door. It was locked. A bolt of irritation went through her tough body and she started knocking on the window so forcefully that the glass nearly shattered.

'Come on, Emil!' she shouted angrily. 'I haven't got time for games today. You're not the only one on my list!'

The house was deadly silent. She listened and knocked on the locked door a few more times. At this point it was purely anger that propelled her as she plonked the plastic box on the steps and went back to her car. He could sulk all he wanted to, she was one step ahead of him. She had her own key to her son's house, obviously. It was in the glove compartment and she fetched it. Resolutely she put the key in the lock. Or rather halfway in. Something was blocking the keyhole. Stunned by this, she remained on the top step while she pushed the key as hard as she could. It would still not go in. At the same time it was difficult to pull it back out again. What on earth was he up to? He had shoved something in the hole; the key was stuck in some-thing viscous. Her face turned red with anger, and fear began its journey through her body. It spread from her abdomen and sooner or later it would reach her fossilised heart. She stepped down, emptied the box of cleaning materials and placed it below the kitchen window. Then she climbed up on to it. The kitchen was deserted. But the light was on. She moved the box to his bedroom window. The curtains were drawn. There was not so much as a tiny gap for her to peer through. She returned to the door and took a look at the three-wheeler. It was covered by the tarpaulin as usual. So he was home. Emil never ventured out on foot. He did not feel safe walking; he felt exposed. People might stop him and say something to him or ask him questions. For the third and last time she banged on the door. Finally she gave up. She left the box and got into the car, where she began sounding the horn. Then she remembered that Emil had neighbours and she was afraid that the noise might attract their attention. She stared at the kitchen curtains, but there was no sign of her son. Elsa's patience was exhausted. She got out of the car and walked over to the garage. She looked for tools, but found nothing suitable. So she drove home, stomped back inside her own house and went over to the telephone.

Just as she heard the dialling tone her chest tightened. It ached fiercely. Perhaps he had fallen down the stairs to the basement. Perhaps he was lying on the floor down there, unconscious. He was very heavy. No, this is nonsense, she thought. Something is stuck in the keyhole. He is keeping me out on purpose. Then the telephone was picked up. He never said anything, simply lifted the handset so her flow of words could begin. No one else ever called Emil.

When he picked up she felt relief wash over her like warm water. Then her rage took over and she was on familiar territory once again. She almost threatened him. She needed to clean! 'You must understand that, Emil!'

Dust and fluff, scum round the sink, crumbs on the floor: they were like demons; they clawed her and she would find no peace until she had got rid of them. She could not sleep at night if his windows were filthy. She could not think clearly if his sofa was covered with broken bits of crisps.

'Now you open that door!' she shouted down the receiver. 'I'm not playing this game with you! If it weren't for me you'd be in a home. Go remove that stuff you've put in the keyhole. I'm leaving now. I'll be on your doorstep in five minutes and you'll let me in!'

'No!' Emil screamed. He hung up. Elsa stood for a while listening to the silence. Then she marched across the floor and out into the hallway. Her sturdy shoes banged on the parquet flooring. It was vital to keep going, don't ever stop to think. Keep busy, keep busy! Get things done, her inner voice told her. Keep going, just keep going all the way to the bitter end; that is where we are all heading.

She found a crowbar in her garage. Then she drove back to Emil's house. Now she was hunched on the top step holding a hammer in one hand and the crowbar in the other. She forced the crowbar in between the door and the frame and started driving it in with the hammer. Elsa was very strong and the woodwork was old and dry. Once the crowbar was a few centimetres in, she started twisting and bending it. Sweat was pouring down her. She wondered if any of the neighbours could see her. It troubled her that they might be watching, but she could not stop. Now she could hear her son inside; he was pacing up and down slamming doors. Her head was throbbing. Suddenly the frame gave a loud crack. The door swung open. She let go of the crow-bar, which landed on the steps with a harsh, clanging sound. Then she went inside.

Emil was standing in the kitchen, his arms hanging down loosely. She tried to interpret the expression on his face, but failed. For her part she was silent. This did not happen often. For a long time they stared at each other.

'Tell me what's going on,' she said, strangely subdued.

Emil turned his back on her. He went over to the worktop and found a bag of monkey nuts. Took one out and snapped it in half. Stood for a while staring at its contents. His mother took a step forward. She snatched the bag from his hands and put it back on the worktop.

'I know something has happened,' she said, louder now. She spun around and went into the living room. She stopped abruptly, baffled.

'What on earth . . .' she exclaimed. 'Are you sleeping on the sofa now? And this place hasn't been aired for days.'

Her eyes flickered round the room and her pale irises glowered with disgust. 'It stinks,' she said. 'You can't leave leftovers in the bin, you've got to empty it every single day or it'll start to smell in just a few hours. How many times have I told you? It'll attract flies too if you don't watch it! And the mess that bird's making! You must hoover underneath his cage at least once a day. When did you last replace the newspapers at the bottom of the cage? Is that where that smell is coming from?'

Then she stared at the door to his bedroom. She did not know why, but she felt compelled to move towards it. Towards this door. One step at a time. Her eyes flashed between the duvet on the sofa and the bedroom door. Emil followed her, his eyes blinking. For a moment she stood by the door, listening. There was not a sound to be heard. She pushed down the door handle. The door would not open. She felt like retching. Her fear grew stronger. It was this smell, so pervasive and strange, so nauseating and sweet. She pushed her fears aside and worked up her rage instead. Went back outside, got the crowbar from the steps and marched back in. Emil pressed himself up against the wall. He was scared too. She resumed twisting, hitting and hammering. Emil's heavy body jerked with every stroke. This door was harder to force than the front door. The resistance of the woodwork drove her insane. Emil ducked. When the door finally sprang open with a crack, he closed his eyes and covered his ears with his hands. Elsa Marie went into the bedroom. Then she stopped, petrified.

CHAPTER 8

The search for Ida Joner was continuing with full force. Of course they would find her. A child did not just vanish into thin air. A child would have to be placed somewhere, hidden completely or partly. Somewhere in the vicinity of where she lived. They kept enlarging the search area, and the search parties found and bagged the strangest items. Later the police would decide what was important. People who hardly knew each other began talking. Ida's disappearance was like a net and it drew them all in. The feeling was both pleasant and scary. They were united in something. At the same time there was one person who knew the truth. They imagined it was a man, maybe two. They believed the worst-case scenario was that he would turn out to be someone they knew. But sick, obviously. Perverted and dangerous. Perhaps he was out looking for another child. Sometimes they felt intense anger; at other times they were overcome by fear. But most of all it had given them something new to talk about. They were no longer talking about the weather or politics. Now the only topic was the identity of Ida's killer. The adults tried to lower their voices whenever children were near but did not always succeed. They were obsessed by it and so were the radio, the television and the newspapers. When the children were at school their teachers took up where their parents had left off. They could not escape it and they did not want to either. They could barely remember what their lives had been like before Ida's disappearance; it had hit their community like a violent earthquake.

Marion Rix was having breakfast. She stuck her spoon in the jam jar and stirred the raspberries carefully. Everything was happening in slow motion. Her thoughts were elsewhere, the spoon stirred itself. Ruth saw her bowed head and felt a dull pain inside. What could she say? How much could Marion cope with? But I don't know anything, she remembered. I don't know what's happened to Ida. All the same, she could not act as if nothing had happened. It was important to talk about things. And Ruth knew the words. She was just scared of using them.

Marion sensed her mother's stare. She was finally satisfied with the consistency of the raspberry jam. Why won't she look at me? Ruth thought. Why are we so afraid to talk? We should be screaming, lashing out, we should be clinging to each other. Holding on to this one thought, that you and I, we still have each other. And that you must not take that for granted, ever. Was this what Marion was thinking? That it had happened to Ida, so it could happen to her?

92

Marion chewed slowly and washed the bread down with milk. She was a chubby girl with dark hair, not fragile or skinny like Tomme. She actually looked a lot like Helga. Ruth studied her daughter's face. Her fringe fell in soft waves either side of her pale forehead. She had a lazy eye, which caused her to squint slightly. She did not want to wear glasses.

'So, Marion,' Ruth began. 'Do you talk a lot about Ida at school?'

Her daughter stopped munching. 'Not so much now,' she said quietly.

'But you're thinking about it?'

Marion nodded down towards the table.

'And your teachers. What are they saying?'

'Some talk about it a lot. Others say nothing at all.'

'But what do you think? Would you like to talk about Ida? Or would you rather not? If you could choose?'

Marion considered this. Her face coloured with embarrassment. 'Don't know,' she said.

'But if I were to ask you what you think?' Ruth said. 'About what's happened? What would you say?'

Marion was silent for a long time. Ruth was almost afraid to breathe for fear that her daughter would censor herself.

'I think she's dead,' Marion said quietly. She sounded so guilty that Ruth winced.

'So do I,' she said.

Finally it had been said out loud. What everyone

was thinking. Everyone except Helga, Ruth thought. Helga had to keep hoping, or her body would explode and all her bones would splinter. Her blood would stop flowing and her lungs would no longer breathe. Her broken body would hit the ground like a sack of bricks. Ruth gasped at her own imagination. She could see it so clearly and felt she had to hug herself tightly in order to keep all her own organs in place. She feared that they would come loose and roll around inside her. Only her heart would stay put and beat heavily.

'I feel really bad about it,' Marion said. 'Because it's almost like I've given up on her. And I haven't. It's just that so much time has passed! They've been looking everywhere!' She pushed her plate away and lowered her head. Her hair covered her face. 'But actually I haven't given up,' she said. 'At night when I go to bed, I haven't given up. But when I wake up and it's morning again and they still haven't found her, then I think she must be dead.'

'Yes,' Ruth said. 'We hope for a miracle while we are asleep. That someone will take over while we rest and fix it for us. But it doesn't happen.'

Marion reached for her plate again. Ruth looked at her chubby cheeks and wanted to burst with emotion. Her love for Marion was so deep that when she thought of Helga, she was consumed by despair. If she lost one child, she would still have one left. Now Helga had neither husband nor daughter. Just her own restless body.

'Tomme cries at night,' Marion said suddenly.

Ruth's eyes widened. What was she saying? Tomme, eighteen-year-old Tomme, crying in the night?

'Why does he do that?' she said without thinking.

Marion shrugged. 'I can hear him through the wall. But I don't like to ask.'

She ate the rest of her food and went to the bathroom to clean her teeth. Then she came back, put on her denim jacket and picked up her school bag. Ruth was still sitting at the table, wondering. Had she misunderstood her son completely? Was he in fact a sensitive soul hiding behind an air of indifference? She was probably not the first person to get it wrong. Yet something continued to irk her, though she did not know what it was. It existed in a place she could not access. Or she did not dare to. Just then she heard Tomme on the stairs. She got up quickly to hug Marion before she left. She always had to do that; this last touch meant the difference between life and death. If she forgot, she would lose Marion. She tried to understand the strange effect fear was having on her and decided to go easy on herself. These were exceptional circumstances.

'You'll stop by Helene's house, won't you?' she said.

Marion nodded.

'You must always go in twos. Don't ever forget that.'

'We won't,' Marion said earnestly.

'If one day Helene is ill, you'll come straight back again and I'll drive you. Do you understand?'

'Yes,' Marion said. 'Please can I go now?'

She disappeared. Grew smaller and smaller as she went down the road, as Ida had grown smaller and smaller as seen through the window in Helga's house. Tomme came out from the bathroom. Ruth went back to the kitchen worktop and busied herself with the breakfast things.

Tomme sat down without saying a word and grabbed the milk. Again he drank straight from the carton, but this time Ruth did not comment. Instead she opened the fridge and took out a packed lunch which she had carefully made for him the night before. He could buy something to drink at college. She did not like him drinking Coke with his food, but she chose to regard it as a minor issue. It was not the worst vice a young person could indulge in. So many temptations, so many challenges. Would he make friends? Would he get himself a girlfriend, a house and a job?

She placed the packed lunch next to him and nudged him affectionately on the shoulder. She wanted to find out more about what Marion had said, that he cried in the night. He did not react to her touch.

'Are you coming straight home from college?' she asked casually. As his car was at Willy's, he had to catch the bus to college and he hated that.

'Going to see Willy,' he said in the same casual tone of voice.

'Today as well? You've hardly been doing any homework.' She instantly regretted nagging him about his homework. On the whole he did well at college and she despised herself when she went on like this. Especially after everything that had happened.

'We need to get it finished,' he said. 'I don't know how I ever managed without a car.'

He put a lump of butter on his bread and then stopped. He started spreading the butter, but then tried to scrape it off.

'Did you call Bjørn like I told you to?' she asked.

He squirmed in his chair. 'I'm going to. But we need to finish the car first.'

'How about Helge?' she continued. 'Do you ever see him?'

'Yeah, yeah. Sometimes.'

'And the car?' she asked. 'Is it going to be all right?' To reach your children, Ruth thought, you have to take an interest in whatever is important to them, and the car was important to Tomme.

'The paintwork is the trickiest bit. Willy hasn't done that before.'

'Oh, I see.'

'Good thing it's black,' Tomme said. 'We need to get an exact match. Black is black.'

'It is.' She smiled, but because he did not raise his head to look at her, he missed her friendly response.

'At least you can console yourself with this: you've been taught a lesson. You'll drive for years now without any accidents. That kind of thing makes you careful. Your dad and I have both dented our cars. I managed it three times. Twice it was my fault,' she admitted.

He nodded and got up from the table. His slice of bread lay untouched.

'I know you're pleased that Willy can fix your car,' Ruth said. 'But I don't like you spending time with him.'

'I know,' Tomme said sullenly.

'It's not that I don't trust you. And I suppose it is a long time since he was in trouble with the police. But it's possible to choose your friends,' she said. 'And I'd rather you chose Bjørn. Or Helge.'

'Whatever,' he said irritably, pushing his chair back.

'So once the car's done, you can just drop him. Can't you?'

'Yes,' he mumbled. 'I guess I can.'

He grabbed his rucksack and went out into the hallway, a little too quickly, Ruth thought. She followed him. She wanted to ask him about what Marion had told her, but he was shutting her out. There was not even so much as a crack she could use to get to him. He took his coat down from the peg and slung it over his shoulder. Glanced quickly at the clock as if he was running late. But he wasn't.

Why don't I ask him? Ruth wondered. Why don't I keep him here and ask him? She realised what a coward she was and felt ashamed. Went back into the kitchen alone and stared out of the window. She saw Tomme's narrow back disappear through the gate. Everything was so difficult. Ida, she thought. Poor, poor Ida. Then she started to cry.

CHAPTER 9

Skarre took a sheet of paper from the printer. He was going to make a paper plane. He listened to the noise from the corridor. His head of department was talking to a reporter from TV2. No one could accuse Holthemann of using his personal charm or charisma to get to the top; he looked severely ill at ease in front of the camera, and to add to his discomfort he had little to say and was forced to fall back on stock phrases.

'Yes,' he said, 'we're treating this as a crime.'

'Does this mean that you've given up all hope of finding Ida alive?' asked the reporter, young and blonde, wearing a black oilskin jacket.

Holthemann clearly could not answer yes to this question, so he said the only thing he could: 'There's always hope.' But he did not look her in the eyes as he said it; instead he focused on the buttons on her jacket. There were three of them and they had an unusual pattern. 'The problem with this case,' he went on, trying to bring the interview to a close as quickly as possible so that he could return to his office, 'is that the number of leads is much lower than usual.'

The reporter was ready with her next question. 'And why do you think that is?'

Holthemann pondered briefly, then Skarre heard his dry voice once more. 'It certainly isn't because the public don't care about this case. Because they do. But no one seems to have actually seen Ida, so we have few leads to follow up.'

He looked more and more reluctant to remain in front of the camera, and the reporter rushed to get through all the questions on her pad.

'Do you have any real leads at all, or any theories as to what might have happened to Ida Joner?' she asked.

'Of course we have our theories,' Holthemann said, addressing her buttons once more, 'but unfortunately we have to admit that this is a case with very few leads.' He paused. Then he concluded the whole charade by saying in his most authoritative voice: 'I'm afraid that's all I have to say for the time being.'

Finally he managed to escape back into his office. Skarre continued folding his paper plane. He knew that Sejer was just as reluctant to talk to the press. However, he also knew that Sejer would have made a different impression. He would have looked the reporter straight in the eyes and his voice would have been firm and assured. He also had such presence, such dedication to his work, that anyone watching the news would feel that the case was in a safe pair of hands. People would see his face and would be able to tell from his steady voice that he was deeply and personally committed. As though he was saying to them: I'm taking responsibility for this case. I will find out what happened.

Skarre had always been a dab hand at making paper planes. But today he was struggling. The paper was too thick, his fingers too big and his nails too short. His folds were not sharp enough. He scrunched up the paper and began again. As he picked up a fresh sheet, it slipped from his grasp and fluttered in the air. His hands were shaking. At that very moment Sejer arrived. He threw a long glance at the reporter and her cameraman, who were just going into the lift.

'I was at a party last night,' Skarre mumbled by way of explanation, because Sejer had spotted a box of paracetamol and a bottle of Coke on his desk.

'Late night, was it?' Sejer asked, indicating the white sheet which Skarre was still trying to catch.

'That's one way of putting it,' Skarre said, attempting a brave smile. 'I ended up jailing one of the guests.'

Sejer frowned. 'But you weren't on duty?'

Skarre continued folding. Suddenly it was vital for him to make the perfect paper plane. 'Do you do what I do?' he asked. 'Leave it for as long as possible before telling people what you do for a living? I mean, socially. At parties and so on?'

'I don't go out much,' Sejer said. 'But I know what you mean.'

Skarre was busy with the paper. 'There was this guy at the party who was just so full of himself.

101

Knew the answer to everything. When I told him I worked here, it was like winding him up and watching him go. He just would not shut up. He was particularly incensed about Norwegian prisons. I've heard it all before and normally I don't get involved. But I just couldn't resist the urge to get my own back with this one.' He turned the paper over and continued folding. 'He was banging on about luxury prisons with showers and central heating and libraries and cinemas and a computer in every cell. About famous bands performing for prisoners, and psychologists and all the other staff who pander to the inmates' every need. About gyms and days out and leave to visit families. It was a never-ending list of perks that he felt no law-abiding, hard-working citizen had access to. In short: he didn't think that staying in such a hotel and getting three meals a day constituted much of a punishment.'

'So you jailed him?' Sejer said. He suppressed a smile. He had grown out of this stage a long time ago.

'The party was at one of my friends' in Frydenlund,' Skarre explained. 'He lives in an apartment block there. He's married with a little boy. Because of the party, the boy was at his grandparents'. His bedroom was empty. Let's play a game, I suggested to this idiot. I'm sentencing you to six years' imprisonment. And you'll spend those years in eight square metres. He thought the whole thing was a laugh. Grabbed his brandy and his belongings and wanted to start right away. I had to remind him that alcohol is not allowed in prison. He did accept that, so he put his glass down and off we went to the boy's bedroom. I guess the room was approximately eight square metres so it was about the right size. I asked for a key to the room and they gave it to me. Then, laughing and joking, we shoved the guy in there. Of course he had no idea what lay in store for him. There was a bunk bed in the room, a small TV, a bookshelf, some comics, a CD player and some CDs. Then we locked the door.' Skarre smiled smugly and discarded another sheet.

'Well?' Sejer said.

'The rest of us carried on having a good time,' Skarre said. He had started a new plane. 'But it didn't take long before he began to make a fuss in there. We were on the second floor,' he added, 'so he couldn't jump out of the window. We let him shout for as long as we could be bothered to listen to him. Then I went to the door and asked him what he wanted. He said he'd had enough of this stupid game!' Skarre smiled contentedly at the memory. 'So you think it a bit claustrophobic in there? I called out. Yes, he admitted that. You still have six years left, I said, but that's all right. You've only done twenty minutes. And you're freaking out already. We heard some bumping noises in there and got a bit worried. I told him not to fight it, that it would only make it harder. Just accept it, I said. Accept you'll be doing time. Then you'll start to feel better. It went totally quiet in there so we unlocked the door. I've never seen anyone look so grumpy.'

'And you think a stunt like this is good PR for the force?' Sejer asked.

'I do,' Skarre said. 'But you know, he hadn't even realised that the police and the prison service are two entirely different bodies.'

'An F-16,' he said, finally, holding up a finished plane.

'It looks more like a Hercules,' Sejer said.

Skarre launched the plane. It flew off in a surprisingly elegant curve and landed smoothly on the floor.

'By the way, what did you want?' he asked, looking at Sejer.

'I want you to talk to Ida's cousin,' Sejer said. 'Tom Erik Rix.'

Skarre got up to retrieve the plane. There was dust from the floor on its belly. 'Do you think it's worth it?'

'Probably not,' Sejer admitted. 'But Willy Oterhals got very nervous indeed when I showed up at his garage. I'm asking myself why. I'm probably on a wild goose chase here, but Tomme left the house in Madseberget around six p.m. on September first. According to his mother, he was going to see his friend Bjørn, who lives in the centre of town. In order to get to Bjørn's house he would have had to drive the same route as Ida was cycling. He could have seen something. As for Willy Oterhals, he has a record. A suspended sentence for taking a vehicle without consent in 1998. He was also suspected of using and supplying drugs, but he was never charged. He drives a large Scorpio and works at Mestern bowling alley. I don't think Oterhals can afford a car like that on his wages. It's possible he's got an additional source of income.'

'Should we really be wasting our time on him when we could be looking for Ida Joner?'

'Until she's found, we might as well spend our time on minor cases such as this one. Tomme goes to St Hallvard's sixth-form college. He's studying electronics. So if you're not feeling too wasted, I'd like you to go and have a word with him.'

Skarre parked in a bay marked for visitors. There was a swimming pool on his left. The smell of chlorine stung his nose and brought back memories from his own school days. The college was made up of several brown wooden pavilions, but Tomme Rix was in the main building. The door to his classroom was opened by a tall, lanky guy in jeans. Skarre's uniform startled him.

'Tom Erik Rix?' Skarre said.

The guy called out into the classroom. You could tell from his expression that he knew what had happened, that he knew Tomme was related to Ida Joner. Shortly afterwards Tomme appeared. His face turned pale.

'I need to have a word with you,' Skarre said. 'Let's go sit in my car. It'll only take a minute.'

A flustered Tomme followed him. He plunged his fists deep into his pockets and got in the car, almost reluctantly. His frightened eyes flickered across the equipment on the dashboard. Skarre rolled down a window and lit up a cigarette.

'You're related to Ida,' he said. 'And you live in the same neighbourhood. Besides, you spend a lot of time on the roads.'

A number of thoughts went through Tomme's mind. He was her cousin. Now he thought the term 'cousin' sounded suspect, that their kinship would be used against him.

'You were on the road on the first of September, too,' Skarre said. 'You drove from Madseberget towards Glassverket around six that evening.'

Pause. Tomme felt he had to answer yes. He thought it sounded like a confession.

'To visit a friend?' Skarre said.

'Yes,' Tomme said.

'What's his name?'

Tomme had no idea why Skarre wanted to know this. Still, it was best to answer. It was not as if it was a big secret. Nevertheless, he was baffled by all the things they wanted to know.

'His name's Bjørn,' he said eventually. 'Bjørn Myhre.'

'I see,' Skarre said. He pulled a notepad from the pocket of his jacket and wrote down the name.

'Would you say you're alert?' he asked.

'No idea,' Tomme mumbled. He stared at a point on the dashboard approximately where the airbag was stored. He wished it would inflate at that very moment. A big ball right in his face, hiding him completely.

'So if I ask you what you saw on your journey, what do you recall?'

Tomme searched his memory, but remained silent.

'Everyone who was in that area on the first of September has been asked to come forward. We need all the information we can get, especially if you saw any cars. But we never heard anything from you.'

'I didn't see anything,' Tomme said simply. 'I've nothing to report.'

'So you saw no cars?' Skarre asked.

'The roads were very quiet,' Tomme said. 'I suppose I must have passed some cars, but don't ask me what make they were. I was busy listening to my music.'

'What were you listening to?' Skarre asked with interest.

'What was I listening to? Do you really need to know that?'

'Yes please,' Skarre said simply.

'Well, bits of everything,' he said. 'Lou Reed. Eminem.'

'I see.' Skarre nodded. He even made a note of this.

Another pause. It was a lengthy one. The silence made Tomme nervous. 'Did you have to drag me out of the classroom?'

'I didn't drag you,' Skarre said. 'You came with me of your own free will.' He changed the subject. 'You were involved in an accident that day. Did it happen in Glassverket?'

Tomme studied his filthy trainers on the floor of the car. 'No, in town. It was a shit thing to happen,' he said sullenly. 'I was on a roundabout. Some idiot forced me off the road, so I ran into the crash barrier and bashed the right wing. The worst thing was that he just drove off,' he said.

'Which roundabout?' Skarre asked.

'Which one?' Tomme exhaled. 'By the bridge. In the centre of town.'

'Is there a crash barrier there?'

'Yeah. Down towards the river.'

Skarre pondered this, trying to recall this precise roundabout. Then he nodded. 'Yes, you're right. Were you on your way out of town or were you heading west?'

'I was going towards Oslo.'

'So we're talking about the section of the crash barrier that follows the bend towards the bridge?'

'Yes.'

'Was there much traffic on the roundabout at that time?'

'A bit.'

'Any witnesses?'

'Witnesses?' Tomme hesitated. 'Well, there were other cars there. But I'm not sure if they saw anything. It was dark,' he explained.

'And the wing? Much damage?'

Tomme nodded. 'A fair bit. A light was smashed. But the dent is the worst part.'

'What was the make of the car that forced you off the road?'

108

'I didn't have time to see. It was large and dark. It looked new.'

'And you say it happened in the evening?'

'Yes,' Tomme said.

'What did you do after the accident? Your mother said you came home very late. Close to one o'clock apparently?'

'I went back to Willy's,' Tomme said.

Skarre paused for a while, trying to digest the information he had just received. The notepad helped him. On the sheet in front of him it read Bjørn Myhre. 'Back to Willy's?' he said. 'Didn't you tell me a minute ago you were going to see Bjørn?'

'Yes, of course,' Tomme said. For a moment he was confused. 'I'm just getting a bit mixed up.'

'We're talking about Willy who's helping you fix the car?'

They talk to one another, Tomme thought; they take notes and exchange information. They know everything.

'And what about the driver who caused you to crash your Opel?' Skarre said. 'Do you want to report him?'

'I told you, he did a runner,' Tomme muttered irritably.

'Really? Why were you going to Oslo?' Skarre continued patiently.

Tomme hesitated. 'I wasn't,' he admitted. 'I just like driving. On the motorway. Where I can put my foot down.'

109

'Of course.' Skarre nodded in agreement. 'Let's talk about something else,' he said. 'The bicycle Ida was riding when she left home. Do you know what type it is?'

'Not a clue.'

'I guess you don't spend a lot of time hanging out with your nine-year-old cousin. That's understandable. But she often visits your family. What about the colour? Do you recall that?'

'It's yellow, I think.'

'Correct.'

'But I actually got that from the papers,' Tomme said. 'They keep going on about the yellow bicycle.'

'And you didn't see her on the first of September?'

'I would have told you,' Tomme said quickly.

'Yes, you would, wouldn't you?'

'Of course!' Tomme was getting angry. The car was a confined space; he felt trapped.

'How long have you known Willy Oterhals?' Skarre asked.

'Quite a while,' Tomme answered. 'Why do you keep on questioning me?'

'Do you find it uncomfortable?' Skarre said, looking at him.

'Well, Willy doesn't have anything to do with this,' Tomme said evasively.

'This?' Skarre said innocently. 'You mean Ida's disappearance?'

'Yes. Not that we're close, either. He's just helping me with the car.'

Skarre flicked his cigarette butt out of the

110

window. Then he nodded in the direction of the college. 'Do you like it here?'

Tomme snorted. 'It's all right. I'll be finishing this spring.'

'What do you plan to do afterwards?'

'You're worse than my mum,' Tomme snapped. 'I don't have any plans. Might try to get a job,' he said. 'In a music store. Or maybe in a video rental place.'

'The search for Ida goes on,' Skarre said. 'Do you think you'll be taking part?'

Tomme turned and stared out of the car window. 'If my mum makes me,' he said. 'But I don't really want to.'

'Many people would find such a search exciting,' Skarre said.

'Well I don't,' Tomme said.

CHAPTER 10

Konrad Sejer swung his car into the car park at Glassverket school. He was met by Ida's class teacher, a tall, blonde and eager woman in her forties. She introduced herself as Grethe Mørk.

'They're expecting you,' she said, 'and of course I've prepared them. I don't need to remind you that they're very young, so you know how easily they scare, and there is a limit to what they can cope with hearing. However, you've probably done this before, I imagine, so you'll know what to say.'

She opened the door for him and walked briskly on very high heels. She was smartly dressed in a skirt and jumper. She wore several chains round her neck and her wrists were covered with bangles.

'I've told them they can ask questions,' she continued as she hurried down the corridor, and Sejer recognised the familiar smell of school, which had not changed since he was a boy. Linoleum. Green soap. Sweaty children. And the smell of damp coats on pegs outside every classroom.

'And I'm sure you'll know how to answer them. They're very keen,' she said. 'Several of their parents have called. Some of them wanted to know if they could be here, but I said no. After all, that's not what we agreed.'

Sejer followed her bustling body and noticed how her skirt swished around her legs. She was nervous.

'When they come home from school today, they'll be pumped for information,' she smiled, 'and I hope they'll be able to rein in their imaginations. Kids tend to embellish. I know all about that.'

Sejer smiled politely, but stayed silent. Then she seemed to become aware of her own flow of words, because she stopped talking abruptly. At last she opened the door to the classroom.

Fourteen children looked at him with curiosity. There should have been fifteen, he thought. Near the window was an empty desk. There was a lighted candle on it. He looked at the desk, at the candle and at the earnest faces of the children. Some stared at him openly. Others looked shyly down at their desks.

'Why don't you take my desk,' Grethe Mørk said, 'and I'll sit here.' She went to the back of the classroom.

Sejer looked at the teacher's desk. He did not feel like standing there. Instead he found an empty chair, placed it between the rows of desks and sat down in the middle of the group.

'Why aren't you wearing a uniform?' an excited boy asked. Then he remembered that he had forgotten to ask for permission. He quickly put up his hand and let it drop and some of the children giggled.

Sejer looked at the boy. 'I've been in the police force for such a long time that I don't have to any more,' he explained.

They clearly did not understand his answer. Why would anyone choose not to wear a police uniform if they were allowed to?

Sejer realised that further explanation was required. 'The uniform is very warm,' he said. 'And the shirt itches.'

More giggling.

'My name's Konrad Sejer,' he said. 'And I have never met Ida. Her mum says she's a lovely girl, very chatty and friendly.'

'I'm her best friend,' said a small girl in a red jumper. 'My name's Kjersti.'

This information caused a debate among the children and a couple of other girls gave Kjersti outraged looks of protest.

'Konrad?' said a chubby boy, waving his hand eagerly.

'Yes,' Sejer said.

'Are you looking for Ida in the river?'

'We're going to,' he said. 'But it's difficult. The river is very wide and deep and the current is strong.'

'So Ida might float far, far away?'

Sejer pondered this. 'We don't know if she has fallen into the river,' he said.

'My dad says so,' the boy stated.

'Really?' Sejer smiled. 'Is he absolutely sure of that?'

This silenced the boy briefly. 'He says there's nowhere else she can be. When you haven't found her on land.'

'I'm hoping we'll find her,' Sejer said. 'In fact I'm quite sure we will.'

'How can you be so sure?' a girl wanted to know.

'Because we nearly always do.'

Ida's teacher was following this from the rear of the classroom. Everyone had something to tell, everyone had a contribution or a story about Ida. They all wanted to be the one who knew her best. They kept looking at the empty desk. They don't really comprehend it, Sejer thought. Only a few days have passed. They don't realise that the desk will remain empty for the rest of the school year. And when it becomes occupied again, it will only be because a new school year has started.

He talked with them for a whole hour. He told them to stay together when going to and from school. They said they took the school bus or their parents drove them. He said that was fine. He asked if Ida had been talking about anything special in the days before she went missing. If she had behaved differently. They thought about this very carefully before they replied. He said that it was good that they thought carefully. A girl wanted to know if Ida would still have a headstone in the churchyard even if she was never found.

115

'I really hope so,' Sejer said. 'But we haven't found her yet, so there's still hope. People do go missing all the time and many of them come back.'

'Children too?' asked a small boy.

Sejer was quiet. No, he thought, not children.

'Miss Mørk has dressed up today,' another little boy proclaimed. Grethe Mørk turned scarlet.

'It's nice that you've lit a candle,' Sejer said.

Holthemann, his head of department, looked at him across his desk.

'Riverbeds are tricky, especially that last stretch out towards the fjord. The divers aren't holding out much hope. They say it's like looking for a contact lens in a swimming pool,' he said darkly.

He got up and went over to the map on the wall. The town was shown on the map in a way that made it resemble an infected wound. The river cut through the landscape like a gash, and residential areas in yellow were marked along the banks.

'Ida's bicycle journey was four kilometres. Where should we begin?'

'Where the road turns right down towards the bank,' Sejer said. 'Where you can access the river by car. There,' he pointed, 'by the old foundry. And there's a cart road leading down to a fishing spot here. That's a start. Along this stretch there's a great deal of vegetation on the bank. She could have got caught up in that.'

'Have the search parties covered these two roads?'

'Several times,' Sejer said. 'Every single building and shed has been turned upside down. As have the ruins of the old foundry. They've moved every stone.'

He was lost in his own thoughts. In his mind he saw a stretch of road. 'How long would it take a man, if he's in a car, to pull up in front of Ida on her bicycle, make her stop, possibly render her unconscious, bundle her into his car, which has to be some sort of van, then throw in her bicycle as well before driving off?'

Holthemann looked at the second hand on his watch. Then he closed his eyes. 'It might be possible to do it in under a minute,' he said, having considered it. 'Perhaps the car was already parked by the roadside. Perhaps he saw her in his rearview mirror. He would have had time to rehearse, so that when he finally came to do it, he would know how.'

Sejer nodded. 'Or he stopped her and got her talking. While waiting for a gap in the traffic.'

'In that case someone would have seen them. Though that part of the road is quiet at six in the evening.' Holthemann pointed to the map. 'That's Holthe Common. There's not a single house on that stretch. The common is nine hundred metres long and curves here, by Glassverket church. There are some houses here. I have a feeling about that common,' he declared. 'I imagine that's where she was picked up.'

'But you can be seen from all directions,' Sejer objected.

117

'It's to the killer's advantage,' said his head of department. 'Suddenly he's alone on the road. There's not a house or a car as far as the eye can see. Then he spots Ida on her bicycle.'

'He would also need time to see who was riding the bicycle,' Sejer reminded him. 'In order to be sure that it was a girl. She would have to be quite close before he decided to strike. Perhaps he drove past her at first and then turned around to come back.'

'Have all her relatives been questioned?' Holthemann asked.

'Not formally,' Sejer said. 'But we're working on it. Ida's uncles have both taken part in the search. Skarre has spoken to her cousin. So far we've discovered nothing about the family that seems worth following up. No alarm bells. We covered the majority of households along the route. Everyone's very helpful, but nobody has seen anything.'

'And there are no rumours?'

'Not to my knowledge. However, it may be days before we find her, so I'm sure they'll start soon.'

Helga had an idea. She would do something completely normal. Several agonising days had passed. If she went about her business, everything would go back to the way it was. If she left the house to get some milk and a loaf of bread, Ida would turn up while she was out. The telephone would ring. All the things that had not happened precisely because she was waiting for them. This was why she had written a shopping list and put on her coat, as she would normally do. She left the front door unlocked. All Ida needed to do was walk right in and sit down on the sofa. She could read a comic while she waited. The comics were still in a pile on the coffee table. Now everything would get better. Now Ida would be waiting for her.

She parked in front of The Joker. Stayed in the car for a while looking through the windscreen. Then she opened the car door and put her foot down on the tarmac. She looked down at her thick ankle and her brown shoe. Raised her eyes. Gazed at the entrance to the shop. At that moment she froze. She was looking right at a yellow bike. Helga started shaking. Her whole body trembled. She staggered out of the car and starting walking towards the bicycle rack. A sudden heat surged through her body. She vaguely noticed that the doors had opened and someone was coming out of the shop. They reached the bicycle at the same time. In disbelief Helga stared at the red-haired girl with the sullen face who grabbed the handlebars with both hands and pulled the bicycle out of the rack. A Nakamura. She pushed the bicycle on to the tarmac and mounted it. Just the way Ida would have done. Brisk and confident.

'No!' Helga screamed. She began to run. Tried to get hold of the pannier rack, but she did not succeed. The girl gave her a mystified look and started pedalling away from the shop as fast as she could. Helga raced after her. She was not used to running, she was heavy and clumsy.

'No! Wait!'

The girl cycled faster. Her skinny body pushed down the pedals as if her life depended on it. Helga started to lag behind. She stopped abruptly and then rushed back to the car and jumped in. Turned the key, revved the engine violently and reversed. A loud crash sounded and she turned round. A shopping trolley had rolled behind her car and she had reversed right into it. She panicked. She got out again to scan the road for the bicycle. Any second now it would disappear around the bend. She shoved the trolley out of the way and let it roll across the tarmac. Got into the car without checking the damage that had been done to it. Turned into the road. Spotted the bicycle just as it swung into a residential area. She knew this neighbourhood well. She had lost sight of the bicycle. She stopped and reversed. Checked her rearview mirror. Where was the girl? Surely that was Ida's bicycle. A brand-new Nakamura, all shiny and yellow! She kept the engine running and got out of the car. Stood for a while, listening. But she heard nothing except the wind and footsteps on the road behind her. Heels clicking sharply against the tarmac. A woman with carrier bags came walking. Helga ran towards her.

'Excuse me!' she panted. 'Do you know if a girl with red hair lives around here? Ten, twelve years old?'

120

The woman looked at Helga and hesitated. 'Eh, red hair? I might know her.'

'I need to talk to her!'

The woman seemed uncertain. Helga looked like a maniac; her eyes were shining. 'Talk to her?'

'I have to. It's important!'

Helga could not control herself, she gripped the woman's coat and tugged it. The woman turned to free herself from Helga's grip. 'There's a girl on Røyskattlia,' she said. 'It's the last house. Her hair's very red.'

She tore herself loose and disappeared with brisk steps. Helga got back into her car. Rolled slowly down the road in first gear. Stopped at the junction. She saw the sign saying Røyskattlia and she noticed the last house. It was wooden, painted in an almost black colour. She stayed in the car for a while with only one thought in her head. The bicycle had to come home. It had to be parked on the drive as it always was. Then she turned the car around, left the area and returned home as quickly as she could. There was no Ida reading on the sofa. She sat down in an armchair and waited for the twilight.

At 10 p.m. it was dark. Once more Helga drove down to The Joker. The shop was closed and the car park empty. She decided to walk the last stretch. She was wearing a dark jacket, and with her dark hair she was hardly noticeable from the windows. There was little street lighting. She found the house again and stood a few metres away, watching the dark

121

drive. The kitchen window was lit up brightly. She tiptoed down a narrow strip of lawn and sneaked around the corner of the house. Two bicycles were leaning against the wall, not visible from the road. A big black gentleman's bicycle and Ida's little yellow one. She went over to it and stroked the saddle. She watched the house with curiosity. Who lived inside it? Would they hear her if she rolled the bicycle across the gravel? Carefully she pulled on the handlebars. They had got caught up with the other bicycle's. She yanked them, and they hit the wall with a thud. Helga held her breath. Had they heard her? Nervously she moved away with the bicycle. She decided to go through the garden. The tyres rolled noiselessly across the grass.

It was light outside The Joker. Helga studied the bicycle in more detail now. It was definitely Ida's. She opened the boot of her car and tried lifting the bicycle up into it. It was heavy and half of it stuck out, even though she pushed and shoved as hard as she could. The boot could only be half shut. Growing increasingly fraught, she started searching for a bungee, but couldn't find one. However, she found a green nylon towrope. She unwound the coil with trembling hands. The bicycle had to come now, it belonged to Ida! The blood roared inside her head as she suddenly heard steps. Startled, she stood up. She felt like a thief. It was an elderly man and he was heading for her car.

'You look like you could do with a hand,' he said gruffly.

Helga gripped the rope tightly in her hands. 'I have to get this bicycle home!' she said.

The man looked into the boot. 'Not enough room,' he stated. 'You drive a Peugeot 306.'

'I'm aware of that,' she said, stressed. 'Some of it'll just have to stick out. But I have a rope.'

He took the rope in order to help her. 'You going far with that bicycle?'

'I'm going home!' she repeated.

'And where's home?'

He was brusque and efficient. He was someone who was used to stepping in and taking care of things as if it was the most natural thing in the world. Helga felt relieved. She let her arms flop and allowed him to take over and deal with it all.

'Glassblåserveien. I'll drive carefully.'

'You'll have to. I'm afraid you might scratch the paintwork if you're not careful. But I see you've already done that,' he said, pointing to the damage done by the trolley.

'I don't give a toss about the paintwork,' Helga said, watching him nervously while he tied the rope. She did not know if he knew her, if he knew what had happened. What he made of the yellow bicycle. But he knew what he was doing. He had done this before and he sorted it out. She looked at the knots and thought, I'll never manage to undo those. But then I'll just use a knife.

The man was finally satisfied. He tugged the handlebars gently; the bicycle hardly moved. She thanked him. Then she drove home quickly and recklessly. Once she got home she cut the rope with a pair of secateurs she found in the garage. She struggled to get the bicycle up the steps. She wanted to bring it all the way into the hallway. Finally she stood there looking at it. It felt good to have the bicycle back home again. All that was missing now was Ida. She went over to the telephone and rang Sejer's number.

'I've found Ida's bicycle,' she said.

Shortly afterwards he was standing in her hallway. He studied the yellow bicycle and tried to be tactful. 'How can you be so sure?' he asked.

She was standing in front of him, trembling but strong. Her face was determined. 'Because I bought it,' she said. 'From Sportshuset. This is Ida's bicycle. I can tell from the height of the saddle, which is on the lowest setting, and from the handlebars, which were adjusted so that she wouldn't be leaning too far forward. I can tell because it's new and unscratched. Ida wasn't allowed to put any stickers on it.'

'If only you'd let her,' Sejer said. 'A single sticker would have convinced me. Did anyone in the house hear you take it?'

'I don't think so.'

He looked at her gravely. 'If this really is Ida's bicycle, and the people who live on Røyskattlia have something to hide, they could deny that it was ever at their property. Do you understand what I'm saying?'

She pressed her lips together and stared at the floor in defiance. 'I was entitled to take it. It belongs to Ida.'

'I'll go talk to them,' he said, more kindly this time. 'But I ask you to be prepared that you might have made a mistake nonetheless. If they can produce a receipt for the bicycle, it means that they bought it for their own daughter. This brand's very popular. And many choose yellow.'

'She had a guilty conscience!' Helga said. 'It was so obvious!'

Sejer had no difficulty imagining the terror the girl would have felt when the desperate Helga Joner had started screaming and chasing after her.

'How about the registration number?' he said calmly. 'Every bicycle's got one. When you bought the bike, I'm sure you got a registration card. Do you remember?'

She frowned. 'Yes,' she said. 'But I'll have to look for it.'

She disappeared into the kitchen. Sejer found the frame number and wrote it down on his notepad. U 9810447. Then he followed her. Helga was rummaging through a drawer.

'It's red,' she said feverishly, 'I remember that the card was red. The receipt was stapled to the inside. It cost 3,990 kroner. They must think we're mugs,' she stuttered as bits of paper and other debris flew around her. 'I remember that they had to take five centimetres off the seat post. Go out in the hallway and see for yourself. It was because Ida needed to have the saddle really low. Go and check!' she called out while she carried on looking. Sejer went out to check the post. He ran his finger over the edge. It had been cut. He returned. Helga had found the registration card. She smoothed it out and handed it to him. Sejer stared at the card and then at his notepad.

He knew the area as a nice middle-class neighbourhood. He found Røyskattlia and drove to the last house. A face appeared in the window. A woman. She looked quickly out on to the drive and noticed the strange car. Then she was gone. Sejer went to the front door and rang the bell. Heard the shrill noise it made. A man appeared, looking puzzled. Sejer read the name below the bell.

'Heide?' he said politely.

The man looked at the patrol car. 'Yes? What's this about?'

He looked the very picture of innocence. But then again, Sejer had not for one moment imagined that he would walk up the drive and straight into the house of the people who had made Ida vanish into thin air. He did not imagine that Heide would have harmed Ida and then given her bicycle to his own daughter as a present. Though he had heard of worse and more incomprehensible cases than that.

'Konrad Sejer,' he greeted him. 'I'd like to speak to you. You have a family? A daughter?'

Heide nodded, but remained standing in the doorway.

126

'May I come in?' Sejer said directly. Heide let him into the hallway. A woman came out from the kitchen. Sejer smiled at her, but she did not reciprocate.

'Why do you want to know about Hanne?' Heide said, looking at him.

'Perhaps she's asleep?' Sejer said, evading the question.

'She's in bed, reading,' her mother said.

'Please would you get her?' Sejer requested.

The parents looked at one another. 'Get her? At this hour? It's almost eleven o'clock.'

'Please would you get her?' Sejer repeated. 'I just want to ask her a question.'

The mother disappeared and returned quickly with a red-haired girl. She was wearing a dressing gown over her nightie and padded anxiously behind her mother. Sejer gave her a friendly smile. It struck him that she looked guilty.

'I'm from the police,' he said. 'But you've got nothing to worry about. I just want to ask you a few questions. Do you own a yellow bicycle?'

She blushed instantly. 'No,' she said quickly. She looked at her father for a long time; her father looked back at her. Her mother was silent.

'Why do you want to know?' her father said, folding his arms across his chest.

'This afternoon your daughter was seen riding a yellow bicycle,' Sejer explained. 'The person who saw her followed her here. She found the bicycle parked outside your house.'

127

'Yes,' the girl said quickly. 'But it's not mine!'

Sejer looked at her and nodded. 'I know,' he said. 'And I'm waiting to hear what you're going to tell me next.'

'I borrowed it from someone.'

'Who lent it to you?' he asked.

'Oh, just a friend.' She stared at the floor.

Her father frowned. 'So what is it about this bicycle?' he said. 'Surely we're entitled to an explanation?'

'You'll get one,' Sejer said patiently. 'But first you need to tell me the name of your friend.' His voice was gentle. At the same time he was agitated.

The girl was having a hard time. Her father looked at her impatiently.

'Go on, tell him the name, Hanne!'

Hanne refused to look him in the eye. Her mother took a few steps forward.

'Surely you didn't take it?' she said nervously. 'Is it a stolen bicycle?' She gave Sejer a troubled look. 'Hanne would never steal. She wouldn't.'

'I'm not saying she would,' he said calmly. 'And I can inform you that the bicycle has just now been removed. By the person who followed Hanne. You did see her, didn't you? She was calling after you?'

'Yes,' the girl said. She was still staring at the floor. Her hands were fiddling with the cord of her dressing gown.

'Why didn't you stop?'

'I was scared,' she said. Her voice was barely audible.

Sejer moved closer to her. 'It's important that you tell me where you found the bicycle.'

Again she was silent.

'What's so special about it?' her mother said. Sejer looked at both parents.

'So neither of you knows how she got the bicycle?'

'She brought it back last night,' her father said. 'She had been to see a friend and was allowed to borrow it. We've told her not to go anywhere without letting us know. That's why we were angry with her. Her friend is called Karianne. She lives a few minutes from here.'

'The bicycle belongs to the missing girl Ida Joner,' Sejer said. 'We've checked the registration number. The woman who followed Hanne was Ida Joner's mother. She recognised it.'

Mrs Heide put her hand over her mouth. 'Oh my God, oh my God!' she said loudly. 'Where did you find it? You said it was Karianne's. Are you lying to us?'

Hanne started crying. Sejer patted her arm.

'Don't get upset. Perhaps you really wanted a bicycle yourself?'

'Yes,' she sniffled.

'Listen to me.' Sejer tried to get her to focus on him; it was not easy. 'You're very valuable to me. It's my job to find out what's happened to Ida Joner. Perhaps you can help me. Tell me how you got hold of the bicycle.'

She began to tremble. 'No!' she shouted.

'You don't want to?'

She hid her face behind a mass of red hair.

Her mother was humiliated and at the end of her tether. 'You have to tell him, Hanne, and you know it!'

Her father stood there not knowing what to do. Conflicting thoughts rushed through his head. 'But how can it be the same bicycle?' he asked in disbelief. 'Are you quite sure?'

Sejer nodded. He looked at the girl's anxious little form. There could be so much resistance in such a tiny body, he thought. Of course we'll make you talk, Hanne. All we need is time. A few minutes at the most.

She had still not moved.

Her mother could not hide her anxiety. 'Hanne! I get scared when you're like this. Did you steal that bicycle? Answer me!'

Hanne was shutting them all out.

'I promise you I won't consider this theft.' Sejer smiled. 'Just tell me where you found it and that will be the end of it.'

'It was just lying there. In the ditch,' she said. 'Behind the substation.'

'Where?'

'At the end of Ekornlia.'

'And you found it yesterday?'

'Yes. At first I thought it might be an old bicycle that someone had dumped. But it was brand new. I was just going to ride it for a while and then put it back. But I changed my mind. So I rode it to the shop today. Then this lady started shouting at me. And I didn't understand why she was getting so worked up about the bicycle.' She sniffed again, this time from relief because everything was finally out in the open.

Sejer nodded. 'Yes,' he said, 'we're all getting worked up because of that bicycle. And now you know why. Do you know Ida Joner?'

'I know who she is,' she said. 'But I'm in Year Seven. We don't hang out with the Year Fives.'

'I understand,' Sejer said.

'You can't go helping yourself to a bicycle just like that,' her father said, trying to regain some sort of control. He hated being put in this position. 'Surely you must have realised that it belonged to someone? You said you'd borrowed it. I don't like it when you lie to us!'

Hanne flinched a little. 'But it was just lying there, in the ditch,' she whispered.

Sejer patted her shoulder. 'Well, I for one am very pleased that you found it,' he said. 'We've been looking for it everywhere.'

He left them and drove around the neighbourhood until he found Ekornlia. He soon spotted the substation. It was situated at the very edge of the housing development. Behind the substation the fields began. It was far too dark to start searching now. Nevertheless, he still got out of the car and walked around the damp grass. What a strange place to leave it, he thought. On the one hand it was hidden behind the grey block of the substation; on the other hand it was so near to the houses that it was bound to be found quickly. There was something careless about it all. An absence of planning. A deed done in haste.

CHAPTER 11

'You've been talking to Tomme Rix,' Sejer said. 'What do you make of him?'

Skarre visualised Tomme.

'Your average eighteen-year-old,' he said 'A bit unsure of himself. A bit defensive, perhaps. And very upset by what's happened.'

'Nothing about him that makes you suspicious?'

'Yes,' Skarre conceded. 'He seems a little confused.'

'What exactly is he confused about?' Sejer asked patiently.

'He left home on the first of September to visit a friend, Bjørn. Later on that evening he decided to take his car for a spin on the motorway. Then he had this accident on the roundabout. When I asked him what he did afterwards, he said: "I drove back to Willy's." It was a slip of the tongue,' Skarre said. 'Presumably he was with Willy the whole time. I'm not sure what it means.'

'His mother is very much against this friendship,' Sejer recalled. 'Perhaps he lied to her about where he was going. And now he can't keep track of what

133

he's said. Did you ask any further questions about the accident with his car?'

'Yes. And I drove over there to check out his story,' Skarre said. 'I thought, if he's bashed his car and damaged the paintwork, there's bound to be traces left on the crash barrier. And there were.'

'I see.' Sejer nodded. 'No one can accuse you of slacking.' He smiled.

They were both silent.

'Where on earth has he hidden her?' Sejer said, having thought it over for a long time. 'We always find them. We find them quickly. In a few hours. Or we find them the next day. We know he has to act quickly. Two hours,' he said, 'that's the margin he has to work with. Abduction. Assault. Killing. And finally there's the task of disposing of the body. He's under pressure. The hiding places are very rarely well chosen. It's about getting some branches together hastily, or digging a makeshift grave, but this presumes that he had a spade to hand.'

'Perhaps he's waiting,' Skarre said. 'Maybe there is something else.'

'How do you mean?' Sejer asked.

'This is how we think: he kills her and disposes of the body in haste. What if he's not in a rush? What if he's keeping her with him somewhere, in a house? A house no one visits.'

Sejer nodded. 'True,' he said. 'That's an option, I agree. But nature takes its course. It isn't easy to get a good night's sleep when you've got the dead body of a little girl under the same roof.'

'But we're not talking about a normal person here,' Skarre objected.

'Oh, we are. He may well be like us in many respects. I'm glad Helga Joner can't hear us now,' he added.

'Oh, she hears us,' Skarre said sadly. 'In her nightmares.'

Sejer went to get a bottle of mineral water from the fridge.

'What about the bicycle?' Skarre said hopefully. 'I thought we'd made a breakthrough.'

'There's nothing to be had from it,' Sejer said glumly. He swallowed some mineral water. 'If my instincts are right, it won't be long before we find her.'

He gave his younger colleague a very solemn look. 'Helga Joner will want to know everything. She'll insist on every detail, every single one. You, who believe in God,' he said, 'you'd better start praying. That when we find the body, it still looks like Ida.'

Ruth pushed the door handle down slowly. Then she stood in the doorway looking at the back of Tomme's head. It lay immobile on the pillow. His breathing was regular, but too light, she thought. He did not want her to know he was still awake. That was fine; she did not believe he had a duty to confide in her all the time or to always be the son she wanted. After all, he was at an age when he needed to free himself and make his own way in the world.

135

She was not allowed to come with him on his journey, and she did not want to either. She had neither the right nor the desire to accompany him.

She sighed quietly and left. Closed the door as softly as she could and went down to the living room where her husband, Sverre, was busy solving a crossword puzzle.

'Grief,' he said. 'Twelve letters.'

'Hopelessness, perhaps,' she suggested quietly.

He looked up. 'Is that twelve letters?'

'Don't know,' she shrugged. Her husband started counting.

'There's something going on with Tomme,' she said, looking at him. Persistently.

'What do you mean?' He put the newspaper aside, having entered the word in pencil. Remained in his armchair fiddling with the rubber.

'Something's bothering him.'

He did not dispute this. He was away from home most of the time. Feelings of guilt showed clearly in his face. Then he held out his hand and motioned her over to his chair. She sat down on the armrest.

'Right, then, my love,' he said. 'Out with it!'

'He's upset about something or other,' she said. 'Marion says he cries in his bed at night.'

'Well,' he said, 'there's a lot going on. You and I and Marion are very distraught. So is Tomme, I suppose. Even though he never had anything to do with Ida.'

'Has,' she corrected him. 'Never has anything to do with Ida. We don't know what has happened.'

He patted her arm. 'Can't we be honest within our own four walls at least? I'm tired of pretending. You don't really think she's still alive, do you? Not after all this time?'

'No,' she said.

They were quiet for a while. Then she looked at him earnestly.

'I want you to talk to Tomme.'

He nodded. 'I will,' he promised. 'I'll talk to him tomorrow.'

CHAPTER 12

Willy Oterhals was older than Tomme, taller than Tomme. He was smarter, too. Had more confidence. He had more money and more plans. And he sampled everything that life had to offer him. However, this was not to say that he was lazy. Right now he was roasting inside his boiler suit. His skin could not breathe through the shiny material and the perspiration made his body sticky. He brushed his hair away from his forehead with an exaggerated, exhausted movement. He wanted to show Tomme just how much strength and skill was required to do this job.

Tomme himself was standing holding a bucket. He looked at the wing. It was finally in place above the right front wheel and curved smoothly and elegantly without a single dent or scratch.

'Fucking hell,' he said happily. He was close to tears.

'Now you can give it a wash,' Willy said, pleased with himself.

Tomme nodded. There was a feeling of silent joy inside him because the car was whole again. He dipped the sponge solemnly in the water and squeezed it so the shampoo foamed. He started soaping the roof of the car, stretching as far as he could to reach the middle of it. This car could have no dents, no scratches in the paintwork, no dirt or mud splashes. He rubbed hard with the sponge, his body embracing the task energetically, his arms tracing huge circles, dirty water cascading down the windows. The fact that the car was whole made him feel whole too. Everything inside him felt at peace.

'Any news, by the way?' Willy asked. He sat down deliberately, rested against the wall and lit a cigarette. It was his turn to have a break now; it was Tomme's turn to work up a sweat. He gave Tomme a searching look. Tomme ceased his rhythmical movements with the sponge but did not turn to face him.

'News about what?' he said curtly.

Willy's cheeks hollowed as he inhaled the smoke. He held the cigarette between his thumb and index finger. 'Well, I'm only asking,' he said. 'You know what I mean.'

'You'd better read the papers then. They know more than I do. But I think they've found her bicycle.' Tomme seemed remarkably unwilling to discuss his cousin. He began scrubbing with the sponge again, faster this time. 'It's not as if there's anything I can do about it, for Christ's sake!' he exclaimed.

These words were said with genuine desperation and a fair amount of defiance. Tomme thought of

139

all the days that had passed. He could cope as long as it was daylight, as long as all sorts of familiar sounds filled his head. In the evening he had the computer. Shelves stacked with DVDs and music of all kinds. There was always something to distract him. But at night, in the darkness and silence, he curled up into a tiny ball under his duvet. When his mind was not occupied, his thoughts would fly off in all directions, to the worst places imaginable. At times he would hear Ida's voice, or her laughter. Every time it was equally strange to imagine that she would never come to their house again. He listened out the whole time he was washing the car. He heard the sound of Willy's footsteps across the garage floor. He was dragging his feet. His shoes were tattered and unbelievably filthy. Tomme's own shoes were wet from the water running off the roof of the car. He felt his pulse throb in his temple. The veins on his arm stood out clearly because he was clenching the sponge so tightly.

'At a pinch I can just about understand men who attack women. Or teenage girls. And just rape them,' Willy said. He was focusing deeply on his train of thought. 'I can even understand the panic. Why they strangle them afterwards.'

Tomme listened and rubbed harder with the sponge.

'But little girls,' Willy went on. 'What do they want with them? Why do they freak out and torture them like that? When we're kids we torment cats and insects,' he said. 'So we get it out of our system that way. Perhaps they didn't get to do that when they were kids. I once heard a story about this guy who dragged a girl into his car. He used all the tools he had on her before he was satisfied. He actually went through his entire toolbox and attacked her with screwdrivers, hammers, wrenches, the lot, to destroy her as much as he could, and she wasn't all that old, the girl, and in very bad shape when they finally found her, to put it mildly. People like that are sick. They can lock them up and throw away the key as far as I'm concerned. Or shoot them in the back of the head. Well, I'm serious.' Willy stopped because Tomme was staring at him with burning eyes. He was crushing the sponge in his hand.

'Just shut the fuck up!' he screamed. The sponge was dripping, as was his forehead, and water seeped into his trainers. He could not see clearly.

'It's my cousin you're talking about!' he roared, his voice hoarse. It had never been powerful, and when he got angry it lost its last residue of strength.

Willy frowned. 'I'm not talking about your cousin. That's not what I meant.'

They stood there staring angrily at each other. Willy had never seen Tomme lose control in this way. He started to back off.

'Some of them get off more lightly,' he said. 'They just get raped and then, well, you know.' He flung out his hand in a gesture of apology.

Tomme was still panting from his outburst. He wanted to scream. Wanted to shove the sponge right

141

into Willy's face. Right into his little gob till the soap began to foam. But he did not dare.

'Take it easy,' Willy said carefully. Tomme was like an unsecured hand grenade. His nostrils were white. 'Let's have a few beers tonight! How about it? I'll get a crate of Corona.' Willy turned his back on Tomme and went out into the light. He needed to create some space between them.

Tomme picked up the sponge once more. He did not feel like drinking, but he felt he owed Willy. 'Yeah, why not? After all, we've got the car sorted,' he said.

Willy felt safer now they were further apart.

'You've got *your* car sorted,' he corrected him. 'Perhaps I'll need a favour from you one day. Then I can ask you, can't I?'

Tomme squirmed. He felt caught in a trap; everything was closing in on him. An absence of freedom he had never previously experienced. Like having to balance with your arms pressed against your body, without being allowed to touch anything: do not stumble, do not fall. Do not fall down, for God's sake! He bent down to wring out the sponge and got up too quickly. He felt faint.

'Drive the car outside when you're ready,' Willy ordered him. 'I'll get the hosepipe.'

Tomme staggered into his room at two o'clock in the morning. There he collapsed like a sack of potatoes and fell asleep with his clothes on. He was still asleep late the following morning. Ruth stood

142

in the doorway, watching him. He was sleeping so soundly that it looked like he was unconscious. That's enough, she thought. He has to stop seeing Willy. It only leads to trouble. She went over and nudged his shoulder. He groaned a little and turned over underneath the duvet, but he did not wake up. It struck her that he was very thin. That he looked so very tired. She opened the window. Her mind was racing. Her son was very quiet during the day. Much more so than normally. So was Marion, but not in the same way. Marion would talk about Ida, but if Ruth tried talking about her to Tomme, he withdrew. I don't suppose he can find the words, she thought. What was there for him to say? And why was he suddenly insisting on spending so much time with Willy? What was the bond between them? She recognised the sour smell of beer and felt impotent. But he's eighteen after all, she thought. He's of age. He is entitled to buy beer. Last night he had a drop too much, but that happens to everyone. Why am I so worried? Because Ida's gone, she thought. Nothing is how it should be. I don't have the strength to think clearly.

She went downstairs. Sverre was sitting in the living room studying a map. He twisted and turned it and put his finger on Madseberget where they lived, and then looked up at Ruth.

'Well, Tomme won't be taking part in the search today,' she said with a smile of resignation, because she did not know how else to behave. 'He'll be in bed most of the day, I imagine.'

'I heard him,' Sverre said, nodding. 'He tripped several times going up the stairs. I think they've finished the car. I suppose they were celebrating.'

'Yes,' Ruth said, sitting down. She did not like the fact that her son was in his bed while their neighbours and everyone else were outside looking for his cousin. Even his friends were there, both Helge and Bjørn. What would they be thinking? She looked at Sverre.

'You will talk to him, won't you?'

Sverre looked up from the map again. 'Oh, yes.' He took off his glasses and placed them on the table. Sverre Rix was blond and broad; neither of the children took after him, Ruth thought.

'But what am I supposed to be asking him?' he said.

'Don't ask him,' she said quickly. 'Just talk about everything that's happened. I imagine he too has a need to talk.'

'Not everyone shares your need to talk about things,' Sverre stated, folding the map. 'Not everyone solves their problems in that way.'

'But they ought to!' Ruth snapped.

Sverre looked at her closely. 'What's this about?' he asked softly.

She looked down at her lap and heard her own thoughts buzzing around inside her head like a swarm of bees. She felt dizzy. 'I don't know,' she replied, her voice as soft as his.

A prolonged silence followed between them, in which Sverre chose to fix his gaze on the tabletop while Ruth rotated her wedding ring on her finger.

'He doesn't usually get drunk.'

'Neither do I,' Sverre said. 'But it happens anyway. On rare occasions. It's as simple as that. Where are you going with this?'

Again she rotated her wedding ring. 'I'm thinking about the car.'

'Why?' he said, looking blank.

Ruth could not explain why. But she remembered the night of the first of September when she had sat by the window in the living room, waiting. She remembered his footsteps when he finally came home; he had practically tiptoed up the stairs. In her mind she saw his back when she opened the door, and she recalled his throaty voice.

'I don't know,' she said.

145

CHAPTER 13

Eight days of intense searching had yielded no results. They decided it was time to call it off. Sejer knew that they would have to stop soon anyway. Hope was fading. People were no longer looking with the same enthusiasm; they almost strolled aimlessly while chatting about everything but Ida and what might have happened to her. They had acquired an air of normality; they were no longer concentrating, and because the chances of finding Ida were dwindling, a few of them had even brought their children along. At least they should have the experience, the adults thought, of feeling they had helped out in their own way.

It was coming up to 9 p.m. on the ninth of September. Sejer tied the laces of his trainers and pulled a fluorescent vest over his head. His daughter, Ingrid, had bought it for him. It was actually intended for horse riders, and printed on the back were the words: *Please pass wide and slow*. Kollberg stayed in the living room. The dog gave him a long look, but did not get up. The yellow vest equated to speed and he no longer had that. Instead he panted for a long time before letting his head sink down on his paws once more.

Sejer was running faster than normal. He thought, if I push myself harder tonight, I will be rewarded. He thought of Ida's bicycle, which was undergoing forensic tests. At first glance there was nothing to be had from it. No scratches, no traces of blood or other substances. The bicycle was quite simply totally unaffected by whatever had happened to Ida. Two young children were coming towards him on the road. At first he was concerned by the fact that they appeared to be out alone. Then he noticed an adult following some distance behind them. A woman. She was keeping an eye on them. The kids were carrying a bag. Now they had stopped and were taking something out of it. They put something in their mouths. Two kids and a bag of sweets. Why were they so insatiable? Ida had been on her way to the kiosk. She never arrived. A frown appeared on his forehead. This woman Laila Heggen who owned the kiosk had said that she never got there. Why had they taken her word for that and not questioned her? Unconsciously Sejer had slowed down; now he increased his speed. Well, he thought, they had taken her word for it because she was a woman. And an agreeable one as well. But did it automatically follow that she was truthful? Why had they spent less than five minutes with the very person Ida had been on her way to see? How many similar assumptions, how many ingrained beliefs had characterised the search? A great many, most likely.

147

It had not occurred to Skarre or to Sejer to check out Laila Heggen. If the kiosk owner had been male, and especially if he had had a record or an outstanding charge hanging over his head – for indecency, for example, even if it had been from a long time ago – how would they have treated him? He ran even faster, doggedly now because he was on to something. A woman could desire a child as well. A woman who served behind the counter in the kiosk day in day out, lifting jars of sweets down from the shelves and counting them out. Jelly babies, chocolate mice and liquorice laces. While watching the kids with flushed cheeks and shiny eyes.

He ran for an hour and a half. Afterwards, as he stepped out of the shower, he felt good, warm and calm, as he always did after a run. It was almost 11 p.m.; it was extremely late to pay anyone a visit. Nonetheless, he drove to Helga's house. He knew she would be awake.

'I've no news,' he said quickly. 'But if you want, we could talk for a while.'

She was still wearing the knitted cardigan. Only the top button was done up. She had wrapped the rest of the garment around herself. It looked like she was trying to close an open wound. 'I didn't think you had time for things like that,' she said. They were sitting in the living room.

He wondered if she meant that he ought to be out in the streets looking for Ida. Or if it was an expression of gratitude. It was hard to know which. Her voice was a monotone.

'How about Anders?' Sejer asked cautiously. 'Does he come round?'

'No,' she said briskly. 'Not any more. I let him off. He's out looking. Every single day.'

'I know,' Sejer replied. He was thinking of what Holthemann would have to announce at tomorrow morning's meeting. We're calling off the search. He did not say it out loud.

'Today I lay down on the floor,' she said. 'I just lay right down on the floor. There's no point in lying on the sofa. Or the bed. I just lay there on the carpet, breathing in and breathing out. That was all I did. It felt good. When you're lying on the floor, you can't get any further down.'

Sejer listened to Helga.

'I was lying on the carpet, scratching it, when I suddenly felt something round and smooth. It was a Smartie.'

He looked at her for an explanation.

'Smarties,' she repeated. 'Chocolate buttons with a sugar coating. They come in various colours. This one was red like the carpet. That's why I hadn't noticed it before. It occurred to me that Ida must have lost it once when she was sitting right where you're sitting now. Because of that tiny chocolate button I almost had a breakdown. I keep finding things of hers. Lots of little things. I wonder how long I'll keep stumbling across them. Be reminded of them.'

'Have you given up hope?' he asked.

She pondered this. 'I have complete confidence

that she'll be found,' she said, 'but I'm scared it'll be too late.'

Helga slumped forward in her chair. It was then that Sejer suddenly became aware of something. A white envelope on the coffee table. He could read the address. It was a letter for Ida. Helga followed his glance.

'I really want to open it,' she said, 'but I've no right. I don't read Ida's letters. She should read it herself, I thought. The letter is from Christine. A girl from Hamburg the same age as her. They've been pen pals for almost a year. I'm pleased about the letters, they help Ida's English.'

'Why do you want to read it?' he asked.

'I have to write a reply to her,' she said, visibly distressed. 'Explain what's happened. I don't know if I have the strength. And I can't write in English.'

'I think you ought to read it,' he said. He did not know why he said it. However, the letter seemed to be beckoning him. Like a little snow-white secret on the coffee table.

Helga picked up the envelope reluctantly. Slid a nail under the flap. Tore it open with her index finger. Sejer went over to the window. Stood there staring out into Helga's garden. He did not want to disturb her. Apart from the rustling of paper, he heard nothing. When he finally turned around it was because she had let out a small, surprised cough. She sat down holding one of the sheets in her hand. Then she gave him a sad look.

'My English isn't that good,' she said. 'But I think it says something about a bird. That Ida knows a bird that can talk. I've never heard anything about that.'

Sejer went over to her chair. He looked down at the letter.

'She's never mentioned anything like that to me,' Helga said. 'Usually when someone has an animal, any sort of animal, she'll talk about it from dusk till dawn.'

She pointed at the letter: *Tell me more about the bird. What can he say?*

Sejer read the sentence over and over.

'Richard, a boy from the neighbourhood, has a horse called Cannonball,' Helga said. 'Ida talks about it incessantly, like she always talked about Marion's cat. We don't know anyone who has a bird,' she stated. 'No budgies or anything.' She clenched the paper in her hand. Her face took on an anxious expression.

'Helga,' Sejer said softly, 'are there any more letters from Christine?'

She got up slowly and went upstairs. Shortly afterwards she came back down again carrying a wooden casket. It was blue with a picture on the lid painted, a little clumsily, by Ida herself. She held out the casket. Sejer took it solemnly. He opened the lid and looked inside. The casket contained a thick pile of letters.

'I'll go through them all,' he said. 'There might be some clues, and we need everything we can get. And

151

if you want us to, we can call Christine in Hamburg and explain.'

It was after midnight when he got back in his car. He placed the wooden casket on the passenger seat next to him. He looked at his watch. Skarre has probably gone to bed, he thought. Nevertheless, he rang his mobile. Skarre answered at the second ring.

Sejer drove into town and parked. He went inside the communal hallway of the block where Skarre lived and looked for his name next to the row of doorbells. Shortly afterwards he heard the familiar buzzing. He half ran up the stairs.

'You've only got seventy-two steps,' he said scornfully, barely out of breath. 'I've got two hundred and eighty-eight.'

'Yes, I'm aware of that,' Skarre said. He held the door open. He noticed the casket.

'Letters,' Sejer explained. 'From Christine Seidler in Hamburg to Ida Joner in Norway. They've been pen pals these past twelve months.' He followed Skarre into the living room.

'There might be some clues? Is that what you're saying?' Skarre asked enthusiastically.

'So far we've found a bird.' Sejer smiled. 'A bird that can talk. We know how Ida feels about animals. However, Helga has never heard anything about a bird and she thinks that's unusual. Consequently this could mean that Ida met someone and neglected to tell Helga.'

152

'It's good that we finally have something to work with.' Skarre nodded in agreement.

'Now, we'll divide up the pile,' Sejer said. 'Christine has written twenty-four letters to Ida and Ida has in all likelihood written just as many in reply. I've put them in chronological order. Look out for anything that might refer to the bird.'

Skarre pulled a standard lamp over to the sofa and started angling the shade so that Sejer would get most of the light. This gesture earned him a disapproving look.

'But you're so short-sighted,' Skarre objected.

They each sat with a pile of letters. The casket remained on the windowsill with the lid open. For a moment they looked at one another, embarrassed at what they were about to do. Letters from one young girl to another were not meant for their eyes. Sejer had read diaries; he had leafed through private photo albums and watched home videos. Been in children's rooms and adult bedrooms. It always felt like a transgression. Even though their intentions were good, even though their aim was to find Ida, it still did not feel right. They both felt they were intruding. Then they began to read. Skarre's living room fell silent; only the rustling of paper could be heard. Christine from Hamburg used several types of stationery. The sheets were decorated with birds and flowers. Sometimes the letters had been coloured in, red or blue. Some were decorated with stickers: horses and dogs, moons and stars.

'We'll just have to guess at Ida's letters,' Skarre

said. They had been reading for a long time. They were both moved.

'Do you speak German?' Sejer wanted to know.

'My German is excellent,' Skarre said proudly.

'How about Holthemann?'

Skarre mentally assessed the qualities of his head of department. 'I don't think so. However, Christine is nine years old. This makes her parents in their thirties or forties. They probably speak English.'

'We'll call them,' Sejer said. 'Please would you take care of that, Jacob?'

Sejer's timid request made Skarre smile. Sejer understood English perfectly well, but he preferred not to speak it. He struggled with the pronunciation.

'*Aber doch. Selbstverständlich!*' Skarre exclaimed. Sejer rolled his eyes.

They read on. The tone of Christine's letters was polite and charming; she was probably very like Ida, conscientious and fond of her school.

'Given that the bird speaks,' Skarre said, 'it's got to be a budgie. Or a parrot.'

'Or a raven,' Sejer said. 'Ravens are quite good at mimicry. There was something else,' he remembered. He placed the pile of letters on the coffee table. 'Laila from the kiosk.'

'Yes,' Skarre said. 'I thought about that. We only have Laila's word that Ida never got there. We took that as gospel. Because she's a woman. That makes us biased.'

Sejer looked at him in surprise.

154

'So I ran a check on her,' Skarre said casually, as if it was the most natural thing to do. 'Laila Heggen's been in trouble with the tax office on more than one occasion. Her books are in a bit of a state,' he laughed. 'She was born in '68, single, no children, and has owned the kiosk for four years now. Before that she worked for the Child Protection Agency in Oslo. In an administrative capacity,' he added. 'Not with clients.'

Sejer was impressed.

'Who leaves a job with the Child Protection Agency to run a sweetshop?' he pondered.

'Laila Heggen,' Skarre said. 'And I want to know why.'

'You're quick off the mark, Jacob,' Sejer said with admiration.

'I've had a good teacher,' Skarre replied.

A short pause ensued.

'Did you bring some tobacco?' Skarre asked.

Sejer shook his head. 'I never carry tobacco. Why do you ask?'

'I've got a bottle of Famous Grouse.'

Sejer considered the offer while staring out of the window into the distance. He thought, one whisky won't hurt. I can leave the car till the morning. I can walk home. Just this one time.

'No, I don't smoke Prince,' he replied as Skarre held out his packet of cigarettes. 'But I would like a whisky.'

Skarre leapt up immediately. He was glad that his boss had said yes for once. As a rule Sejer tended not to be very sociable. Skarre was pleased that they could sit together in the darkness, thinking. His admiration for Sejer knew no bounds. There were even times he felt downright chosen to be working with him. The inspector had simply taken him under his wing. Encouraged him and given him responsibilities. It was a gesture he took great care to be worthy of.

'What is it with girls?' Sejer said. 'They correspond for a whole year and everything's about animals? They've barely mentioned any people. Just rabbits, horses and dogs.'

'She writes about a reptile, too,' Skarre said, walking across the room to get two glasses. 'An iguana named Iggy Pop. That's quite witty, I think.'

'Is it because they think so little of people?' Sejer raised his voice because Skarre was further away.

'It's a girl thing,' Skarre said. 'Girls like fussing. They like caring for someone and feeling useful. Boys are into other things. Boys like stuff they can control. Like cars. Planning the design, constructing it, assembling it, influencing it and manipulating it. Girls have different values; they invest in caring for someone. And they're less afraid of failure.'

He fetched the whisky bottle from the cabinet. It was three-quarters full.

'Since when do you drink whisky?' Sejer asked.

'Since I met you.'

Sejer took his whisky. He raised the glass to his nose. Skarre took out a Prince cigarette from the packet and lit up. Sejer reached for the casket on the windowsill to replace the letters. By chance he happened to glance at the bottom of it. There was something there, something soft and light.

'A feather,' he said, holding it up in wonder. 'A red feather.'

Skarre stared at the feather that Sejer was holding in his hand. A beautiful feather, ten centimetres long. 'That doesn't belong to a budgie,' he stated. 'Something bigger. A parrot. Macaws are red. Perhaps it's from a macaw?'

'She hasn't shown it to Helga,' Sejer said, wondering. 'Why not?'

Skarre met his eyes across the coffee table. 'I would have done so when I was nine. If I'd had a feather like that. I would have even shown off a crow's feather,' he declared.

'So would I,' Sejer said. 'I'll check with Helga just to be sure. But this feather seems to be a secret.'

Skarre gave Sejer an envelope. Carefully he put the feather in it and placed it in his inside pocket. Later on he walked briskly through the streets, exhilarated by this new discovery. Then he had to smile once again. A red feather. Something so minor. Kids collect all sorts of stuff. They're closer to the ground, he thought, and they notice much more than we do. He saw his own shadow beneath the street light; it grew to the size of a monster, then shrank to the size of a dwarf. Over and over, from lamppost to lamppost. Tomorrow it'll be ten days, he thought. Tomorrow Helga Joner's nightmare will have lasted two hundred and forty hours. She

157

lies in bed, waiting. She stares out of the window, waiting. The telephone sits on the coffee table, an ardent hope one moment, a black and hostile object the next.

Ida was not waiting for anything. Her tiny body was wrapped in a white duvet. Just as Sejer opened the door to his flat on the thirteenth floor, a car stopped a few kilometres out of town and the driver placed a bundle by the roadside. It was very noticeable against the dry, withering grass. It was just waiting for the dawn.

CHAPTER 14

It was 7 a.m. Sejer was standing by the window in his living room, looking down at the car park. He had just knotted his tie and was pushing the knot upwards towards his collar. Suddenly his telephone rang.

'We've found her,' he heard. It was Skarre's voice. Professional and firm. 'She's wrapped in a duvet.'

'Where?' Sejer said. At that moment something inside him wilted. He had been preparing for this, but he must have been secretly hoping after all, because now he felt a great sadness.

'By Lysejordet. Drive out to the Spinning Mill. Follow the road inwards some four to five hundred metres. That's where we are.'

Despite the huge gathering of people, the crime scene was very quiet. Everyone moved around noiselessly, everything was measured and focused. Everyone's voice was subdued.

Sejer closed his car door. Softly he walked the last few metres.

'Who called us?' he asked, looking at Jacob Skarre.

'A lorry driver. He was passing. Then he stopped and reversed. He says himself he's no clue as to what made him do that.' He pointed across the road. 'He's over there, having a cigarette.'

Sejer stopped at the tiny bundle. Everyone made way for him. He thought, this is what we have been waiting for. Now it is here. He knelt in the grass. The small white parcel had been carefully opened at one end. Ida's face was visible in the opening. Her eyes were closed. The skin on her cheeks was very pale. At first glance there was no sign of injuries or cuts. No red bruises, no cranial fractures, no blood anywhere, no evidence of damage. But something was wrong. He felt perplexed. This child has not been dead for ten days, he thought. A day, perhaps, or two. A technician found a craft knife in his bag and cut through the brown tape that was secured around the bundle. Then he unwrapped the duvet. Sejer shook his head in disbelief. Her clothes, he thought, looking around, where are the clothes she was wearing? Her tracksuit and her trainers. Ida lay there on the duvet wearing a white nightie. She was barefoot. He got up again. A strange sensation came over him. I've never seen anything like this, he thought. Never in all my life. He looked around Lysejordet. It was an isolated spot. Not a single house as far as the eye could see. No one would have seen anything. Whoever had brought her here had done so under the cover of darkness. She had been placed, not thrown, it struck him; she was lying flat on her back. He was deeply moved by the sight of the little girl in her nightie. The whole scene was like something out of a fairy tale. He thought of Helga Joner and was relieved that it would be possible for her to see her dead daughter. She was almost as lovely now as she had always been. So far they had no idea about what her body might reveal. He knelt down again. She had a tiny little mouth. It was drained of colour now, but on the photos it was dark red like a cherry. Her eyelids had swelled up over the sunken eyeballs. There were no marks on her face, but the blood had started to form minute red dots on her hands. Her hair, which was thick and curly in the photos, was lank and lifeless. But apart from that . . . Almost like a doll, marble-like and delicate.

'The body has been frozen,' said Snorrason, the pathologist. He had got up to stretch his back. 'In fact, she is only partly defrosted.'

Sejer raised his eyebrows.

'In other words, she could have been dead for ten days. She just doesn't look like it.'

'Why would he freeze her?' Sejer wondered, looking at Jacob Skarre. This was exactly what he had suggested, that the killer might not have been in a hurry, but could have kept her somewhere in his house.

'To gain time, possibly. Perhaps he lost his nerve. I don't know,' Snorrason said.

'Gain time. For what? He hasn't attempted to hide her. She was lying right by the side of the road. He wanted us to find her.'

Sejer noticed something in the grass and bent down to pick it up. It was tiny and white as snow. 'Down?' he speculated and looked at Skarre. 'From the duvet?'

Skarre frowned. He rubbed a corner of the duvet between his fingers. 'Possibly,' he said reluctantly. 'However, I don't think this duvet is made from down. It's a cheap synthetic one from IKEA, the kind you can machine wash and tumble dry.' He had located the washing instructions and was pointing to them.

Sejer searched the grass. He found several tiny white feathers. They were mostly sticking to the duvet, but some had attached themselves to the nightie. When he tried to catch them they flew off like dandelion seeds.

He called out to the photographer. 'Photograph her nightie,' he said. 'Make sure you get the neck opening with the red edging and the lace on the sleeves. Take pictures of the duvet. Get a close-up of the pattern. Look out for more down.' He gestured with his hand. 'Be careful with the duvet. Do not shake it or disturb it in any way. Any particles found on it could be important.'

Then he pulled Skarre aside and walked a few metres in the damp grass. He kept the white duvet in the far corner of his eye. He surveyed the horizon, taking in every ridge and treetop. A low, earnest murmur could be heard from the large crowd of people working on the crime scene.

At that moment more cars arrived. The press was descending.

162

'When does it start getting dark in the evening these days?' Sejer asked. 'Around eight thirty?'

'Thereabouts,' Skarre said. 'It gets light at seven. So between eight thirty last night and seven o'clock this morning, a car drove along this road. It would only have taken a few seconds to move her from the car to the roadside.'

'Everything is so neat,' Sejer said. 'The nightie. The duvet. The way she's lying. Why did he do that?'

'Don't know,' Skarre said.

'Perhaps he's read too many crime novels,' Sejer said. 'All we need now is to find a poem under her nightie.'

'You're saying we can eliminate young men from the investigation?' Skarre asked.

'I would have thought so. This is the work of a more mature person. A teenage boy wouldn't have arranged her like this.'

'There's something feminine about it.'

'I agree,' Sejer said. 'I hate IKEA,' he added. 'They make everything in such vast quantities, we'll never be able to trace it.'

'We have to pin our hopes on the nightie. It looks expensive.'

'How can you tell?' Sejer was impressed.

'It's old-fashioned,' Skarre declared. 'Girls today wear nighties with Winnie-the-Pooh or something like that. This looks like it came from another era.'

'Who buys nighties from another era?' Sejer was thinking out loud.

163

'People from another era, perhaps? Old people,' Skarre said.

'Old?'

Sejer frowned. They looked at the crowd once more. 'I hope he's made a mistake,' he said. 'Nobody gets everything right.'

'This doesn't look rushed,' Skarre said.

'I agree,' Sejer said. 'We'll have to wait for forensics.'

He went back to Snorrason. The pathologist was working quietly and methodically. His face was inscrutable.

'What do you think about the down?' Sejer asked.

'It's strange,' the pathologist said. 'The feathers stick to the duvet and yet they float away once they're loosened. There are some stuck to her hair, too.'

'You found anything else?'

Snorrason lifted up Ida's nightie carefully. 'I don't like to speculate,' he said. 'And you know it.'

Sejer looked at him urgently. Snorrason began rolling the white nightie up Ida's body. You could tell he had done this several times before. He had his own technique, a special gentleness about his hands. Sejer saw her thin thighs emerge. He saw the bare stomach. She was not wearing any knickers. A sudden nervousness gripped him as her torso was revealed. And there it was. Her chest. It was oddly caved in and slightly discoloured. Snorrason placed two fingers on her lower ribs. As he pressed, her entire ribcage gave way.

'She's been subjected to a blow,' he said. 'Or a kick. But it looks like it was a forceful blow.'

Sejer looked at Ida's chest. Fragile like a bird's nest. He was silent.

'Several ribs have been broken. I know even saying it sounds bad, but I wish her skin had broken or that we'd found some external injuries,' Snorrason confessed. 'Then we would have had a better chance of determining what caused them.'

Sejer needed to process this information. The damaged chest was too much for him.

'Whatever hit her did so with great force,' Snorrason said. 'Something big and heavy. No sharp edges.'

Sejer looked at Ida once more. He outlined the damaged area with his eyes and tried to imagine what could have caused this massive blow.

'A very big stone?' he suggested.

Snorrason did not reply.

'A stick? A boot?'

'Not a stick,' the pathologist said. 'Something bigger. And not a boot either. That would have left a heel print. Guessing will get you nowhere, Konrad. I need to open her up.'

Sejer was silent. Snorrason looked at him. 'What are you thinking?' he asked.

'I'm thinking about Helga Joner,' Sejer confessed. 'About what I'm going to tell her. She will have so many questions.'

'Tell it like it is,' Snorrason said. 'We don't know what happened.'

'I'd rather she didn't see Ida's chest,' Sejer said.

'You have to let her if she asks,' Snorrason said. 'And don't forget: she's prepared. I don't mean to sound insensitive, but it could have been worse. It could have been much worse.'

Sejer knew the pathologist was right. He merely nodded in reply. He did not know what Helga had imagined in her own mind, but perhaps it was worse than the body lying at his feet. She looked like a sleeping doll. And the nightie, which did not belong to her, was poignant and beautiful in its simplicity. What had happened? Where had she been? He had to go to Helga's house now. Perhaps she was sitting in her chair by the window. Perhaps her eyes were fixed on the telephone. He thought about how scared she was. He thought: she is prepared. But she still lives in uncertainty. A few more minutes, he thought, in screaming uncertainty.

The crime scene was carefully secured. They worked on Ida and the area surrounding her body for several hours. Later Sejer and Skarre met up at the office. Finally they had something to work with. Concrete physical evidence, which could be examined and might lead them somewhere. In the midst of everything they felt a kind of relief. They had been waiting for this moment; now they had got past it and they could move on.

'The nightie is made by Calida,' Skarre said. 'In Switzerland. This country imports large quantities of nightwear and underwear from there. It's available in most shops.'

Sejer nodded. 'Good work,' he said. 'Any news from Hamburg?'

'Some.' Skarre perched on the desk. 'Christine's mother is called Rita Seidler. She found Ida's last letter and faxed it to us. I've translated it. And made a few corrections so it's easier to understand. Nine-year-olds these days know a lot of English. I didn't know they would be this good,' he said.

'Read it to me,' Sejer asked him.

'Dear Christine,' Skarre read. 'Thank you for your letter. Today is Monday and I always watch a programme on TV called *Pet Rescue*. There is a team that goes out and saves animals. Today it was about a fat dog. It almost could not walk.'

Sejer thought of Kollberg, who almost could not walk either. He held his breath as he listened because Skarre read so tenderly, and he found the words so charming.

'The people from *Pet Rescue* came to get the dog and the owner got really angry. He said that he could feed it as much as he liked because it was his dog. Then they told him that the dog could die from a heart attack unless it lost weight. So they gave him three weeks. But when they came back, the dog had died.'

Skarre paused. Then he continued.

'I know a parrot that can talk. I am trying to teach it new words, but it takes a long time. Mum does not know about it. The parrot is called Henry. It is

167

very irritable and bad-tempered, but it does not bite me. I am going to ask Mum if I can have my own bird. I will pester her for ever. In the end she will say yes. Tell me more about your rabbit.'

Skarre looked briefly up at Sejer and then returned to the letter. 'I am going to be ten years old soon. September tenth. Love, Ida.'

He folded the letter. 'It's her birthday today,' he said solemnly. 'Today, September tenth.'

'Yes, I know,' Sejer said.

Skarre put the letter down on the desk. 'And Helga?' he said softly. 'How did she take it? What did she say?'

'Nothing,' Sejer said. 'She just fainted.'

CHAPTER 15

Elsa Marie did not knock. She used her own key to let herself in and stomped into the kitchen. Emil had done his best to mend the door. He was standing by the worktop fumbling with a cloth. The crumbs refused to stick to it, he was just moving them around the surface. Finally he swept them away with his bare hands.

'Go for a ride on your bike,' his mother ordered him. 'This is going to take time.'

He no longer protested, exactly as she had predicted. Emil heard the trembling undertone in his mother's voice and it made him nervous. He left the kitchen and grabbed an old coat from a peg in the hallway. He pulled his leather cap over his head. His mother watched him. She looked at the ridiculous leather cap. Her body was very tense and every movement caused her pain. She reminded herself that she was facing an important task. She would become a cleaning machine. She would work her way through his rooms and leave behind a strong smell of Ajax and bleach. It was the whole house this time. The curtains were going to be taken down; the bed linen was going to be washed. Her jaw was clenched. Emil slunk out on to the drive and got on his three-wheeler. It would not start. He made some irritable grunting noises and noticed his mother's face in the window. He tried to get angry but did not succeed. It took a lot for Emil to get angry. Finally the engine started coughing. He revved it, a little more than was strictly necessary, and his mother's pale face vanished. He saw the curtain settle back into place.

Emil always kept to a steady speed of forty kilometres an hour. He had nowhere to go, no one to visit. No money in his pocket either. But he had half a tank of petrol. He could drive a long way on half a tank, all the way into town and back and perhaps even up to Solberg. The waterfall appealed to him. He decided to drive out to it. He wanted to sit on his three-wheeler and feel the spray from the waterfall on his face. He often did that. It was not a cold day and his coat was warm. Buttoned all the way up. He was wearing brown gloves and thick boots.

Five minutes later he passed The Church of Jesus Christ of Latter-Day Saints. He was able to read a few short words, but he did not always understand what they meant. Emil was tired. His mother had been screaming at him for days. 'I want you to talk to me!' she demanded. 'I don't understand!' And he wanted to. He knew that the words lay somewhere at the back of his head. He could arrange them and line them up in those rows people called sentences. But he was afraid to let them out. He worried that they would come out the wrong way and make everything worse. Things had never looked as bad for him as they did now. The racecourse was on his left. He was constantly being overtaken. He was used to it, used to irate drivers tailing him, beeping at him. He was faster than bicycles, but slower than motorbikes and he took up more space. Everyone was in a hurry these days. Emil never was. He wondered what it was they all had to do. Once he had witnessed a car crash just as it happened. A deafening bang, the sharp sound of metal and steel, bending and snapping, glass splintering and raining down on the tarmac. He remembered the silence that followed, and the smell of petrol. Through the windscreen he had seen a head resting on the steering wheel and blood pouring out on to knees in grey trousers. He drove off when he heard the sirens.

Ahead of him now he could see the exit to Solberg. He began indicating in plenty of time and managed the turn expertly. Further up he needed to turn right again and soon he could see the waterfall. He changed down into second gear and parked in a lay-by. Got off the three-wheeler and walked over to the railings. Leaned forward. He liked the deep roar of the water, liked hanging over the railings. 'No,' he said, out into the air. He felt the vibrations in his chest. He tried to form an 'o' with his mouth. A noise that sounded like an owl hooting emerged through the drone of the waterfall. He bent his head and stared into the eddy. He could say anything

171

inside his own head. He could say: 'Have you no shame, have you gone completely mad?' Or: 'What on earth am I going to do with you?' He heard the words inside his head and the voice was agreeable to listen to, a pleasant male voice. Not his own gruff 'no'. He thought of his mother busy rushing around turning drawers and cupboards upside down and inside out. She always asked him endless questions about everything. But his silence protected him. He was made of granite. For fifty years his mother had tried to make contact with him using every possible means, in an attempt to chip away at the granite. She had tried being kind, she had tried ignoring him, and she had tried provoking him with sharp words. But he was silent. He would always be silent.

While Emil Johannes was staring into the roaring waters, Ruth and Sverre Rix sat waiting for Tomme. They had tried reaching him on his mobile, but there was no reply. Ruth had called both Helge and Bjørn, but he was not with them. Marion was leafing through a photo album displaying pictures of her and Ida. The cat featured in several of the pictures. It had been run over by the school bus and they had found it in a snowdrift. It was flattened, with its own intestines smeared all over it. Now Ida was gone too. There's just me left, Marion thought. She put her finger over the cat and Ida and saw her own face shine white and lonely in the picture. Finally they heard the Opel on the drive. Ruth and Sverre looked at each other.

They heard the sound of the garage door being opened and then shut with a bang. Now he was opening the front door. Then they heard his footsteps; he was not coming into the living room. He hardly ever does these days, Ruth thought. He was becoming more like a lodger who came and went independently from the rest of the family. They got up and followed him upstairs. Marion looked after them for a long time. Then she bent over the album once more.

Sverre Rix knocked on the door to his son's bedroom, then opened it. Tomme had turned on his computer. A series of strange sounds could be heard from the speakers, tiny beeps making up an uneven rhythm, like playful raindrops, Sverre thought. As he and Ruth stepped inside, a deeper sound that pitched itself below the beeps could be heard. For a moment this distracted Sverre. It had started to rain, lightly for now, but it would soon increase in strength.

'Tomme,' he said, looking at his son. 'They've found Ida. She's dead.'

Tomme, who had been watching them calmly, suddenly looked petrified.

'Where?' he asked quickly. 'Where did they find her?'

His father looked at him earnestly. 'Oh, where? Some place near Lysejordet. By the roadside. She's dead,' he repeated. 'Helga has had a breakdown.'

'Lysejordet?' Tomme lowered his head. He studied the pattern of the carpet for a while.

173

'But – how did she die?' he said quietly. His face was strange, they thought. His voice was alien.

'They don't know yet,' his father said. 'But they'll find out, obviously. We don't know any details,' he added.

Tomme was very pale. He could not think of anything to say at all. No one had ever come into his bedroom to announce a death. Then he remembered his aunt. 'And what about Aunt Helga?' he asked.

His father looked at Ruth. 'We don't really know yet. They've pumped her full of sedatives,' he said.

'We won't be able to talk to her for the time being. Could we sit down for a moment?' Ruth sat down on the bed. Sverre remained standing in the doorway. Tomme turned down the sound on the computer. He squirmed in his chair and felt uncomfortable.

'So now there will be a funeral. I thought you could be a pall-bearer,' Sverre said. 'You and I. Uncle Anders, Tore and Kristian. And a teacher from the school. Is that okay?'

Tomme nodded automatically. Then he realised what it would involve. He would have to stand up in the church and walk over to Ida's coffin. It would not be very big, he thought. Then he would have to grab a handle and with the others raise the coffin. He would feel the weight of her. If he were at the front, his own head would be very close to Ida's. He would have to walk at the same pace as the others and be careful not to stumble or lose his grip. The coffin would have to be kept level at all times or she might slide from one end to the other. He was not

174

entirely sure how it worked. But the reality of it hit him and an intense churning sensation started in the pit of his stomach.

'Is that okay?' his father repeated.

Tomme nodded again. Then he thought that carrying Ida's coffin to her grave might be a turning point. Because he would see the body disappear into the earth for good. Then perhaps they could finally put all this misery behind them. He nodded once more, looking directly at his father this time.

'Tomme,' his father said, returning his gaze, 'there's something I have to ask you. Something completely different.'

Tomme looked guarded and his young body braced itself. He fiddled with the keyboard.

'You've started seeing Willy again,' Sverre said, 'and you know we don't approve.'

'But the car . . .' Tomme began.

'Yes, but it's finished now.'

'It's looking really good,' Tomme said, pleased.

'Then I expect you to stop seeing Willy once and for all,' Sverre said.

'It's been years since he stole that car,' Tomme objected. 'Are you going to hold that against him for ever?'

'No,' his father said. 'But we do for now. And anyway, you've got other friends. We need to sort this out once and for all. So much has happened. We've got to get things under control again.'

The room fell very quiet. Tomme refused to look his father in the eye.

175

'And this accident with the Opel,' Sverre said. 'You hadn't been drinking, I hope?'

'And what if I had?' Tomme said in a subdued voice.

His father looked at him insistently. The low hum from the screen was audible, as was Ruth's heavy breathing.

'You heard the question,' his father said quietly. 'Why are you driving around the streets in the middle of the night anyway? Why don't you come home? That's what I don't understand. That's why I'm asking . . .' He paused. 'Marion says you've been crying in the night,' he continued. 'Is there something wrong?'

Tomme's eyes widened. Then he lost his temper. 'That's a load of crap!' he shouted.

'That's what she says. That she can hear you.'

'Well, is there a law against crying?' Tomme said. He turned his back to his father and stared furiously at the screen.

'No, of course not,' Sverre said, backing down a little. 'I'm only asking. Surely you can give me an answer?'

Again Tomme fell silent; only the hum from the screen could be heard. Ruth was shaking like a leaf and she did not understand why. She heard her son get up from his chair. He stopped right in front of his father, he was ten centimetres shorter than Sverre. 'I'm going out,' he said defiantly.

'You've just come back,' Sverre objected. 'Why are you getting so angry?'

'I'm not angry,' Tomme said, trying to get past him. 'But you're always on my case!'

His father blocked his path. 'We care about you,' he said firmly. 'I just want to be sure that everything is all right.'

Yet again Tomme tried to squeeze past him and get out of the room. His father continued to block him and stood broad and heavy, barring his route to the door. Ruth sat on the bed watching them. She hid her hands between her thighs.

'Ida is dead,' she said. 'Could we stop arguing, please?'

Reluctantly Sverre moved away from the door. Tomme shot down the stairs; they heard the front door slam and then the engine of the Opel as it started up.

'This is too much for us,' Ruth said, cradling her head. 'What's going to happen to Helga? Perhaps she'll just stay in her hospital bed. What's the point of her getting up and carrying on as before? I wouldn't,' she said, wiping away her tears. 'I would just stay there for ever.'

Sverre sat down next to her. They sat like that for a long time in total silence. The computer emitted a luminous blue glow.

CHAPTER 16

'What does the lab report say?' Skarre asked.

Sejer turned around slowly in his chair. He was holding a fax in his hand. 'You were right about the duvet,' he said. 'The filling is synthetic. The down we found on the duvet and the nightie must have come from somewhere else. A bird, for example. This means there must have been a bird in the house where Ida was kept when she was wrapped in the duvet.'

'What kind of bird?' Skarre asked quickly.

'They can't say. These are minor coverts. They don't have follicles, so they can't be classified. They could belong to a chicken for all they know,' he said.

'Or a parrot,' Skarre said eagerly. 'What else did they find?'

'A great deal, in fact,' Sejer said. 'Including traces of peanut shells, strands of Ida's hair and other unidentified substances. They're still working on those.'

'That red feather, where do you keep it?' Skarre said.

Sejer pulled open his desk drawer and found the white envelope.

'There's a pet shop three blocks from here,' Skarre said. 'Mama Zoona's. Perhaps they sell parrots. Perhaps the bird which Ida wrote about was bought from Mama Zoona's. They're valuable birds; not everyone can afford them. Maybe they keep a sales record. There might even be some kind of caged bird society that he's a member of. Or he goes there for bird supplies. They don't just need food. Birds like that need all sorts of things. Toys. Vitamins. Things you can't buy from the super-market.'

'You're very well informed.' Sejer was impressed.

'I'll go check it out,' Skarre said, jumping up. 'Can I get you anything?' He was already halfway out of the door. 'A white rat, perhaps? A couple of goldfish?'

Sejer looked rather alarmed at his suggestion. 'I'll call Snorrason,' he said. 'He says Ida died from internal injuries. How do you sustain internal injuries?'

'A fall from a great height?' Skarre suggested. 'That's one possibility.'

'Blows or kicks,' Sejer said. 'Or from a collision.'

'But her bicycle was undamaged.'

'Perhaps she wasn't on her bicycle at that moment.'

'Why wouldn't she be?'

'Dear God, I don't know. But surely people do get off their bicycles sometimes,' Sejer said. At that very

179

moment he started scratching the back of his leg. His psoriasis was bothering him. Then he rubbed his eyes hard for a long time. Looked up at his young colleague, who was still waiting in the doorway.

'You've just burst several blood vessels,' Skarre said.

The name Mama Zoona's made him think that the shop would belong to a brisk and efficient woman. But a man of about thirty introduced himself as the owner.

'Bjerke,' he greeted Skarre. The distinctive smell of animals and animal feed, pungent, but not unpleasant, filled the whole room. It was hot in there and the humidity was high.

'You sell birds?' Skarre asked, listening to the noises coming from another room. Bjerke nodded. Piercing screams and an excited twitter could be heard.

Skarre went into the room. He stopped. There were yellow, green and blue budgies. Cockatoos. Macaws, a raven, several nymph parakeets in a variety of colours, tiny black mynah birds with yellow beaks, and a grey, less flamboyant, parrot he did not know the name of. The presence of the two men in the room caused the birds to increase their volume. Skarre stared immediately at the two red macaws. But they were an intense and warm shade of red, whereas Ida's feather had a softer, cooler shade. For a moment the noise disorientated him.

'Quite a racket,' Skarre said, looking at Bjerke. 'Don't people realise?'

'No.' He smiled. 'But they're not all that bad. And there are a lot of them in here. The cockatoos are the worst,' he admitted. 'They give out this piercing cry. And they aren't very friendly either.'

'But they sell?' Skarre said.

'No,' he said dourly.

'But you've got two of them here? The gold-crested ones.'

'They're mine,' he said. 'They're not for sale. Even if you offered me a hundred thousand kroner.'

Skarre shook his head. 'I haven't got a hundred thousand. Are they really that valuable?'

'They are to me,' he said. 'They are the most beautiful birds in the world.'

'So how about the macaw?'

'Macaws are okay,' he said, 'but the gold-crested cockatoos are finer.'

Skarre went from cage to cage admiring the birds. 'What would you advise me to get if I were to buy one? I'm a beginner.'

The chance to show off his expertise put Bjerke in a good mood. 'Nymph parakeets,' he suggested. 'Or one of those.' He pointed to the grey parrot. It was then Skarre realised the parrot had red tail feathers.

'The colour's a bit dull,' he said. 'But the tail feathers are nice.'

'An African Grey,' Bjerke said. 'One of the best talkers. Very alert. But parrots aren't like cats or dogs. They're unpredictable and eccentric. Personally

181

I don't like dogs,' he said, growing more talkative, delighted at the interest his visitor had expressed. 'They're so needy. And they have to be taken for walks all the time. But parrots have great personalities. You can leave them a whole weekend if you need to, they'll be fine. Their cage is easy to clean out and their diet is straightforward. Some seeds and an apple sliced into boats. Perhaps a few peanuts on a Saturday night,' he joked.

'Peanuts?' Skarre said, suddenly alert.

'Unsalted ones in their shells,' Bjerke said. 'They crack open the shells with their beaks. They can inflict a lot of damage with those beaks. I've been on the receiving end of that a few times over the years,' he confessed.

Minor coverts from a bird and traces of peanut shell, Skarre thought. He went over to the grey parrot and studied its red tail feathers. The bird was the size of a dove, with beautiful grey-blue plumage. It was a lighter shade around the eyes, almost a pale rose. Its crest had smaller, rounder pearl-like feathers in various shades of grey. The feathers across its back were a darker grey, like slate. It approached the bars and tilted its head inquisitively. Then it started to sing beautifully. Skarre stared into the shiny eyes. They baffled him a little. Two black buttons void of expression.

'I need to ask you some questions about parrots,' he said. 'Those feathers at the bottom of the cage, they're called minor coverts, am I right?'

'You are,' Bjerke said. 'Birds lose minor coverts

all the time, for example when they preen them-selves. The down drifts like snowflakes and sticks to everything. A clean form of waste, I think, com-pared to dog hair and so on.'

'I bet you don't sell one of those every week,' Skarre said. 'How much does it cost?'

'Around six thousand.'

'Do you keep a sales record?'

'Of course.'

'Do you make a note of the customer's name?'

'No,' he replied. 'Not their name. Why would I? But I obviously remember some of them. This is not an impulse buy. People visit the shop many times weighing up the pros and cons. They read bird books and talk it over with their families. Things like that.'

'Is there a local parrot society?'

'Yes, but it's hardly got any members. I'm the chairman, incidentally.'

'That's convenient,' Skarre said. 'So if I ask you how many parrots you've sold this year, can you tell me without having to look it up?'

Bjerke contemplated this, counted on his fingers.

'Three, I think.'

'That's not many.'

'That's not how I make my money. I make my money selling animal feed, guinea pigs, goldfish and rabbits. That's what people want. It's a pity, because they have such a short life span. If you buy a parrot, you have it for life.'

Skarre smiled in disbelief. 'They live that long?'

'Up to fifty years. There are stories about some parrots living till a hundred and twenty,' he laughed. 'That's probably not true, but my point is that it's a lifelong commitment. And thus worth six thousand kroner. Why do you want to know so much about parrots?' he said suddenly, unable to suppress his curiosity any longer.

'I'm looking for someone,' Skarre said. 'Someone who owns a parrot. It's a reasonable assumption that he lives in this area, and if he does he could have bought his parrot from you.'

'That makes sense,' Bjerke said.

'What kind of person buys a parrot?' Skarre said. 'Can you tell me that? Do they have something in common?'

'I doubt it. Parrots are for adults. However, it's usually the kids who drag the adults in here in the first place. People don't realise how difficult parrots are to handle. When they get them home they're disappointed when they discover they can't take the bird out of the cage and stroke it. This is not exactly a pet,' he said. 'Some people even get so fed up they return them.'

'Do you allow that?' Skarre was surprised.

'Obviously. If the parrot's not really wanted, I'd rather take it back.' He opened the door to the cage and lifted out the grey parrot. It perched on his hand, completely still. Its feathers quivered.

'An African Grey,' he said, rapt. 'A female. Five months old. Personally I prefer the males. They grow bigger, their tail feathers have a more intense colour and their beaks are more impressive. But they are more difficult to tame than the females. On rare occasions you come across very aggressive males. They're no good for breeding and so their value is reduced. They kill the female instantly instead of mating with her.' He giggled, as if he found the thought of this somehow entertaining. 'But if I'm selling one of those, I always warn the customer about it. The problem is that when people have had the bird for a while they lose interest. They start ignoring it and later try to soothe their guilty conscience by buying another bird to keep the first one company. The result can be a bloodbath.' He smiled, and started stroking the bird's head.

'Why doesn't it fly?' Skarre wondered.

'It can't. Its wings have been clipped.'

Skarre instantly lost some of his respect for the shop owner.

Bjerke explained. 'Just while it's here. The feathers grow all the time and they will grow back.'

'Oh, I'm glad,' Skarre said, relieved. He pulled the red feather out of his pocket and held it up in front of Bjerke's eyes.

'This one,' he said. 'What do you think it is?'

Bjerke returned the bird to its cage and took the feather from Skarre with two fingers. 'I believe this feather comes from an African Grey,' he said. 'A tail feather. Probably a large bird.'

'Do you know when you last sold one of those?' Skarre asked.

'Ah . . .' he hesitated. 'It's been a long time. I don't

actually remember. People prefer parakeets. They're more colourful.'

'Have you named all the birds?' Skarre asked.

Bjerke shook his head. 'The gold-crested ones are called Castor and Pollux. None of the others have names. People want to name their own pets, so there's no point in me doing it.'

Skarre understood. 'Would you keep an eye out for people who buy supplies for their parrots?' he asked. 'Question them a bit, show a little interest? Especially when it comes to the name of their bird? I'm looking for one called Henry.'

Sejer was getting nowhere with the piles of paper on his desk. He had stared himself blind at all the reports, searching high and low for something they might have missed. He had tried to find a clue or a link, tried to form an idea of the crime. What type of crime are we actually dealing with? he wondered. There's something bizarre about this whole case. Something unknown. This is different from any of my previous cases.

He left the office and got into his car. Drove steadily down Drammensveien and thirty-five minutes later parked outside the Institute of Forensic Medicine.

'You just won't take no for an answer, will you?' Snorrason said. 'Ah well, you'd better come in anyway. Sit down.' He spoke to Sejer the way you would speak to a child who will not stop pestering you. Then he switched off his reading light and spun his chair around to face him. 'As I've already told you,' he began, 'Ida died from internal bleeding. She was subjected to a blow from something extremely heavy or she was struck violently, we don't know which. Yet she could have been alive for some time afterwards.'

'Any idea how long?'

'An hour or two perhaps.'

Sejer took off his jacket and sat down. 'I need more details, please. What caused the internal bleeding, and why did she die from it?'

Snorrason folded his hands in his lap. 'She sustained multiple rib fractures. One of her lungs has been perforated and her liver ruptured. As a result she started bleeding from her liver into the abdominal cavity. Eventually her blood pressure started to drop. The body of a girl of that size contains approximately two and a half litres of blood. Once one litre has seeped into her stomach she'll be close to death. Slowly she'll start to lose consciousness. If her blood pressure falls below forty or fifty, she's dead.'

'Would she have been in any pain?' Sejer asked. He was thinking of Helga Joner.

'With a perforated lung? Absolutely. It cuts like a knife whenever she inhales. She'll have been queasy and felt very ill. She would have been pale, nauseous and thirsty.' Snorrason's face showed no emotion while he spoke. It was almost as if he was giving a lecture and as long as he stayed within his area of expertise it was easier for him to keep his feelings out of it.

187

'It could have been a collision,' he continued. 'The headlight of a motorcycle, for example, would have been the right height for her chest. However, there is one problem with this theory.'

'Which is?' Sejer said.

'Let's start by imagining that it was a car,' Snorrason said. 'If Ida was walking along the road and was knocked down by a car, it would have hit her lower legs first. They would have been broken. If she was knocked down from behind, her head would have hit the tarmac or the bonnet if she was facing the car. And if she'd been knocked down while riding her bicycle, then the bicycle would have been damaged. And it isn't. It almost seems as if she were lying down when she received these injuries. And this points more towards some sort of assault, such as blows or kicks. In which case she never put up her hands in self-defence. There are no cuts or other injuries to them. And if she was kicked, her attacker must have been barefoot. Shoes would have left marks. However, he's clever. He changed her clothes. Her own clothes would have given us more clues.'

'So you think that's why she was found in the nightie? The nightie itself is of less significance, the point being that it was a clean item of clothing, no traces?' Sejer said.

'Don't you?' Snorrason asked him. He reached out for a blue thermos flask and poured coffee into a mug. Sejer declined.

'He could just as well have put her naked inside

the duvet. There's something sentimental about this,' Sejer contemplated. 'Something feminine.'

'She was very neatly wrapped,' Snorrason said. 'We don't normally find them like that. But nothing about this case is normal.'

'Was she assaulted in any other way?'

'I haven't found any evidence to suggest it. But you can do a great deal to a child that leaves no physical traces. Incidentally, the duvet has been patched up,' he said. 'Someone's mended it, very meticulously.'

'Someone who can sew,' Sejer said. 'Another feminine aspect.'

'The patch is made from a piece of plain fabric, which could be a sheet,' Snorrason said. 'However, there wasn't a single drop of blood to be found, not on Ida or the nightie or the duvet.'

'What about the tape used to wrap her?' Sejer asked.

'Ordinary brown parcel tape, found in every household.'

'And her stomach contents? What did they tell you?'

'That she hadn't eaten for several hours. The nightie,' he carried on, 'you haven't made any progress with it?'

'We're still working on it. A female officer thinks it wasn't bought in a chain store. So we'll check lingerie shops.'

'There can't be that many of those.'

'Five in our town alone. Those five shops have

189

twelve staff in total. That will be a fun job for Jacob Skarre,' Sejer said. 'By the time he's done, he'll know his way around every single lingerie shop in southern Norway.'

'Well, he's single, isn't he?' Snorrason laughed. 'Perhaps he might learn something. Underwear is practically a science these days.' He smiled. 'Did you know that much of what women wear now is a by-product of space-age technology?'

'No,' Sejer said. 'I know nothing about such things.' He had got up again and started putting on his jacket.

Snorrason drained his coffee mug in one gulp and pushed it aside. 'Well,' he said. 'So what are you thinking right now?'

'Right now I'm thinking of this,' Sejer said. 'A huge percentage of people killed in this country are killed by someone they know.'

CHAPTER 17

Tomme heard the doorbell ring downstairs. He rushed down to open the door. The sight of the unknown man on the doorstep made him nervous straight away.

'Konrad Sejer. Police.'

Tomme tried to pull himself together. 'My parents are at the hospital,' he said quickly. 'Visiting my aunt Helga.'

Sejer nodded. There was something fearful and jumpy about the young man. This roused his curiosity.

Tomme stayed in the doorway. He was seriously regretting opening the door.

'I presume you're Ida Joner's cousin?' Sejer asked.

Tomme nodded. 'I was just going out,' he declared, looking at his wristwatch as if he was in a rush.

This urgency puzzled Sejer. It was as if the ground was burning beneath the young man's feet. 'Spare me a few minutes, please,' he asked on impulse. 'After all, you knew Ida well.'

Of course, Tomme thought, I'm her cousin. They

191

always suspect uncles and cousins. He stepped back into the hallway. Sejer followed him.

'I'm so very sorry about your cousin,' he began. They were in the living room. It did not occur to Tomme to ask Sejer to sit down. So they remained standing, looking at one another.

'Thank you,' Tomme said. He looked outside for his parents' Volvo. If only they would come home now and rescue him from this agonising situation. He could find no words to talk about Ida and everything that had happened recently.

'There is something I've been meaning to ask you,' Sejer remembered. 'It's about your car accident.'

When he mentioned the car, Tomme grew nervous once more. Sejer picked up on it. He did not know why Tomme was reacting like this. He assumed the boy might have been driving under the influence. That had to be the reason he had turned so pale.

'You bashed your car,' Sejer said, 'and it happened on the roundabout by the bridge. September first. The day Ida went missing.'

'What about it?' Tomme said.

'Your car received a dent and some damage to the paintwork. One of our officers found traces of paint on a crash barrier by the bridge that may have come from your car.'

Tomme had had his back to him all this time. Now, however, he turned around.

'In other words, there is every reason to believe that the damage happened in exactly the way you described,' Sejer said. 'Nevertheless, I would like to know more details about the incident. Exactly how it happened. You have stated that you were forced off the road, to the right, by another car?'

Tomme nodded. 'Some guy entered the round-about the same time as me. But he was in the wrong lane and going too fast. I had the choice between hitting him on the left or swerving to the right and hitting the crash barrier.'

'But you didn't report the other driver or give a statement to the police?'

'He drove off,' Tomme said quickly. 'I didn't get the chance.'

'Did he?' Sejer said. 'What make of car was he driving?'

Tomme thought. 'Now what was it? A dark blue car, fairly large. An Audi or a BMW, perhaps.'

'Why do you think he drove off?'

'Dunno. Perhaps he'd been drinking.'

'Had you been drinking?'

'No, no! I never drink and drive.'

'Did he actually hit your car?'

'No.'

'Have you done anything to find him?'

'How would I?'

'What about witnesses, Tomme? Someone must have seen it.'

'Guess so.'

'But no one stopped?'

'No.'

Sejer allowed the room to fall silent. He kept

looking at Tomme. 'Do you often go out driving late at night for no particular reason?'

'Do I need a reason?' Tomme said warily.

'You look nervous, Tomme,' Sejer said. 'It makes me wonder why.'

'I'm not nervous,' he said quickly.

'Oh, you are,' Sejer said. 'You're pale and nervous. You've no reason to be if it's simply the case that a bad driver on a roundabout forced you off the road, only to speed off without taking responsibility. You ought to be furious.'

'And so I am!' Tomme burst out.

'Not really,' Sejer said. 'You're upset.'

'The Opel has already been fixed,' the boy said abruptly. 'It's as good as new.'

'That didn't take you long,' Sejer said. 'Straight from the roundabout and into Willy's garage.' He smiled. 'Did he do it as a favour?'

'Yes.' Tomme nodded.

'He must be a very good friend,' Sejer said slowly.

Tomme hesitated. His explanation was beginning to falter. It was not a very plausible story. He had not thought it through in his mind, and now it was all starting to sound rather unlikely.

'What precisely was the time when it happened?' Sejer asked.

When? Tomme thought as hard as he could. He did know when it had happened. It had been close to midnight. It had been dark. Could he say twelve o'clock? After all, that was the truth. But then what would Sejer's next move be? No matter what he replied, Sejer could come up with a new angle Tomme had not considered. He was standing there now waiting for an answer and Tomme could not drag it out any longer, so he told it like it was, that it was twelve o'clock at night. And Sejer listened and drew his own conclusions. Tomme hardly dared move, but he feared the worst. That the truth, that he had bashed his car at that particular place and at twelve o'clock exactly, would ultimately prove fatal for him.

'You left this house at six p.m.,' Sejer spoke slowly, as if he was picturing it all.

'Aha,' Tomme said. And it was true. It was nearly all true; that was precisely the problem, he realised.

'Where were you going?'

'To see Bjørn,' he explained. 'But he wasn't in. So I went to see Willy instead.' Again this was true. Completely true.

'And you stayed there for how long?'

'Almost till twelve.'

'And then you drove into town. At twelve o'clock at night?'

'Yes.' Again this was true. Unbearably true.

'Then you had the accident on the roundabout. What were you doing in the town centre so late at night?'

'Nothing, I was just driving for no particular reason,' he said defiantly.

'You've said you were heading in the direction of Oslo. Is that right?'

'I just wanted to do some motorway driving,'

Tomme said. 'I didn't intend to drive all the way to Oslo itself.'

'You got home at one o'clock in the morning,' Sejer said. 'What were you doing between midnight and one?'

'I drove back to Willy's,' Tomme admitted. This, too, was entirely true.

'After spending the entire evening from six to midnight with him, you drive back to him again?'

'Yeah. Because of the damage to my car. I was really wound up about it,' Tomme confessed. 'I had to show it to someone. I wanted Willy to check it out, see if he could fix it for me.' It all sounded highly suspicious, he thought miserably. Even though what he was telling him now was the truth.

'How long have you known Willy Oterhals?' Sejer asked.

'A few years.'

'You spend a lot of time together?'

'Not any more. My parents don't really approve,' Tomme admitted.

'Do you know anything about his past?' Sejer wanted to know.

Tomme was not sure how to answer this question. He knew a bit. He had never asked Willy for details, precisely because he did not want to get involved with anything illegal. In spite of everything he wanted to be a responsible young man. But then again, he thought it might appear suspicious if he pretended to know nothing. It was impossible to decide what this man would consider a genuine answer.

'I have to admit I don't always know what he gets up to,' Tomme said eventually. 'But I never get involved with any of it.'

Sejer backed off a little. However, he gave Tomme a long, hard look. Though the boy looked very nervous, he also had an air of innocence. There was something decent about him.

'Choose your friends carefully,' he said sincerely. Then he left.

They were pinning all their hopes on the nightie. It was the strongest lead they had; it could be traced back to the shop where it had been bought and from the shop back to the customer. If they were lucky. Skarre strode purposefully down the high street with a carrier bag in his hand. He was looking for a lingerie shop called Olav G. Hanssen. It was just across the road from the department store. Jacob Skarre had never been inside a lingerie shop. He found it very exotic. There was an abundance of beautifully domed cups, ribbons and lace, rosettes and bows. Wonderful colours. Corsets with impressive lacing, slips and suspenders. A mature lady was standing behind the counter, sorting out a box of silk stockings. She noticed the curly haired man in uniform and greeted him with a friendly smile. Skarre wandered over to the counter and looked at the stockings. They were self-supporting ones with rubber at the top to hold them in place.

He looked at the sales assistant. Refined, well dressed and mature. The shop probably had a number of regular customers, most likely women like the sales assistant herself. She had extensive knowledge of people's buttocks, breasts and thighs, and the years behind the counter had probably taught her a great deal about the kind of person who frequented the shop. Their likes and dislikes, and of course she knew what they looked like in their underwear.

Skarre placed the bag with Ida's nightie on the counter. Carefully he took it out. It was dry now and completely clean, obviously brand new. It was white, made from high-quality cotton, with red ribbon around the neck. A narrow, modest lace trim ran along the hem and the sleeves. That was all. On the inside was a label stating that the nightie was a child's size fourteen years. It had come down almost all the way to Ida's toes.

'Do you recognise this nightie?' he asked, laying it out carefully on the counter.

The sales assistant reacted immediately. 'Oh, yes. Of course I do.' She nodded and Skarre could tell from her face that she was sure of it. 'We've been selling it. We bought in four, from sizes ten to sixteen years. I've got one left, the biggest one,' she said.

Skarre nodded. 'So it could have been bought here?'

The sales assistant was eager to help, but she wanted to be accurate so she concentrated on answering his questions.

'Absolutely. But other shops could have stocked

it. It's made by Calida. Mercerised cotton,' she said knowledgeably. 'They make some very fine things.'

'I've visited the other four lingerie shops in town,' Skarre explained. 'They didn't stock this one.' He smoothed out the nightie a little. 'And I'm sure you've got other staff here,' he went on, 'but do you personally remember selling a nightie like this, and if so, who bought it?'

She considered this. 'There are just the two of us. I work ten to four every day. Then I've got another lady who only works Saturdays. I know I've sold two. Let me see. One to a man in his thirties. It was a birthday present,' she recalled. 'He wanted it wrapped. The other was bought by an elderly lady. Someone's granny most likely. I think she bought a size fourteen years, so it could have been that one.' She took another look at the nightie. 'She was not at all sure about the size. Didn't really spend time browsing, just took the first nightie she saw and didn't want it wrapped. So it was probably not a present.'

Skarre's curiosity was kindled. 'Can you describe her in more detail?' he asked.

'She was in her early seventies, I think. Well dressed. Didn't say very much.'

'What was she wearing? Do you remember?'

'A coat. Dark and anonymous, you know, the type with a fur collar. She paid cash.'

Bother, Skarre thought.

'The price was 590 kroner,' she said, 'but she didn't want a receipt. I thought that was strange. I

199

told her she would need to show her receipt if she wanted to return or exchange the nightie, but she said she wouldn't be exchanging it. She didn't even want the box. She said it was just more waste. And I remember her purse. She had one of those crocodile-skin ones.'

'Can you find out the date?' Skarre asked, even more curious now.

'I can go through the till receipts. However, I'll need some time.'

'Had you seen her before?'

'She's been here a few times, buying stockings and underwear. Normally she's very chatty.'

'So you would recognise her face? If I needed you to?'

'Oh, yes,' she said with confidence. 'I should think so.'

Skarre smiled contentedly. It was possible to get this woman to open up and remember all sorts of details if he gave her time. However, he also knew people's unbridled helpfulness when it came to recollections. Too much encouragement could easily lead to errors or sidetrack them. So he stopped and changed the subject.

'You said you'd sold another one. Or maybe it was the lady who works Saturdays? How can I get hold of her?'

Skarre was given a number he could call. He folded the nightie and got ready to leave. 'Thanks for your help.' He smiled. 'I might be back. Please would you call this number when you find out the date?'

He gave her his card. Then he walked up the pedestrian precinct to the police station. His telephone started to ring just as he sat down in front of his desk.

'The size ten nightie was bought on the twenty-ninth of August,' she informed him. 'And the other one, the older woman, bought hers on the third of September.'

'I'm most grateful to you,' Skarre said.

Sejer had just listened to a message on his answering machine.

'Hi. It's Sara. Are you ever at home? I miss you. Not all the time, not every hour of the day, but every now and again. Especially at night. Especially just before I fall asleep. And especially if I've had a glass of red wine, which I admit I have treated myself to every single evening. I've just been reading the papers on the Internet. Find out who killed Ida, please. Don't let this guy get away with it! New York's great, but it's hard work. Take care.'

He sat by the window with his glass. He had listened to the message twice and he had a funny smile at the corner of his mouth. The dog was resting by his feet. In the background he could hear Tracy Chapman's deep voice. 'Baby Can I Hold You'. On the wall was a photo of his late wife, Elise. He looked up at her, let her fill the room and allowed himself to feel all the emotions he normally suppressed. Nothing good ever came from prolonged mourning, it was merely exhausting.

'You're still beautiful,' he mumbled, taking a sip from his glass. He rested his eyes on her face. 'And you're keeping well,' he added. 'Much better than me.'

He put the glass down and reached for the packet of Tiedemann Mild Number Three. Started rolling a cigarette. He liked selecting a pinch of tobacco and ripping it; he felt the thin fibres cling to one another, felt them loosen so he could lay them in a row on the paper and then carefully roll one fat cigarette with maximum draw. He lit up and inhaled deeply, all the time listening to Tracy Chapman. He was tired and would have been able to fall asleep the moment he lay down in his bed, but he was too comfortable in his armchair to move. A woman, he pondered, trying to put together a sequence of events in his head. An older woman might have bought the nightie. Was she covering for someone? And the duvet could have been mended by a woman. Why this careful wrapping? A pretty white duvet. Brand-new nightie. Nearly six hundred kroner, according to Skarre. This had to mean that whoever was responsible for Ida's death was a responsible person in general. Concerned about Helga Joner. Who could finally bury Ida and fill her coffin with soft toys. Was that what she would have been thinking? Or he? Or they?

He looked out over the town from the thirteenth floor. Living this high up gave him a feeling of literally being on top of things. And control, he admitted. He always enjoyed the drive from the police station via Highway 76, exiting and heading for the ridge and later conquering the thirteen floors by foot to reach the very top of this stone tower that was his home. He had always liked observing people from a distance. However, there were times, and now was one of them, when it filled him with a sense of isolation. He remembered his childhood home on Gamle Møllevej outside Roskilde in Denmark, where he used to sit by the living room window looking out at a tree at eye level. Life on the ground floor.

He finished smoking and stood up. Took his glass to the kitchen. Rinsed it carefully under the tap. The dog struggled to get up and padded into the bedroom where his blanket lay next to the bed, as he always did. Sejer turned off all the lights. Caressed Elise's photo, turned around and went into the bathroom. He splashed his face with cold water and spent a long time brushing his teeth. He used an ordinary toothbrush even though an electric Braun was plugged in. It was a present from his daughter, Ingrid, but he never used it. He did not dare tell her. He opened his bedroom window. His alarm clock was set for six. He switched off the bedside light and closed his eyes. There were fifty-two flats in the whole tower block, occupied by more than one hundred and fifty people. But there was not a sound to be heard.

CHAPTER 18

Tomme decided not to answer when he saw Willy's number light up on the display of his mobile phone. However, it did mean that at some point in the future he would have to deal with the message Willy was leaving. After a while he started to sweat. It might look as if he was trying to avoid Willy and he knew he could not keep that up for ever. Eventually he got in the Opel and drove over to Willy's place. Willy was in his garage as always. The bonnet of the Scorpio was up and Willy's backside was visible.

'Did you drop off the face of the earth or what?' he asked as Tomme walked in.

'No, no,' Tomme replied. 'It's my mum and dad.'

'But you're eighteen,' Willy said. 'You can see whoever you like.'

'Of course,' Tomme declared. 'Anyway, I'm here now, aren't I?'

Willy dived back into the engine. He said nothing. Tomme waited.

'Why were you calling me anyway?' he asked. Right now he would much rather be driving back home or nipping over to see Bjørn or Helge. But he could not reject Willy just like that. He knew it. Not after everything that had happened.

'I fancy a trip to Copenhagen,' Willy said. He got up and pulled a cotton rag out of a bag on the floor. Then he spat into his palms and started rubbing grime off his fingers. 'I thought you might want to come along.'

'To Copenhagen?' Tomme hesitated.

'On the MS *Pearl of Scandinavia*,' Willy said. He pulled out a leaflet from a pocket in his boiler suit. Then he started listing the ship's amenities.

Tomme had never travelled on the ferry to Denmark. And he had no money either.

'Brand-new boat,' Willy said eagerly. 'A regular cruise ship. I've got some business to do in Copenhagen. Why don't you come along?' he repeated. He said it like it was an order. Tomme did not like the sound of it. He took the leaflet.

'It's not new at all,' he said, having read for a while. 'It's just been done up.'

'Same thing, isn't it?' Willy said.

'You know I can't afford it,' Tomme said. He put the leaflet on the worktop. It stayed there with the Polyfilla and the tools.

'I'll lend you the money, you know that,' Willy said.

Tomme thought about it. 'Business?' he said dubiously. 'I don't want to be involved with your business dealings and you know it.' The invitation worried him. Perhaps Willy had ulterior motives.

Willy shrugged. 'You've got nothing to worry

about. I just need to pop into a bar. It's called Spunk,' he said. 'It'll just take a couple of minutes. You can wait for me someplace else, if you're scared of getting into trouble. And then we'll hit the town.'

'I don't want to get mixed up with anything,' Tomme said with all the authority he could muster. If Willy got himself involved in something, he could end up taking Tomme with him. Tomme had never had a girlfriend, but he imagined that it would be easier to break up with a girl than get rid of Willy.

He instantly realised his own hypocrisy, how convenient it was for him that Willy always had money. That he was now prepared to fork out for a ticket for him, a return ticket to Copenhagen. That he had fixed his car for free. On top of that, running away from it all was quite tempting. The oppressive atmosphere at home. The police suddenly on his doorstep. His mum and her probing looks.

'Friday to Sunday,' Willy said persuasively. 'And we'll have a few hours in Copenhagen.'

Tomme tried to buy time. 'I need to check with my parents. They'll probably say no.'

'Tell them you're going with Bjørn and his mates.'

'They're bound to find out,' Tomme said.

'Bjørn and his mates will cover for you,' Willy said. 'Just tell them what to say. You're eighteen, for fuck's sake. Do you need to get permission for everything?'

'But I live there. It's their house.' Tomme tossed his head, humiliated by his situation at home. Then he remembered that Willy was older. When I'm twenty-two, Tomme thought, I won't be living at home.

'I'll book the tickets,' Willy said. 'We'll get a cheap cabin on the lower deck.'

Tomme felt as if he had trodden in glue. He wanted to free himself, but he was stuck with Willy. That same evening he asked his mother for permission to go on the boat to Copenhagen with Bjørn. She said yes. 'I'm pleased that you've started seeing him again,' she added. 'I like Bjørn. He's a nice boy. And you need to get out a bit more.' Tomme nodded. Bjørn had promised to cover for him should it become necessary. 'I can't not go,' he explained to his friend. 'Willy fixed my car. He really wants me to come with him.'

On the afternoon of the twentieth of September they joined an endless queue at the check-in desk for the MS *Pearl of Scandinavia*. They had taken the bus to Oslo. Neither of them wanted to leave their cars in the capital over the weekend. They had bags slung over their shoulders. Tomme's was a blue and red Adidas. Willy's a black and white Puma. The bags were approximately the same size with roughly similar contents. A toothbrush. A spare jumper. A jacket. When they got on board, Tomme had a look at the cabin. He didn't like it.

'A right crypt,' he mumbled, grimacing at the narrow room.

'We won't be spending much time down here,' Willy said enthusiastically. 'We'll be in the bar, won't we?'

They tossed their bags on the floor and headed for the bar. The weather forecast for the weekend was bad; Willy thought it sounded great.

'A gale, Tomme, that would be something, eh?'

Tomme ordered a pint. He had no desire for a gale. He looked across the table at Willy. His upper lip flattened every time he inhaled his cigarette. He was downing his beer at an impressive speed. Tomme suddenly felt completely alone, at the mercy of this other person. It was difficult enough at home, but there at least he had his own room. He always had choices. He could sit in the warm and cosy living room eating his mum's cakes. Or be on his own in his bedroom with some DVDs and his computer. Now he was sitting here with Willy and would continue to do so until Sunday.

'The ship weighs forty thousand tonnes,' Willy informed him, reading from the leaflet. He looked around, rolled his eyes and then looked out at the sea. 'It can carry two thousand people. Fancy that.'

'It would be a terrible disaster if it sank,' Tomme said, sipping his beer slowly. 'I intend to find out where they keep the life jackets. Might as well do it sooner rather than later.'

'Top speed twenty-one knots,' Willy stated. 'How fast is twenty-one knots?'

Tomme frowned. 'No idea. Forty kilometres per hour, perhaps?'

'Forty? That's not a lot.' Willy stared out of the window at the lazy grey waves. He was holding his pint with both hands. 'On the other hand,' it occurred to him, 'this forty-thousand-tonne baby cutting through the waves in the middle of the sea at forty kilometres an hour. And in rough weather too! That's not bad when you think of it.' He drank more beer.

He's nervous, Tomme thought. He has done this loads of times before and it has always gone without a hitch, but now he's nervous. So am I. The police have been to his garage. But they were looking for me. Perhaps they're out to get both of us. He shuddered and gulped down his beer.

'So what's up?' Willy said, glancing at him sideways. 'Any more news from the cops?'

Tomme considered his answer carefully. He would prefer not to talk about his cousin Ida and everything that had happened recently. However, it was hard to avoid. 'An officer turned up at our house the other day. Bloody tall guy!' He looked up at Willy. 'He's heading the investigation. I've seen him on TV.'

'He's the one who came to my garage.' Willy nodded.

'He wanted to know how I bashed the car. Exactly how it happened.' He was watching Willy closely. 'They've even checked out the crash barrier at the bridge. Would you believe it? They sent a man out to look for traces of black paint from the Opel!'

'Yeah?' Willy said; he was so fascinated by this that his eyes looked as if they were about to jump out of his head.

'And they found them,' Tomme said. 'I was shitting myself.'

'But it's true!' Willy stated. 'You're only telling them the truth!'

'I know. But I was still shitting myself.'

'And what else? What else are they doing?' Willy said.

'I think they've got a lead. I wish I knew what it was. I don't understand any of it,' Tomme concluded, rubbing his neck with a clammy hand. Despite the thick carpets, the floor was throbbing underneath his feet. It was weird to think that they were on a ship. It didn't feel like it; it was more like a huge restaurant with a strong humming sound coming from the basement. A power station or something like that. Tomme touched his neck with his hand again and started massaging it. He was sitting with his back against the wall and a chilly draught was coming from the window behind him.

Tomme did not dream. He fell asleep quickly and the low hum from the engines kept him company throughout the night. The next morning they went ashore. It felt good to have solid ground underneath his feet once more, but the gale was strong. The boys walked sideways against the fierce wind and warded off the worst gusts with their shoulders. Tomme's jacket had a hood; he pulled it over his head and tightened the toggles. When you looked at him from the side, his narrow nose stuck out like a fragile beak.

On Saturday Willy carried out his bit of business at Bar Spunk. That was how he phrased it. It was no big deal, just a bit of business. He had no intention of getting anyone hooked. He never forced his drugs on anyone, people came to him. Adults. Regulars always. This was how he looked at it, a welcome bit of extra cash. His wages at Mestern bowling alley were measly, and as far as he had been able to work out, none of his regular clients had ever ended up with a serious drug habit.

'But there's no way you can know that,' Tomme said. 'Kids might get their hands on the drugs. Terrible things could happen.'

'That's not my problem,' Willy said. 'I sell to responsible adults. What they do with them has got nothing to do with me.'

Tomme was in a café eating chicken and chips. Willy had gone off purposefully with the Puma bag over his shoulder. It did not look noticeably heavier when he returned just under an hour later. Afterwards they drifted round the streets, people-watching. Later that day Tomme called his mother to assure her everything was all right. With him and with Bjørn. Then it was time to go home.

They returned to the bar, to the same cabin below. Willy did not say anything about what his business had involved, he just tossed his bag casually into the cabin. True, once during the evening he nipped out to check something, as he put it, but he was back quickly. Tomme wondered if the bag, which looked entirely innocent, might have a false bottom or a secret compartment. In fact it was an ordinary sports bag made from cheap nylon.

211

Willy seemed on top of the world. During the evening he got quite drunk. Tomme was nursing his third beer and feeling clear-headed. Another gale was brewing. However, it hardly affected them; they were comfortably ensconced in their armchairs. Suddenly Willy went over to the bar and bought three pints in one go. He started downing the first one.

'Why did you do that?' Tomme said, baffled. He stared at the three glasses.

'The gale is about to hit us,' Willy said. 'If it gets too severe, they'll stop serving.' He took a huge gulp. 'I travel a lot,' he explained, 'so I know these things.'

Tomme shook his head in disbelief. He sipped his beer carefully and accepted that he would end up carrying Willy back to their cabin later on.

'There's something I've been meaning to ask you,' Willy said. His speech was beginning to slur and his face had taken on an ugly expression, which unnerved Tomme.

'Aha?' Tomme said. He tried to sound indifferent. All the same, he could not help feeling scared. He had been expecting this.

'I mean, let's face it,' Willy said. 'You owe me a favour. Or two.'

'And why's that?' Tomme said. He suddenly felt sober, and he pushed his glass aside to indicate that he was in another place. That he was in control.

'To begin with, there's this weird story of yours,' Willy said. 'Though your secret's safe with me, that

212

goes without saying. And then there's the fact that I fixed your car for free.'

'But now you want paying, is that what you're saying?' Tomme said acidly. Christ, he wished he had not come with Willy. He reached for his glass and drank fiercely. He was angry. It felt good; everything was easier when you were angry. Anger sped things up, made the blood run faster.

'Now, now, don't be crude,' Willy said. 'I'm not talking about money.'

'I didn't for think for a moment that you were,' Tomme said.

'Just a small favour in return,' Willy said. 'A little job. It'll only take a few minutes.'

Tomme waited for him to continue.

'When we go ashore,' Willy said, 'we'll swap bags.'

Tomme jumped in his chair and his eyes widened with fear. 'No way,' he said, clutching his glass.

Again Willy smiled his vicious smile and leaned across the table. 'Please, let me finish,' he said.

'I'm going back to the cabin,' Tomme said. 'I don't want to hear another word about it. And don't you go thinking that telling my weird story to anyone will get you very far.'

'Won't it?'

'Think about it, for Christ's sake. I don't even understand a single word of it myself. So why would the police?'

'Perhaps they're smarter than you?' Willy suggested.

'I don't think so. You're blackmailing me,' Tomme accused him.

Willy looked at him and pretended to be hurt. 'Aren't we as bad as each other? I've got something on you. You've got something on me. I wouldn't call that blackmail. I would call it a standoff. It'll only take you a few minutes. All I want you to do is carry the gear through customs for me.'

'Do you take me for an idiot? You're drunk,' Tomme declared. 'Let's go to bed. It's late, and they're shutting the bar soon anyway. I've had enough of this.'

'Still got some beer left,' Willy slurred. 'I just thought you might want to help me out. Given that I helped you.'

'You're asking a lot, I think,' Tomme said bitterly.

'As were you. If you think about it. If you really think about it,' Willy said, pronouncing each word with exaggerated clarity.

Tomme kept staring out of the window, hoping to see the sea. No use. It was almost impossible to believe that the sea was on the other side, right on the other side. Inside it was bright and cosy. Inside there was music and good times to be had. Now and again bursts of laughter rang out and the clinking of glasses could be heard. It was like a different sort of sea, waves of warm bodies, music, rhythm, and all of it lit up so strangely that it reminded him of the undulating surface of the ocean. He suddenly felt worn out. So tired and fed up with it all.

'Take your beer outside and let's get a bit of fresh air,' Willy said.

Tomme yawned. 'It's the middle of the night.'

'I want to see the gale,' Willy said. He drank three huge gulps so the glasses would not spill when he carried them. They left the bar and climbed up the stairs. The wind got hold of them the moment they opened the door to the stormy deck.

'For fuck's sake,' Tomme said. 'We'll get soaked.'

'Fantastic,' Willy screamed with elation. He stood with his arms stretched out to the sides and the icy wind hitting him straight in his face. It was totally exhilarating. 'The perfect storm!' he yelled.

Tomme crouched as he felt the wind grab hold of him. He held on to the railings and moved cautiously towards the stern of the ship.

Willy followed him on unsteady legs. 'Fresh air!' he hollered. 'Christ, this should sober me up,' he muttered into his glass.

Tomme felt the salty spray stick to his face. He bent over the railings. Far below he could see the black swell with the foaming white peaks. Suddenly he hated Willy. His story would haunt him for ever as long as he knew Willy. It would rear its ugly head whenever Willy wanted something from him. Whenever he wanted him to walk through customs with a bag full of drugs. He shuddered and stared down at the waves. Willy came over to the railings. Climbed up on to them and gazed down at the black water. He was taller than Tomme, but skinny as a rake. His hair was soaked through.

'Just what exactly did you buy?' Tomme said eventually.

'Eh?' Willy screamed. The roar of the sea drowned out all other sounds. The sharp rain pricked their faces.

'What's in your bag?'

'Well, it's not exactly sweets,' Willy giggled. He drank from his glass again. Suddenly it slipped out of his hand and disappeared into the waves. Amazed, he followed it with his eyes.

'Perhaps I hit a fish,' he mumbled optimistically. 'Right in the middle of its fishy head.'

'Tell me, for God's sake!'

Willy turned and faced him. 'What a way to carry on, man. I asked you to do me a favour and you said no. That's fine, you've made your point. But I wasn't being serious; I just wanted to test your loyalty. You didn't pass,' he declared.

It was said in jest, but Tomme knew him better than that. There was a bitter ring to the drawling voice. Suddenly he felt uneasy.

'I'll speak to a garage,' Tomme said, 'and get a quote for the work. Then I'll pay you back when I get some money.'

Personally he felt this was an honourable attempt at re-establishing the equilibrium between them. Willy didn't reply. He was hanging over the railings. His eyes were distant, as if the rush from the beer and the roar of the sea had carried him far away. Tomme suddenly imagined the skinny body toppling over and disappearing into the waves.

Imagined Willy sinking and taking his story with him. And that he himself would take it with him to his own grave when the time came. And that no one else knew. Only Willy. He was so drunk and reeling. So unprepared. Not a soul could see them up here.

Tomme was horrified by his own fantasies. He pulled back from the railings and sat down on a crate. His clothes were wet. It was raining harder. He remembered that he had no other trousers apart from these damp ones he was wearing now. Only a dry jumper in his bag.

He heard Willy starting to hiccup over by the railings. He hiccupped loudly four or five times then turned around and looked at Tomme. In the darkness and the rain their faces were lit up like dim lanterns and a silence grew between them that neither of them wanted to break. Tomme studied his friend's face and saw it as a moon-coloured oval; the eyes and the mouth appeared as blurred shadows. It seemed to float in the air, detached from the rest of Willy's body. Every time a gust of wind came, his hair was forced over his face, dividing the oval into two halves. White fingers appeared and glowed in the darkness only to disappear as if spirited away by a magician.

'What are you looking at me like that for?' Willy said.

Seven hours later Tomme woke up in agony from a severe headache. He could barely move his head. He stayed in his berth for several minutes without

217

opening his eyes. His mind was in turmoil. Had it all been a dream? Something evil, something utterly incredible surfaced as snippets of light and sound. He did not know whether it was still night or early morning. If they were in the middle of the fjord or nearly in port. There was no porthole in the cabin. He could raise his left arm and look at his watch if he wanted to. However, that seemed to him to require too much effort. The steady hum from the diesel engines was still there. Its pleasant vibrations spread to his body and he felt a strong reluctance to get up and lose this sensation. He could not hear any voices or footsteps. Finally he opened his eyes and stared at the ceiling. Tried to swallow. His mouth was dry. Perhaps we're in port, he thought. Perhaps all the other passengers have disembarked. There's only you left, Tomme Rix, all alone in a berth in a cabin at the bottom of the ship. At the very bottom. He could stay on and travel back to Copenhagen. And later return to Oslo. He could sail across the sea for ever and ever. Lock himself in the cabin. Bolt the door. He did not want to get up, did not want to leave the ship, did not even want to be conscious. But he was unable to go back to sleep. There were voices in the distance after all. They brought him out of his trance. He sat up drowsily and planted his feet on the floor. He had slept in his clothes. His jeans were still wet from his time on deck. He staggered over to the small sink. Splashed cold water on his face without looking in the mirror. Dried himself with the towel. The towel was stiff, he thought; it scratched his skin.

He grabbed his Adidas bag and went out. Walked through the endless narrow corridors. There was no one around. Then he reached the foyer and was suddenly surrounded by a crowd of tired people, by smells and the murmur of voices. He placed himself right in the middle of them. Tried to lose himself in the crowd. He stared at the floor. It was carpeted. He traced the pattern with his eyes and began a new one as soon as he reached the end of it. Circle, circle, square and straight line. Bow, square and straight line. The crowd started to move towards the exit. He allowed himself to be pulled along, no will of his own. Walked through customs, where no one even glanced at him, and up towards the city. At Egertorg he stopped for a minute. He stared at the entrance to the underground; saw the white sign with the blue 'T'. Tried to create an image in his mind that he could share with others later. Wasn't that Willy just disappearing down the steps? The bony shoulders he knew so well. The dark blue jacket? He saw it quite clearly. So clearly that later he would be able to retrieve it, should it become necessary. Something inside him started ticking. It made him feel like he was going to explode. The ticking would continue for a while until finally everything would blow up. He continued onwards to Universitetsplassen. There he joined the queue for the bus.

219

CHAPTER 19

The newspapers carried a photo of Ida's nightie. Two people came forward immediately and were eliminated. The nighties they had bought were the wrong sizes. However, the elderly woman who had visited the shop on the third of September and bought the size fourteen years did not contact them.

'Let's try an artist's impression,' Sejer said.

A drawing was produced in accordance with instructions from the sales assistant at Olav G. Hanssen and published in the papers. The drawing showed an elderly woman with large ears and protruding round eyes. Her face was elongated and marked, and if it expressed anything at all it was scepticism. Her mouth was straight and narrow, her hair thick and full. Next to the woman's face was once again the photo of the nightie. Now all of Norway knew how Ida was dressed when she was found by the roadside out at Lysejordet.

The chances of someone calling in with clues to her identity were high. The readers loved artists' impressions and the illustrator was gifted.

The third caller caught Sejer's attention instantly.

'I know a lady very much like her. She turned seventy-three last spring and she doesn't have a grandchild or any other relative who would wear a nightie that's a size fourteen years,' the voice said confidently. It sounded like it belonged to an elderly woman. She introduced herself as Margot Janson.

'Now she's a generous size forty-four,' she carried on. 'I've known her for twenty years. She does my washing. I've broken my hip, you see, and God only knows what I would have done without her. She comes here every single week and she's thorough, trust me. She lives at Giske, in one of the flats out there. Her husband died many years ago.'

Sejer was taking notes as she spoke.

'Of course it's unthinkable that she would have anything to do with Ida going missing, and I've no idea why her picture is in the newspaper. She's the most decent person I know. But it does look very much like Elsa. Elsa Marie Mork.'

Sejer made a note of her name and address.

'She helps out with all sorts of things, she is even a member of the Women's Institute. A capable lady, trust me, and very hardworking too. On top of that she has enough on her plate in her private life. Not that I can tell you anything about that, I don't want to gossip,' said Margot Janson.

Sejer was now seriously interested. He thanked her and hung up. Perhaps the nightie had been bought by Elsa Marie Mork. And if she officially had no one to buy it for, then that in itself was suspicious. He found it hard to believe that the killer

221

would turn out to be a woman in her seventies, but she could be covering for someone. Margot Janson had said that Elsa Marie Mork's husband was dead. What other person would make an elderly woman run such risks? The answer was obvious. A brother. Or a son.

The drive to Giske took fifteen minutes. Four two-storey blocks were neatly positioned on a sunny slope. Not high enough to treat the residents to a pleasant view of the river; however, they were shielded from the wind by the ridge that lay behind them. A cosy and comfortable location. There were no sandpits or tricycles to be seen. These flats were inhabited by elderly people who no longer wanted to live within earshot of kids playing. He read the names on the doorbells, found hers and pressed the button. Women in their seventies could be hard of hearing, or the ultra-efficient Elsa might be busy hoovering. Whatever the reason, she took her time. Perhaps she was checking him out from behind the curtain first. Or she was simply not in. Sejer stood on the steps, waiting. Finally he could hear her footsteps coming from the inside. A sharp clicking as if she was walking across a wooden floor. The last thing he had done before leaving his car was to take another look at the artist's impression. It was burned on to his retina. The stern face with the narrow lips. Suddenly she was standing right in front of him. Her body was already pulling away, she was trying to shut the door again as she did when faced with people wanting to sell her things.

222

Konrad Sejer bowed deeply. The bow was his trademark; an old-fashioned gesture, rarely used by people these days and then revived only for special occasions. It made an impression on Elsa Mork, so she remained standing in front of him. She had strong views on manners.

'Konrad Sejer,' he said politely. 'Police.'

She blinked in fright. Her face took on a gawping expression and her eyes strayed towards the grey plastic carrier bag he was holding in his hand.

'I've got a few questions,' Sejer said, looking at the elderly woman with interest. She was wearing trousers and a jumper. Her clothing was typical of elderly people, for whom comfort takes priority. They were non-iron, colourfast and plain. The trousers had an elasticated waist and stitched creases. It would be unfair to describe Elsa Mork as vain. There was not a hint of jewellery or anything like that. Her face was scrubbed and not a hair was out of place. He could see why Margot Janson had called. This woman looked exactly like the artist's impression. At last she opened the door completely and let him into the hallway. It had parquet flooring just like he had imagined, and Elsa Mork was wearing clogs. He noticed the smell. It struck him that her flat had a distinctive smell; that you could actually smell that the whole block was inhabited by old people. However, he could not pinpoint exactly why he thought that. Perhaps it was more the absence of smells. There was something very reserved about her, but that did not necessarily mean anything. She was a woman living on her own, and

223

she had just let a strange man measuring one metre ninety-six into her home. She looked like she was already regretting it.

She showed him the way to a kitchen, which was painted green. She nodded towards the table and Sejer sat down on the edge of a chair. Then he placed the carrier bag on the table. A grey carrier bag with no printing or logo. He took out the nightie and laid it on the tabletop. All the time he was watching her. Her face was closed.

'This nightie is important,' he explained. 'And I need to speak to the person who bought it.'

She sat rigidly on her chair as he spoke.

'We have reason to believe that you went to a shop and bought a nightie like this. On the third of September. From Olav G. Hanssen in the high street. Is that correct?'

Her mouth tightened. 'No. Surely you can see it's too small for me,' she said, giving him a look that suggested his eyesight needed examining.

'The papers carried a photo of this a few days ago,' Sejer went on. 'We asked people to contact us if they had seen or bought a nightie like this. Two people called us. However, the shop sold three in total,' he said. 'And I'm here because the sales assistant in Olav G. Hanssen gave a very detailed description of the woman who bought the third one. And it so happens that you fit that description.'

Elsa Mork was silent. Her nails dug into her palms as she rested her hands on the Formica table. She had become mute.

224

'Have you seen today's paper?' he asked kindly. He even smiled. He wanted to say, don't worry. I don't blame you for Ida's death.

'Yes,' she said slowly. 'I read the papers.'

'And the artist's impression?' He smiled patiently.

'What artist's impression?' she said defiantly. She no longer dared to look at him.

'An artist's impression of a woman. She looks like you, doesn't she?'

Elsa shook her head blankly. 'She doesn't look like me at all,' she said firmly.

'So you've seen it?' he went on.

'I flick through the pages,' she said.

Sejer listened out for the sound of birds chirping in the flat. He heard nothing. Perhaps a blanket had been laid over the cage; he believed that would make birds stop singing because they would think it was night-time.

'The Ida Joner case. Are you familiar with it?'

She thought about this for a few seconds before answering him with the same firmness. 'Like I said, I read the papers. But things like that I just skim over. I think all those details are so gruesome. So I don't read about crime. Or sport or war reports either. That doesn't leave very much,' she said sarcastically. 'Just the telly pages.'

'Do you own a bird?' he asked curiously.

She was startled. 'No,' she said quickly. 'Never owned a bird. Why would I want one of those?'

'Many people have caged birds,' he said. 'I'm asking because it's relevant to the case.'

225

'I see,' she said. She sat by the table looking tense, staring fixedly out of the window. 'No, I don't keep birds. Please, help yourself, take a good look around. Why would I want to keep birds,' she went on. 'It's too much mess. Seeds and feathers all over the place. I can do without that, thank you very much.'

Sejer thought about what she had just said. About seeds and feathers all over the place. She sounded as if she knew a great deal about what keeping a bird involved. Had she already got rid of it?

'Perhaps you know someone who keeps a bird?'

'No,' she said quickly. 'People my age don't keep that type of pet. A friend of mine's got a cat. Her whole house stinks of it. It's for the company, I suppose, but personally I don't need that. I don't spend my days sitting in here staring out of the window like a lot of people I know.'

'That's good,' he said. He started folding the nightie, but deliberately made a mess of it. She was watching him out of the corner of her eye.

'So you don't recognise this nightie?' he asked once more.

'Absolutely not,' she claimed. 'What would I want with it?'

'You might have bought it for someone else,' he suggested.

She did not answer and used all her strength to maintain her rigid posture by the table, as if a change of position would give her away.

'But it's pretty, don't you think?' Sejer smiled,

226

putting it back in the carrier bag. Then he tied the handles into a knot. 'We can agree that whoever bought it had an eye for beauty as well as quality. Well, that's what one of our female officers said.' He smiled.

'Absolutely,' she said quickly.

'Expensive, too. Four hundred kroner,' lied Sejer.

'Oh,' said Elsa Mork. 'I would have thought it was more.'

Sejer got up from the table. 'Please forgive me for disturbing you,' he said. 'I realise you don't have children of that age. It's a size fourteen years. But it might have been for a granddaughter. I have an eleven-year-old grandchild,' he added.

She relaxed somewhat and smiled. 'Well, I do have a son, but he's over fifty,' she said. 'And he'll never have kids.'

She wanted to bite her tongue. Sejer pretended nothing had happened. The fact that she had a son meant nothing in itself. But she had seemed alarmed by the admission. As though mentioning her son would give Sejer cause for thoughts he had not been thinking so far. He left the green kitchen quietly. He did not want to frighten her by asking her for the name of her son. And anyway, it would be easy for him to discover. She followed him out.

'Just a small thing,' he remembered. 'Do you own a dark coat?'

Elsa Mork smiled her ironic smile once more. 'Every woman over seventy owns a dark coat,' she said.

'With a fur collar?' he asked.

She squirmed in the doorway. 'Well, it's some sort of fur collar,' she muttered. 'Not sure what it is. It's an old coat.'

He nodded; he understood.

'But I still don't know why you came here,' she said in sudden despair; she had to put words to her confusion, she could no longer control herself.

'Because you look like the woman in the artist's impression,' he said.

'But you've never met me before. Someone must have called you!' The latter came out as a cry of indignation.

'Yes,' he said. 'Someone did call. I'm going to visit the next person on my list now. Or rather the next woman. That's what I do. Door-to-door enquiries.'

He walked the few steps to his car and looked at her once more. 'Thank you for your time,' he said, bowing again. Her eyes flickered slightly. She realised it was finally over. She was free to go back into her kitchen, where she could sit by the window and wait. Sejer was back in his seat. He opened the paper once again and looked at the artist's impression. He knew she was standing behind her curtain, watching him.

CHAPTER 20

Emil Johannes' throat was getting sore. He had been standing by the waterfall, grunting, for a long time. The roar from the water, which he needed before he had the courage to start, also made it difficult to hear if he was successful at making a sound or not. If he had managed individual words, or an 'o' or an 'a'.

Now he was back in his house. He went to the mirror in his bathroom and pursed his lips. There was no waterfall here, but he could turn on the cold tap and lean towards the mirror. How would he ever explain it? Suddenly he had so much to say. He had never needed to speak, never needed to explain himself to anyone. Fancy standing by the waterfall shouting, he thought, and blushed. A grown man behaving like that. Despondently he stared down into the sink, where the slightly discoloured water had stained the porcelain. There was rust in the pipes, but his incapacity benefit would not stretch to having them replaced with new copper ones. Not that he cared. Only his mother cared. She gathered together all his whites

229

and washed them in her own machine. Otherwise you'll end up with tea-coloured bed linen in a few weeks, she nagged. Emil wasn't in the least interested in the colour of his bed linen. He didn't think such things mattered. His mother would turn up with citric acid and tell him to add it to the water when he washed up. It'll make the water clear, she explained. But he couldn't make out how to use the powder. And he couldn't see that his plates had changed colour.

He stared stiffly at himself in the mirror. He didn't usually do that; he avoided looking at himself. Nor did he look properly at other people when he drove around on his three-wheeler, or wandered around the shelves in the shops. However, he liked watching television. Liked being able to stare at people without them knowing it. He could laugh at them, or threaten them with his fists, and there was nothing they could do about it. Sometimes he pulled terrible faces, and occasionally he would stick his tongue out at them. However, they were inside a box and could not get at him; they would not care what he did, and they would never ask him questions. Still, they were good company. He watched a lot of television. Political debates. Agitated people calling out and gesturing, people who got excited and flushed and heated, who banged the table with their fists and flung out their arms like squabbling children. He liked that.

Through the splashing from the tap he suddenly heard the telephone ringing. He made an involuntary movement with his head and let it ring. It rang eight times, then it stopped. From experience he knew that it would soon start to ring again. It was his mother. She would not give up.

He turned off the water and went out into the living room. Threw a hostile glance at the telephone, which was the old-fashioned type with a rotary dial. The bird instantly tripped along its perch and tilted its head. Perhaps food was about to appear between the bars. Emil felt caught between a rock and a hard place. He wished his mother would leave him alone and stay away from him. At the same time he knew he needed her. There were things he was incapable of sorting out. Once, his power had been cut off. He had no light, no television. Yet still he had sat in front of the television all night, watching his own silhouette. That had been a really boring evening, Emil thought. His mother had had to call the electricity company on his behalf. He thought it was good that she talked, that she dealt with things and got them fixed. The telephone rang again. He waited a long time. Instinctively he turned his back to the telephone as he answered it. A rejection she would not be able to see.

'Emil?' He could hear that her voice sounded very strained. 'Have you seen today's paper?'

Emil looked across the room to where the newspapers lay untouched on the table. 'No,' he replied truthfully.

There was total silence at the other end of the telephone. Emil realised that this did not happen very often. It intrigued him enormously. It also made him feel scared. There was something ominous about his mother's voice, normally she sounded so self-assured.

'Well, just leave them then. It's almost too much to bear,' she groaned, and Emil heard how impotent her voice sounded. He realised for the first time that his mother was frightened. He had hardly ever experienced that. Not since he was a boy.

'The police were here,' she whispered. 'Have they been to see you?'

He shook his head in terror. At the same time he looked out on to the drive. There was nothing to see.

'No,' he said.

'I'm scared they might turn up,' she said. 'If they come knocking, then don't let them in!'

'No,' he said.

'If they stop you on the road, shake your head and drive on. Just be yourself,' she pleaded. 'Don't try to explain anything; you won't succeed, so it's best if you keep quiet like you always do. They'll give up when they realise what you're like. Just roll your eyes or stare at the ground, but don't let them in the house. And for God's sake don't sign anything!'

'No,' he said.

'If they turn up, you must call me. It might be best if I come over right now. They've just been here. If I'm with you when they turn up, I can speak for you. You won't be able to handle this on your own; we both know that. We just have to keep them at bay as best we can. And this time you'll do as I say, Emil. I hope you realise how serious this is. I don't know how much allowance they'll make for you, but I wouldn't automatically assume that they'll let you get off more lightly than others.' Her voice was close to breaking.

Emil poked at a scratch in the table with his fingernail. Oh, he always got off more lightly than others. He simply refused to answer. Then they gave up. They always gave up. No one ever had the patience.

'Dear Lord,' he heard her voice down the telephone, 'this will be the death of me. You know I'm strong, but this is getting to me, even to me. What's going to become of you, Emil?' She sighed deeply.

Emil often got fed up with his mother's complaints, but what he was hearing now was worse than ever.

'Have you thought about what all this is doing to me?' she said. 'I'm seventy-three years old, Emil! Have you thought about that?'

'No,' he said. To be honest he had no idea how old she was. She had always been the same, he thought. He wanted her to hang up, so that everything would be quiet.

'So,' his mother said with another deep sigh, 'don't talk to anyone. And don't sign anything. Do you hear me? And don't you dare cross me!'

'No,' he said.

He hung up. Went over to the kitchen table and found some old brown wrapping paper in a drawer. There was a pencil on the windowsill. Slowly he wrote his name in large, clear letters. There it was in all its glory. Emil Johannes Mork.

He looked towards the window. His face took on a defiant expression, like that of a child who insists on showing you something, who will not be thwarted. I can explain it all, he thought.

The sun was shining outside. SUN. He wrote that down. Some words were easy. He wrote FOOD because he felt hungry. Other words were harder. He thought of the word 'misunderstanding', but had to give up. Whereas the word DEAD was easier. After a few minutes he scrunched up the paper. He stood for a long time squeezing it, compressing it into a tiny hard ball. Then he pulled himself together and went into the living room. First he opened the door to the cage. Then he held the ball of paper out to the bird. The bird instantly lifted its claw and snatched it. It began tearing the paper into shreds with its beak. Sharp ripping noises could be heard as the paper fell to the bottom of the cage in fine strips.

Emil opened the newspaper. He turned the pages slowly, then froze as he saw the artist's impression. Oh no, he thought, shuddering. The drawing was horrible because it resembled his mother and yet at the same time it did not. He worked his way through the text. Many of the words were too complicated for him, but he understood the gist of

234

it. He let the newspaper fall and rubbed his head nervously. This is all going wrong, he thought. They don't understand anything.

CHAPTER 21

Tomme arrived home at Madseberget. He opened the door to the hall and put his bag down. Immediately he heard his mother's footsteps. A second later she was standing there giving him a searching look. She wanted to know how his trip had gone. The kind of things mothers always wanted to know. They think they've got a right, Tomme thought. Have they?

He peeled off his jacket, the ticking inside his head continuing all the time. I could tell it like it is, he thought, I could spin round and scream it right in her face. That something truly awful has happened. Something she wouldn't believe. Whereupon everything would explode inside both him and his mother. He did not do so. He chose the ticking. Heard his own voice saying it had been a nice trip. The words came easily and he was amazed to hear his own account of the weekend in Copenhagen, which included the weather, which had been windy, the tasty sandwiches they had eaten at the café, and their tiny cabin. Then he went to the bathroom. He desperately needed to clean his teeth.

Ruth looked after him for a long time. She did think he seemed pale and drawn, but boys will be boys, she thought. Bjørn, the friend he had gone with, was a very sensible boy, she was sure of that. Tomme was still in the bathroom. She thought he might have fallen asleep in there, on the heated floor, like Marion used to when she was little. He was taking a long time. It was very quiet.

'You haven't fallen asleep, have you?' she called through the door. He coughed briefly and she heard the sound of the taps being turned on.

'Oh, no,' he replied.

She retired to the kitchen. He's practically a grown-up, she thought. Why should I expect him to report back to me whenever he's been away from home? They had to try to get back to some sort of normality. However, Ida's death had upset the whole family. There was strain and tension everywhere, she felt. And wasn't he strangely pale? His voice sounded mechanical, like he was delivering a rehearsed speech. She had never questioned Tomme's honesty. She took it completely for granted. She thought the same of her daughter, Marion, and her husband, Sverre. That they always told the truth. Yet she felt uneasy whenever she thought of her son and the way he was acting. Something kept on nagging her. She had a strong feeling that he was struggling with something. A deep-seated instinct was telling her that he was lying. It's just because I'm tired, she thought, I'm not thinking straight. It's a vicious circle. From now on I have to trust that he's telling me the truth. From now on, she thought.

Cheered by this decision, she faced the evening. She thought, life goes on. Ida has been buried. The police will find her killer. She calmed down. Made coffee and heated up some waffles in the microwave. Called to Marion.

'Come downstairs,' she said, 'and let's watch the news.'

They sat close together on the sofa. Ruth put her arm around Marion's shoulder. Again they showed the photo of the white nightie.

'It's a pretty nightie,' Marion said.

'Mm,' Ruth said quietly. 'It must be strange for Helga to see it on the telly.'

'Why do you think they did it?' her daughter asked, looking at her.

'Did what? Kill her, you mean?' Ruth said.

'No. Why did they dress her in a nightie?'

'Why do you want to know?' Ruth asked.

'Don't know,' Marion said gravely. 'I don't really know.'

'Everything can be traced,' Ruth speculated. 'They can find out everything about that nightie. Life's strange like that. It's practically impossible to hide anything. The truth will always out. It just takes time.' She stroked her daughter's chubby cheek. 'Are you scared?' she wanted to know.

'No,' Marion said.

'I mean, when you're out walking and a car drives past you?'

'But I'm hardly ever outside now,' Marion reminded her.

'No,' Ruth said. 'I'm sorry if I'm going on about it. It'll get better.'

'Yes.'

Marion put jam on a heart-shaped waffle. Tomme came downstairs and sat in an armchair. This did not happen often. Ruth appreciated it. Everything was so peaceful. His dark head was bent over a magazine. Marion ate waffles till she was sated and then started on her homework. Sverre was abroad again, in London this time.

Then the telephone rang. Tomme did not seem to want to answer it. Ruth went over. Baffled, she listened to the voice at the other end. It was a woman. She introduced herself as Anne Oterhals, and Ruth realised that she was Willy's mother. She stared at her son in disbelief; she could not take in what she was hearing. For a moment she felt dizzy. She could see Tomme sitting there, terrified at what was happening right now; she could tell from his shining eyes that something very complicated was going on inside his head. He kept his eyes fixed on the magazine, but he was no longer reading.

'Tomme,' Ruth said reluctantly. 'Do you know where Willy is?'

He looked at her with glassy blue eyes. 'Willy? He's with a friend, I think.' His voice was so faint, Ruth thought. He held her gaze for two seconds, then he hid behind his magazine once more. Ruth recognised it as *Illustrated Science*.

239

Tomme was staring right at a photo of the Egyptian god Anubis. It looked like Willy, he thought. The lean face with the protruding chin. Like a dog. He heard the ticking again. He thought his mother could hear it too, and his sister, who was sitting over by the dining table. It filled the whole room; it was like a prickling sensation in his ears.

His mother was still on the telephone. She was bewildered. 'I don't understand this,' she said down the telephone. 'Tomme went to Copenhagen with Bjørn. Bjørn Myhre.'

She listened to the other woman. Her face is so naked, Tomme thought. He was peering up at her. He did not like seeing her like this. Marion was bent over her books. She was listening too. There was something wrong with the mood in the whole room; she dared hardly breathe or cough or stir over by the table. In her maths book were illustrations of squares, triangles and cubes. She decided to make this her own private universe and lose herself in it. So that was what she did.

'Aha?' Ruth was saying. She was yanking the telephone cord while her eyes flickered. 'Yes,' she said. 'Hold on. I'll just ask.' She pressed the receiver against her chest and looked at her son. 'It's Willy's mother. He hasn't come home after his trip to Denmark. You said you were going with Bjørn. Did Willy come too? What's going on?' she hissed.

'It was just Willy and me,' Tomme said. The words were barely audible. The ticking faded for a moment, but increased in volume when he stopped talking.

'You lied to me?' Her voice was quivering.

'Yes,' he said flatly.

'So where is he then?' she said, louder this time. 'His mother is saying he's not back. Did you get on the same bus?'

'We went our separate ways in Oslo,' Tomme said, studying Anubis. 'He got on the underground. At Egertorg.' He visualised the dark blue jacket as it disappeared down into the depths. He had rehearsed this image earlier.

His mother passed this information on to Willy's mother. Her eyes still had a naked expression. Most of all she felt like slamming down the receiver and hurling herself at her son. Instead she was forced to listen to the endless flow of words coming from the other end. Willy's mother wanted to know exactly where they had said goodbye. What Willy had said. She went on and on.

'I caught the bus at Universitetsplassen,' Tomme said truthfully. 'Willy didn't tell me who he was going to see, he just went off. Said he was meeting a mate.'

His mother passed on this information as well. Finally she hung up. She remained standing, looking at him.

'You owe me an explanation,' she said, her voice eerily calm now. She knew that Marion was listening, but she could not stop herself.

Tomme nodded. 'He asked if I wanted to come,' he admitted. 'I didn't think I could say no. He spent days working on the car.'

241

'I think it's about time you started making your own decisions,' Ruth said firmly. 'You've got to stop letting him order you about like this. But the worst thing is that you've lied to me.'

'Yes,' Tomme said feebly.

'There will be no more lies!' she said furiously. 'You've let me down!'

'Yes,' Tomme said. He let it all rain down on him, he did not try to escape.

Suddenly Ruth started to cry. Tomme sat in the armchair, motionless, and Marion hid behind her maths book.

'I'm just so tired,' Ruth sobbed.

As neither of the children said anything, she tried to pull herself together. 'But why hasn't Willy come home?' she asked.

Tomme was still staring at his magazine. 'I suppose he had some stuff to do,' he said. 'I wasn't really that interested. It's not like he's my boyfriend.'

'No.' She hesitated. 'I just think it's strange. That he didn't go straight home.'

Tomme finally turned to the next page. Ruth thought about Willy. After all, he was twenty-two. Surely there was no need for her to worry about him. But once again something made her anxious. She could not calm herself down. She paced up and down the house and started tidying up. Her rage was rekindled and it struck her that Tomme was getting off far too lightly. She would have no more lies in this house; they made her feel sick. In the hall

242

she found Tomme's bag with his jumper and his jacket. And some brown plastic bags. There were four of them, the size of ground-coffee bags. Baffled, she held one of them up and squeezed it. Its contents felt like tiny pills. Her words were coming faster than her thoughts as she marched back to face her son. She was raging like a volcano at the point of eruption. Her whole body shook and her face was scarlet.

'What on earth did you buy in Copenhagen?'

Tomme looked at the bag. For a while he just sat there gawping. Slowly the truth dawned on him; it crept up his body like wriggling worms, starting from his toes. Willy had slipped the drugs into his bag. He understood it now and wanted to explain, but no words came out.

Ruth lost it completely. She was very scared, but her fear had sunk deep down inside her, only to surface as violent rage. Now her very worst fears had been realised, and this time she would not hold back. She marched over to the coffee table where Tomme was sitting and tore open the bag with her fingernails. Hundreds of tiny pills spilled out. They rolled past the coffee cups and the teaspoons, they spilled over the edge and down on to the carpet. She forgot that Marion was sitting at the dining table doing her homework, forgot everything about discretion and sensitive approaches, because this was serious! Now she could finally confront her son; every single one of her suspicions had turned out to be well founded.

Tomme was still gawping. The magazine had slipped out of his hands. He saw Marion like a shadow at the table.

'Now I get it,' he said feebly.

Ruth was white as a sheet. 'Well I don't!' she said through clenched teeth. 'And this time I want you to tell me exactly what it is you and Willy are up to!'

When people tell the truth, the whole truth, the truth straight from their heart, a special light appears in their eyes, a glow of innocence that is mirrored in their voice, which in turn takes on a distinctive and sincere tone, a persuasive force it is quite simply impossible to ignore. When people are scared the way Tomme was scared now, only the unadulterated truth can save them. That is why truth will always out in the end. When everything has gone too far. When too many awful events have happened. And when death has touched a house, then only a hardened and habitual liar would risk inventing another story. That was what Ruth was thinking as she listened to Tomme and his tale. And she believed him. Not because I'm his mother, she thought, but because I know him and I can tell when he's lying. And he has done that so many, many times. But he is not lying this time. He had let go of the magazine and held his fists clenched in his lap. He looked at her, his blue eyes shining with the light of innocence and a fervent plea, a passionate supplication that now, at this very moment, after many dubious stories, he was finally telling her the truth.

244

Ruth nodded. Willy had tricked Tomme in the most horrible way. He had forced him to carry the tablets through customs. She wiped her tears and sensed how the exertion had made her warm. And she was strong. She laid down conditions. He was to break off all contact with Willy and see other friends. Together they would flush the tablets down the toilet. They really ought to take them to the police, but he deserved one last chance. And when Willy turned up to get his drugs, Tomme would have to face him and tell him the truth. That they had been flushed down into the sewer.

It was Tomme's turn to nod. He looked his mother straight in the eye and nodded his dark head emphatically. All the while remembering the moment when Willy had nipped out from the bar and gone down to the cabin 'just to check something'. It all made sense to him now. Ruth believed him. His behaviour towards Willy matched her knowledge of him; he was not strong enough to stand up to someone who was four years his senior. She could forgive this. And she was convinced that Tomme himself had never taken drugs. She would have noticed. They spoke for a long time about many things. Tomme realised that he could not leave; he had to stay there until his mother had finished. When she finally stopped talking he would go upstairs to his room and lie down on his bed. Then he would stare at the ceiling, lost in a world of his own. And the ticking would continue. It's so strange, he thought, that this is happening. That I'm sitting here in this armchair, nodding. There are waffles and jam on the table. If I wanted to, I could help myself to some. When she stops talking. I think I fancy a waffle. In his mind he could conjure up the taste of sweet jam and salty butter.

'Now I don't want any more trouble from you for a very long time,' Ruth said. 'Do you hear?'

Tomme nodded. Poor Mum, he thought, and felt like laughing, but he controlled himself. There would be plenty of time for laughing. Later.

Ruth suddenly remembered that Marion was still at the dining table. Giddily she ran over to her and hugged her tightly.

'Marion!' she said. 'Willy's the one who's broken the law. He's trying to drag your brother into this, but we won't let him succeed. Do you understand?'

Marion nodded into her book and concealed her face with her hand. It was impossible to work out what her answer was. Ruth sniffed again and mustered a brave smile to lighten the mood.

'It's going to be all right,' she said, hugging Marion's plump body. Marion was practically crushed by her arms. 'Everything is going to be fine. I promise you!'

246

CHAPTER 22

I've always been open-minded and tolerant. I'm not normally biased. I'd stake my reputation on that, Konrad Sejer thought. Everyone deserves a chance. Pigeonholing people destroys any possibility of seeing them as they really are. Yet the information on the screen had got him thinking. It was technically correct that Elsa Marie Mork had a fifty-two-year-old son who was unmarried. He was also receiving incapacity benefit. He'll never have kids, she had said. As though he was different in some way and should not expect the same blessings in life as everyone else. When speaking of Elsa, Margot Janson had hinted that she had problems of her own. Perhaps she was referring to the son. For a while he stared at the name. It was unknown to him, but it had a pleasant ring to it. A name given in love, not allocated casually. He wrote it down on a scrap of paper and went over to the map on the wall. Slowly and carefully he stuck red and green pins into significant locations. Ida's house on Glassblåserveien. Laila's Kiosk. The substation at the end of Ekornlia. Lysejordet where Ida was found. Elsa Marie Mork's house and finally her son's. Then he stepped back and studied the result. The pins circled an area with a diameter of ten kilometres. He left the office, found Skarre in the meeting room and handed him the scrap of paper.

'Emil Johannes Mork,' Skarre read aloud.

'Brenneriveien 12,' Sejer said. 'You know your way around up there?'

'Well, I've got a map,' Skarre said, putting the note in a pocket of his uniform.

'I want you to go and check him out,' Sejer said. 'Keep your eyes open. Note what type of car he drives, if he does drive. He's on incapacity benefit,' he added. 'We're probably looking for a van. At any rate it has to be a vehicle with plenty of room for a girl and a bicycle.'

Skarre drove off. He knew the area roughly, but ran into difficulties nevertheless. For a while he drove around completely lost, but eventually he found Brenneriveien. The numbering on the short road was hopeless and he had no idea what kind of house he was looking for. Finally a boy came walking past. Skarre rolled down his window.

'Number 12?' he asked through the window. 'Emil Johannes Mork?'

The boy was carrying a skateboard. He tucked it under his arm and pointed across the road. 'The green house,' he said, staring at Skarre's uniform with curiosity. 'With the garage next to it.'

'I see.' Skarre thanked him.

'So what are you doing here?' the boy asked him cheekily.

'Nothing at all.' Skarre smiled. 'I just wanted a word or two.'

The boy laughed. 'That's not a lot,' he said.

'No, it's not, is it?' Skarre said.

The boy pulled on his skateboard. It kept sliding down his nylon jacket. 'That Mork guy, he can't talk!'

Feeling bewildered, Skarre stayed in his car with the engine running. 'Really?' He hesitated.

The boy was still laughing. 'But you can always have a go!'

Ah well, Skarre thought. I don't suppose I'll get a bigger challenge in my career in the force than questioning a man who can't talk. He put the car into gear and drove on. He noticed the house, no number on the door. He stared at the garage, which presumably was full of junk, since the owner's vehicle was parked on the drive. Not a van. A three-wheeler with a body. Skarre got out of his car. A large piece of tarpaulin was tied to one end of the body. He stood there for a time staring at the three-wheeler, because it seemed familiar. And he remembered that during the search, when everyone had met up at Glassverket school, this very vehicle had been parked next to the bicycle shed. A man had followed them at a distance. Skarre sensed a budding apprehension spreading through his body. He glanced towards the house and thought that whoever lived inside it would already have heard the car and would be expecting him. The house was small, with two windows facing the road. It was an older property, from the forties or fifties, and reasonably well maintained. Through the curtains he could see a yellow light in the kitchen. The door frame was splintered as if someone had attempted a break-in.

As he stood there staring, he began to wonder. Had Ida been in this house? If so, would he be able to sense it? He knocked three times and waited. The door opened quietly. A man stared out through the gap. His hair was thinning; he was compact and heavy, with a broad, solid face. His clothes seemed old-fashioned; a blue-and-green-checked brushed cotton shirt and old terylene trousers. He was wearing Levi's braces and they were tight. The waistband of his trousers was pulled well up over his stomach. His expression was closed and the gap in the door was narrow. Skarre gave him a friendly smile.

'Hello,' he said, 'Jacob Skarre. I hope I'm not disturbing you?'

Emil saw the uniform. He glanced over his shoulder into the house. His mother's words echoed in his ears. 'From now on we'll keep quiet!'

'No,' he said. His voice was unexpectedly powerful.

Skarre took a step forward. That boy with the skateboard had clearly been wrong. Of course this man could talk.

'Is your name Emil Johannes Mork?' he asked, expecting a nod. It did not come. But that was the name on the letterbox. Skarre had checked. 'I'm going around the neighbourhood asking questions,' he continued. 'So if you're not too busy?'

'No, no,' Emil said once more, rocking backwards and forwards in the doorway. Skarre kept on smiling. The man was on his guard and did not look particularly welcoming, but he was talking. Presumably he rarely got visitors. He continued to block the doorway and gave no indication of wanting to move.

'Could I come inside for a moment, please?' Skarre asked him directly.

Emil stared down at the doorstep while he thought hard about this. His mother had said no. No, don't let anyone in. But he had so much to explain. He wanted to and yet he did not. Frustrated, he began tugging at the door frame and the floorboards under his feet started to creak.

'It's a bit chilly out here,' Skarre tried, while making a shivering movement with his shoulders at the same time. Emil was still silent. He tucked his thumbs under his braces and started pulling them.

'Nice braces,' Skarre said, nodding at his chest.

Emil finally made up his mind and opened the door all the way. Skarre thanked him and followed him inside. They came into a small kitchen. It was clean and fairly tidy, yet it contained a series of unmistakable smells. Skarre tried to distinguish them and detected a blend of coffee, leftovers, green soap, sour milk, and sweat from a mature man who did not wash regularly. He looked around with curiosity: at the kitchen table with the

251

chequered wipe-clean tablecloth; the artificial plant on the windowsill – a pink begonia with luminous green leaves, the wall calendar where a red magnet indicated today's date. The twenty-fourth of September. Emil went over to the cooker. There was a kettle on it, blackened by age. He started fumbling with the lid. Skarre watched his broad back. His build was heavy, but he was not particularly tall: one metre seventy-five, perhaps. The policeman was just about to ask if he could sit down when the silence in the small house was torn apart by a piercing scream. It cut through the room and culminated in a howling, hoarse climax so unexpected and so alien that it made Skarre jump. His heart leapt to his throat and his blood froze in his veins. The scream hung suspended between the walls; it was so powerful that Skarre felt actual pressure on his eardrums. For a moment he stood swaying from the shock while staring at the man by the cooker. Emil, by contrast, had not even blinked.

Slowly the penny dropped. It dawned on Skarre with a mixture of horror and joy that it was the scream of a bird. He laughed, a little embarrassed at himself, and went into the living room to explore. And there in front of the window stood a large birdcage. Inside the cage was a grey bird. He tried to relax his shoulders. He was starting to tense up. They had been looking for a man with a bird. Now he was here, in the living room of Emil Johannes Mork, staring straight at a grey parrot. A remarkable bird of an unremarkable colour. Apart from the tail feathers. They were red.

'You scared the living daylights out of me,' he said to the bird. The bird blinked its black eyes and tilted its head. Skarre could not believe something that small could scream so loudly.

'Can it talk?' he asked Emil.

Emil was standing some way behind him. He watched Skarre with considerable vigilance, but did not reply.

Skarre moved closer. He stared at the bird and looked down at the bottom of its cage. It was lined with newspaper on top of which rested a removable tray, full of tiny white feathers. Minor coverts, he thought. In addition to the white feathers there were a fair number of bird droppings, some larger grey feathers and a lot of shells, which Skarre recognised as peanut shells. Some feathers had attached themselves to the bars of the cage. He picked one of them off. It felt sticky. Exactly like the ones they had found on Ida's duvet. He turned to Emil again.

'It's an African Grey, isn't it? What's its name?' he asked, mesmerised.

Emil still did not reply. But he nodded in the direction of the cage. Skarre noticed the brass plate fixed to one of the bars: 'Henry the Eighth', it said.

'Henry,' Skarre whispered. His head was spinning. He was here! Here, in the house where Ida had been. She had got the red feather from the bird called Henry. It had to be so.

'Henry the Eighth,' he said, louder this time. 'He

was King of England, wasn't he? He was the one who chopped the heads off all his wives.'

He grasped the implication of this just a little too late. The man standing behind him could be Ida's killer. Skarre began to feel uncomfortable. He was standing closest to the window, and the broad, silent man was blocking the exit to the kitchen and the hall. He stood passively, with his hands behind his back. He kept looking at Skarre. He did not know much about English kings. Then he went back to the kitchen. Skarre quickly scanned the tiny living room. He saw a television and a sofa. There was an old-fashioned teak coffee table. The sofa was green, with curved feet. On the wall hung a rug in loud colours; it was large and held in place by a cast-iron rail. On the floor was a polyester rug. Left of the cage he was looking straight at a door leading to another room, a bedroom perhaps. This door, too, was splintered, as if someone had attacked it with a powerful tool. He was trembling with excitement as he followed Emil. Calm down, he told himself. You've got to stay professional. He realised that his conduct during these next few minutes would determine the rest of the case. At the same time it seemed unthinkable that this man might try to run off. He seemed rooted to the floor; he was part of the furniture, something that had always been there. He matched the ancient teapot covered by a crocheted tea cosy sitting on top of the fridge. He matched the patterned wallpaper in the kitchen and the hanging lamp with the curly cable.

Emil had sat down by the kitchen table. Now he was staring out at the drive. He was interested in the police car. He rarely had the chance to study them at close range. His expression was peculiar, Skarre thought. Not vacant, not unwilling either; he looked like he had a great deal on his mind. Perhaps he was overwhelmed by the fact that he had a visitor. And that the visitor was in uniform. He turned around twice to study Skarre's jacket. Skarre sat down directly opposite him. He ought to make a telephone call immediately, but he felt that this moment was precious and would never come back.

'Some of these birds kill the females,' Skarre told him. 'Instead of mating with them. So I've been told. Is he one of those? Is that why he's called Henry the Eighth?'

'No,' Emil mumbled. He did not seem to follow where Skarre was going with this. Now he just looked sad. What kind of man is this, Skarre thought, who only says 'no'? Is that all he can say? He decided to test him.

'Do you live here with your family?' he asked.

'No,' Emil said. He would not want that. His mother was more than enough; he did not want any more people trampling around his house.

'Any children?' Skarre persisted.

No, Emil did not have children, though to be honest he preferred them to adults. They pestered him, but they told it like it was. Such as whether his three-wheeler was smart or ugly. Sometimes they asked for a ride in the body. But he said no.

Skarre thought for a while. 'But your mother visits you sometimes. Elsa Marie?'

Emil was silent. Skarre patted the pocket of his jacket and tried again. 'Do you mind if I smoke?'

No, Emil did not mind. The smell was unfamiliar to him, but it also offered him a novel experience. He did not remember anyone ever sitting by this table blowing fine smoke out into the air. He followed it with his eyes. Skarre watched the broad face as he searched for his next question.

'Perhaps you might have an ashtray?'

Emil did not. But he got up and opened a cupboard above the kitchen worktop. Skarre could see the patterned shelf paper, which was fraying around the edges. Emil selected a chipped saucer.

'So where do you work?' Skarre said casually, pretending he did not know that Emil was on benefits.

Silence. Yet again the sad expression in his eyes.

'Perhaps you don't have a job?'

'No,' Emil said.

Skarre touched his pocket. 'Do you want a cigarette? I forgot to ask you.' He held out the packet.

'No. No!'

A violent shaking of the head, followed by dismissive waving with one hand.

Skarre stared at the tablecloth for a moment. Did he really only know this one word? Could it be true?

'Do you have many visitors?' he said lightly.

'No,' Emil said.

'But your mother comes, doesn't she?'

Emil turned around again and stared out of the window. His head was hurting. Skarre did not know what to do. The man might be the turning point in this impenetrable case. He owned a bird with red tail feathers called Henry. A man who only said 'no'. Or stayed silent. An oddball. Who might be able to read and write, or might not. Who was mentally disabled. He seemed to have some understanding, but lacked the words to express himself. A man who might have killed Ida Joner. He looked at Emil again. Why on earth would he want to do that? It just did not make sense.

Emil was being very defensive. He turned a broad shoulder to Skarre. Again he tucked his thumbs under his braces, and kept staring out on to the drive.

'Are you expecting someone?' Skarre asked carefully.

'No,' he said abruptly. But this was not entirely true. He was scared that his mother's car would pull up in front of the house. Seeing the police car might make her panic and drive off so quickly she would send the gravel flying. Suddenly the word was repeated by a similar but metallic voice from the room next door. *No!*

It took Skarre a second to work out that it was coming from the bird. 'Henry the Eighth can talk,' he said excitedly.

Emil wiped his nose on the back of his hand. Skarre returned to the living room, Emil followed him. He clearly wanted to know what Skarre was doing. Skarre on the other hand had not yet recovered from the shock. The human voice from the bird and the force behind it. He went over to the cage. Emil followed him with his eyes. Skarre sensed him like a shadow behind his back, where he stood legs apart, silently tugging at his Levi's braces. The bird pressed itself against the bars and puffed up its feathers. This made it look bigger. Skarre did not know what this signified. He stuck a finger in between the bars to stroke its head. It offered itself lovingly and he felt the tiny cranium underneath the soft feathers. Suddenly there was a snapping sound and he felt a sharp pain. Perplexed, he pulled his finger back. The bird withdrew rapidly and gave him an almost vicious stare, Skarre thought. He studied the cut in disbelief. A circular hole was visible on the tip of his index finger. Slowly it filled with blood. He spun around quickly and looked at Emil.

'That taught me,' he said, wiping his forehead. 'He doesn't like strangers. Does he like you?'

'No,' said Emil. He was staring at the floor. Perhaps he was hiding his laughter.

'You just feed him, is that it?'

Emil wanted to get back to the kitchen. Skarre kept watching the bird. His finger was throbbing fiercely.

'Hey.' He followed Emil. 'You wouldn't happen to have a plaster in the house, would you?' he said, waving his bleeding finger. Of course Emil did. He had a whole box of them. He held out the box so that Skarre could help himself.

'Never attach a plaster in a circle, and don't ever tighten it,' Skarre recited; he recalled this from his first aid training. 'But I'll just have to. Not many other options when it comes to fingers.' He looked to Emil for a smile. It never came.

'I need to ask you something,' he said eventually. He observed Emil carefully. It was crunch time. Nevertheless, he kept thinking it had to be the wrong house. It could not be this one, not like this. 'Do you know a girl called Ida?' he asked.

There was no reply from Emil. Only a downcast look.

Skarre struggled to move on. 'Has she ever been to this house?'

Still no reply. How was he supposed to do this?

'Emil,' he pleaded. 'Emil Johannes. Listen to me. Ida was in this house, I'm sure of it. Do you deny it?'

'No,' said Emil Johannes.

CHAPTER 23

Once Skarre had left, Emil was overcome by misgivings. He had believed that he would be able to handle it and put it right; but no, it was an impossible thought. Now he regretted it deeply. At the same time he experienced a pleasant feeling because this man had sat at his table. The smell of cigarette smoke still hung in the air. The box of plasters lay on the kitchen table. The telephone started ringing again. He did not want to answer it now. He rushed out of the house, started his three-wheeler and drove off towards the waterfall. It felt good to be back on the three-wheeler; when he was driving it he was in control. It felt good to grip the handlebars and feel the wind on his face. It was a grey day, but the light was pleasant. His green driving jacket was unzipped. He pulled out into the right-hand lane as soon as he got to the church. Before long the church disappeared from view. When he reached the waterfall, he parked, turned off the engine, pushed his cap backwards and walked the last few steps to the edge. It had rained a lot during September; the waterfall was huge and thundering. When he stood there he felt the roar of the water spread through his body. There was no one else around. Everyone was at work now.

Emil had had a job once, in a sheltered workshop. He sorted screws and nuts and put them into boxes. It was easy but boring, and the pay was lousy. However, the hardest part was the other people who worked there. He never got on with them. They were all like kids. And I'm an adult, Emil thought. But because he never spoke, no one ever noticed that, or he was simply ignored. He preferred being alone in his own home, all alone rather than with company. He deliberately started making mistakes with his boxes. He mixed up screws and nuts and put too many in. They asked him to stop. His mother was furious, he recalled. It was humiliating for her to have a son on benefits. It was one thing that he would never get married. Another that he could not talk. But she would have been so proud if she could have talked about his job. Emil, my son, he's in full-time employment now, she would say when the sewing circle met, without mentioning precisely what he did. To be able to say this one important thing. That he got up in the morning like other people and went to work. Emil always got up early. He certainly did not stay in bed all day. He never had any problems passing the time.

He walked to the edge of the waterfall. Stood so near that he could feel the cool mist on his face. The waterfall did not have just one voice. After a while he could detect several. There was the deep hum from the bottom and there were other, higher notes from the top. Even a tinkling from the shallow water that trickled over the stones on the bank far below. It's a whole orchestra, Emil thought, playing a neverending, wondrous tune. The deep one said, 'I'm coming, I'm coming, I'm unstoppable and strong', while the high notes hurried after it crying 'Wait for us, we're coming too' and the fainter ones near the bank busied themselves with other things, hiding away and dancing across the pebbles, mixing with the vortex, the yellow and white foam. All those colours, Emil thought. From the grey-black deep to the white foam. A steady and violent stream heading for the ocean. He thought of the moment when the water arrived. When it poured out and merged with the big blue sea. Sometimes he drove down to the sea just to watch it. If he got there early, the sea lay calm as a mirror. He thought that in itself was a miracle every time. That so much water could lie so still.

He pursed his lips and tried a word. He wanted to say 'impossible'. He forced air from his diaphragm out through his mouth. He remembered that sound was formed by the tongue and the lips. Faintly he heard something resembling a grunt. He tried again, opened his mouth wide and listened intently through the roar of the waterfall. A long, coarse sound emerged from his throat. He became annoyed and tried once more. His voice was so gruff; he did not understand why. 'No' was easy. 'No' lay at the roof of his mouth, ready to be spat out like a cherry stone. How about 'yes'? Could he say that? However, he did not like that word as much, it felt like surrendering to something and he did not want to do that. How would he ever manage to form long words? Such as the difficult word 'misunderstanding'? It was quite impossible. He gave up and felt sad. His face was wet. Then he remembered 's'. This was a sound he could form at the front of his mouth; no tone, just a hiss, like that of a snake. He could manage that! This cheered him up. Quit while you're ahead, Emil Johannes thought. He padded back to his three-wheeler. Pulled his cap back down. Started the engine and swung out on to the road. He did not realise that two kids had been lying behind a rock watching him the whole time. They were laughing so much it hurt.

Later he was back in his living room. He could not stay by the waterfall till night-time. He could not escape either; he had nowhere to hide. It was a question of waiting. Thirty minutes later he heard a car door slam out on the drive. Emil planted his palms on the windowsill and rested his whole body weight on them. It was considerable. The windowsill groaned and squeaked like the floorboards. It was not his mother's car. He looked at the bird. Stuck his finger into the cage. Instantly it started nibbling him and licking his finger with a warm black tongue. It was coarse, like sandpaper. Then came the knocking he was anticipating, three sharp knocks. Emil took his time. Checked that the bird had food in both its cups, water and cubes of apple. Softly he walked to the door. At first he was puzzled. The police officer was a woman, he had not expected that. He made no sound, just stood still watching her. She actually looked friendly. Another officer stepped out of the car, the same one with the curly hair who had visited him earlier. Emil saw the plaster on his finger. What an idiot, he thought. But his expression was kind. At the same time they appeared serious. Emil sensed this seriousness, but he could not tell them that.

'Emil Johannes Mork?' the female officer said.

He did not nod, just waited.

'You need to come with us, please.'

He stood for a while considering this. She was asking him nicely. Emil went back inside the house. There was something he had to take care of first. He put a towel over the birdcage and checked the radiator below the window. Opened up the curtains and made sure that they did not overhang it. There was all this talk of fire precautions; his mother went on about it all the time, so he was aware of such things.

Then he went back out into the hall and found his green driving jacket. They waited by the car while he locked the front door. He thought about his mother, wondered if they had picked her up too. He thought so.

Jacob Skarre held out his hand. He asked for the key to the house. Emil hesitated. His mother had cleaned it. Thrown away the rubbish and tidied

264

everywhere. He handed over his key. They held open the car door for him and helped him get seated in the back. He rarely went in a car. He felt enclosed; it was airless. The female officer took the wheel. She had a long blonde plait down her back. It was fastened tightly and shone like a nylon rope. Emil kept looking at it. It was one of the most beautiful things he had ever seen, but it would have looked nicer if she had tied a bow at the end of it.

Elsa Mork was arrested simultaneously. She wanted to see Emil and became quite difficult when they refused. As if denying her access to her own son was completely unheard of and thoroughly reprehensible. Is it legal to treat people in this way? she asked. And they answered, yes, it's legal. She said that Emil Johannes could not be questioned at all, because he simply could not speak, and they said, yes, we know. They asked her if her son could write. Her reply was evasive. The ground beneath her feet, which had been solid for more than seventy years, crumbled away. She reached out to the wall for support.

'His name,' she said. 'I've taught him that. But as for anything else – I don't really know what he can or cannot do.'

And her ignorance made her feel terribly ashamed.

'He has a newspaper delivered,' she remembered. 'But I don't know what he does with it. Perhaps he has fun taking it out of the letterbox every morning like other people. Perhaps he likes the pictures. Perhaps he can manage the headlines. I really don't know.' She ventured a bitter suggestion. 'You'll just have to find out for yourselves.'

Everything seemed unreal to her. They took her coat and her handbag, which she was clinging to tightly. A female officer reached out for it; Elsa held on to it. At the same time she could see how ridiculous the situation was. But she felt naked without the bag. She watched as they emptied the contents on to the table. Mirror, comb and handkerchief. And a mock-crocodile purse. She stood still, her hands unoccupied for once, taking in the strange surroundings. People came into the room and left again. She felt they were staring at her. It was just as well that Emil was the way he was, she thought. All he had to do was what he had always done. Keep quiet.

CHAPTER 24

She was waiting in the interrogation room. Sejer walked slowly along with a folder tucked under his arm. Oh, she's good at cleaning, he thought. But not that good. If Ida was in her son's house, we'll know about it.

What was going on inside her head? He thought she was mainly concerned about Emil. Even though he did not know her, he did not underestimate how strong and determined she might be. She had lived her whole life with a son who was different. A son she had cleaned up after, washed for and taken care of for more than fifty years. How well did she know him? How disabled was he? Had it been his own choice to withdraw from all contact? People did, sometimes for good reasons. What kind of life had they lived? Perhaps she had no life of her own because she had never wanted or been able to have one? She got involved with the lives of others instead and cleaned up after them. He thought of her with humility as he walked down the corridor. She was a person who had never previously broken the law. At the same time he was thinking of Ida.

She was sitting with both hands in her lap. It would be wrong to describe Elsa Mork as a beautiful woman. But everybody has got something, Sejer thought. Now he noticed her posture. Her back was effortlessly straight. There was fighting spirit in her strong face. Her hands, hidden under the table, were red and dry from cleaning. He remembered this from their first meeting. She was wearing a thin jumper with a round neck and a straight skirt with no pleats. It reached halfway down her calves. She wore low-heeled, sensible shoes with laces. No perm in her hair, which was short and the colour of steel, not unlike Sejer's own.

He greeted her kindly and pulled out a chair. She nodded briefly, but did not smile. Her face was expectant. Beneath that calm exterior she had to be under great stress, Sejer thought, but she was hiding it well. This might mean that she was used to hiding things, used to keeping up appearances, like the one he was observing now. But this is about a dead child, he thought. An adorable child with brown eyes, who looked like Mary Pickford. Elsa Mork had a child of her own. It had to be possible to reach her.

He poured himself a glass of Farris mineral water. The fizz from the water was the only sound in the quiet room. It seemed very loud. Elsa waited. Sejer drank from his glass.

'The air in here is dry,' he stated. 'I'm just telling you. It helps having something to drink, should you begin to feel tired.' He indicated the bottle next to her seat.

She did not reply. He was friendly, but she was on her guard. She was used to it, she was always on her guard.

'Do you understand why you're here?' he began.

Elsa had to think about that. Of course she did. However, it was important to articulate this in the best possible way.

'I think so,' she said stiffly. 'Emil and I have both been brought here in connection with that case. The girl you found by the road.'

'Correct,' he said, watching her. Her gaze was steady for the time being.

'Do you recall her name from the papers?' he said.

She was reluctant to say the name out loud, but it came anyway. 'Ida Joner,' she said in a subdued voice.

'Have you ever met Ida Joner?' Sejer asked.

'No.' The answer came quickly. It might also be partly true. Perhaps she had only seen her once she was dead.

'Do you know if your son ever met Ida Joner?'

Again this no, again the same firmness.

'He owns his own house?' Sejer said.

'No, it's a council house,' she interjected.

'I see.' Sejer nodded. 'But he lives on his own. You often go there to help him, but most of the time he is on his own. Is it totally impossible that Ida might have been in his house without you knowing?'

Elsa had to think about that. She could not appear too certain. Sejer could tell that she was searching desperately for plausible lies. On top of that she was quite rightly anxious about the evidence they had already collected and of which she knew nothing. It was likely that they had searched Emil's house as well as her flat.

'Of course, I can't swear on it,' she said eventually, having thought about it for a long time. 'I'm not there every hour of the day. But to be honest, I find it hard to believe that a little girl would go home with Emil of her own accord. No one would dare.'

'Please would you clarify?' he asked cautiously.

'He doesn't talk,' she said. 'And he's very slow. And he looks gruff. Even though he isn't. That's just how his face is.'

Sejer nodded. 'But we can't disregard the fact that your son might have had Ida in the house?'

'There are so many strange things going on in my life right now that I'm not disregarding anything,' she said brusquely.

She was close to boiling point. She calmed herself. Sejer looked at her earnestly. For a second he had caught a glimpse of the forces that raged inside her: despair and fear.

'Sometimes people like Emil find it easier to form bonds with children,' he said gently. 'They feel less threatened by them. It wouldn't be the first time.'

She did not comment on this. She chose silence. It struck her that silence was effective. And that Emil had realised this long ago.

'Your son keeps a bird?' he said, changing the subject.

270

'Yes. A parrot.'

'Do you think he benefits from that?'

She felt that this was a safe topic and gave herself permission to reply. 'I hope so,' she said. 'It chirps and sings and is a sort of companion to him. It doesn't need more care than Emil can manage.'

'When I questioned you about it earlier, you denied knowing anyone who owned a bird. Do you recall that?'

'Yes,' she said, biting her lip.

'Why did you deny it?'

'Don't know,' she said defiantly.

'Well,' Sejer smiled, 'it certainly isn't friendly. One of my officers is walking around with a fair-sized hole in his finger.'

She was listening, but his remark failed to produce a smile in her. 'It'll never be tame,' she said by way of explanation.

'Why not?'

'Don't know. I know nothing about birds. It was ten years old when I bought it. It's nearly sixteen now.'

She looked like she wanted to run away. Her whole body was trembling. She did not want to answer his questions, but she liked him. This confused her. She did not often speak to men. Only with Margot from next door and the women in the sewing circle. Everywhere she went, nothing but women. Now she listened to his deep voice, a professional and very correct voice, agreeable to listen to.

271

'It's very quiet in his house,' she said. 'After all, he never has any visitors. In the shop they told me that the bird could talk. I thought it would do him good to hear a few words every now and again. I had hoped it might trigger something in him.'

'What does the bird say?' Sejer asked with interest.

'Well . . .' She shrugged. 'Hi. Hello. Good morning. Things like that. It mainly sings tunes. It picks them up from the radio and the television. Jingles and so on.' She stared at the table. Out of the corner of her eye she spotted the bottle of mineral water. The glass was cloudy with condensation. 'I don't know how long you're thinking of keeping us here,' she said, 'but the bird is going to need feeding and watering.'

Sejer nodded to indicate he had taken this on board. 'We'll take care of the bird, should it prove necessary,' he said.

He knew he would make Elsa Mork talk eventually. He knew that he was stronger than her. He felt sad when he thought of this. Because right now she felt she was the strong one. She had made the decision not to talk. But she did not know what he knew. Therefore she could not fabricate a story, because she could not see which cards he held. He held many. Ida's purse, for example, which they had found inside a box of crispbread in Emil's kitchen cupboard. Perhaps Emil had liked the purse and Elsa had missed it when she cleaned the house. So he had thought of a hiding place for it. There was also the old chest freezer in the basement. Several dark hairs found on the bottom of it had been sent off to forensics. Elsa had not remembered everything; hardly anyone does. Now she was waiting calmly in her chair, determined to win one trick at a time, endure the pain it caused her and think up new answers. After a while, hours or days perhaps, she would start to tire. She was a bright woman. When she realised she was beaten, she would surrender. He allowed the silence to continue for a time and looked at her sideways. Her shoulders were tense, expectant. She can handle a great deal, he thought. A very tough old woman. A real fighter.

'You'll get a female defence counsel,' he said. 'She has a child too.'

'Really?' Elsa said.

'I just wanted you to know that,' he added.

Elsa disappeared back into her silence. I should have done this more often, she thought. I've been talking my whole life. God only knows what I've been saying.

'Please tell me if there's anything you need.' Sejer said it with such kindness that she felt it like a caress. She looked at him blankly. Her face opened up for a moment, then it closed suspiciously.

'I don't need anything,' she said. 'I can manage on my own. I always have done.'

Sejer knew it. He could attack now, suddenly and unexpectedly, just to watch her stumble for a moment. He did not do so. It had to be possible to defeat her in such a way that she kept her dignity. He shrank from pressurising her, shrank from luring her into a wilderness. He would take no pleasure from seeing her shame when he caught her contradicting herself. Most of all he wanted to reach the point where she would tell him everything. Where she would finally unburden herself and confess.

CHAPTER 25

The press had been hovering, cruising listlessly while there was little progress in the Ida Joner case. Now the journalists nose-dived from a great height towards their rather exotic prey. A seventy-three-year-old woman and her fifty-two-year-old son with learning difficulties. This led to much speculation. What exactly had happened to little Ida Joner, what exactly had they done to her? Even though there was nothing to suggest that Ida had been sexually assaulted, and this was made clear in all the papers, it did not stop the journalists. Surely he must have done something with her? They knew the art of implying. They wrote nothing explicit, but encouraged their readers to use their own imagination, which in turn they duly did. At this point in time it was extremely unclear what precisely had happened to Ida. As a result the journalists had to focus on other things. This was a juicy story. The rumours about the bird with the portentous name, Henry the Eighth, made an impression. Not only did Ida's suspected killer own a bird that could talk; it also bore the name of a murderer. This story had legs.

Elsa Mork was strong. Like her son, she answered 'no' to everything: I've never seen Ida Joner. No, I never bought a nightie. You'd go far for your child, but not that far. If I know how to mend clothes? Repairs and sewing? Of course I do. All women of my age know how to do that.

She was confident and firm. They took her back to her cell.

Sejer went into his office to go through the interrogation in his head. He tried to imagine how Elsa Mork would handle prison, if she were convicted. She would be busy washing the walkways, he thought; she would rush around wiping the ashtrays in the smoking lounge. He was interrupted by the sound of agitated knocking on his door. Jacob Skarre popped his head round.

'Just a quick message,' he said, ready to burst with excitement. Sejer tried to turn his thoughts away from Elsa and everything to do with her.

'Aha?' he said, looking up at him.

'Willy Oterhals has been reported missing.'

Sejer did not understand why Skarre was so excited by this. At the station that kind of report was known as an overprotective parent's report, given that Oterhals was twenty-two and would most likely turn up of his own accord. Sejer did not reply straight away. He recalled Oterhals from their conversation in the garage. He remembered that he

276

had a record and that he was friends with Tomme. Tomme Rix who was Ida Joner's cousin.

'Missing? Missing how?' he asked, confused.

'His mother, Anne Oterhals, has just called the duty officer. Willy travelled on the ferry to Denmark together with Tomme on Friday, the twentieth of September. More precisely, they were travelling on the MS *Pearl of Scandinavia*. Tomme returned home Sunday afternoon as he was supposed to. But Willy never showed up.' Skarre let himself fall into a chair. 'She called the Rixes to ask if they knew where he was. Tomme said they had gone their separate ways at Egertorg. That Willy had disappeared into the underground, going to see a mate apparently. Perhaps there was a reason for the trip to Copenhagen,' Skarre said. 'If he's still selling drugs it might be the case that he buys them in Denmark. He might have gone to deliver them to someone in Oslo. However, that shouldn't have taken him very long.'

'I wonder what this means?' Sejer said. 'How anxious is his mother?'

'She says that occasionally he's gone for a night or two, but that he usually calls her. And he's not answering his mobile. Normally he always does. It's like he's vanished into thin air.'

'Or the sea, perhaps?' Sejer said on impulse. 'No, I was thinking about the ferry,' he admitted. 'People have been known to fall overboard. We need to have another word with Tomme. How very strange,' he added, resting his elbows on his desk.

'Strange how?' Skarre said.

'Well, these two lads,' Sejer said, 'who clearly stick together even though Ruth and Sverre Rix are trying their hardest to stop them: perhaps they're up to something and maybe we ought to look into it?'

He checked the date on his watch. When he was not busy interrogating Elsa Mork, he would focus on these two. It was as if the boys beckoned him. However, if they were selling drugs, it was not his area, especially not now. It was more important to find out what had happened between Emil and Ida. So why did he have this strange feeling that something did not add up? Why did the boys keep on intruding on his thoughts like some constant distraction? Gripped by a sudden impulse, he called the ferry company's office in Oslo. He was on the telephone for a long time. After having clarified a few details about that particular crossing, he hung up and got in his car. He did not announce his arrival. He drove straight to Tomme's house.

The Rix family had just finished eating their dinner. Ruth scraped the leftover roast chicken into the bin under the sink. Skin and bones slid down the plates and mixed with other smells. It reeked under the sink; they had had fish the night before. It stinks of decay, Ruth thought. Tomme was in his room. He was halfway through watching *The Matrix*, but he was not really paying attention to the plot. Marion was on her bed, reading.

Ruth heard a car pull into the drive. She resisted the temptation to look out of the window. They were not expecting anyone. It could be someone selling something. Or local kids out selling lottery tickets for the handball team or the school orchestra. It might even be one of Tomme's friends, Bjørn or Helge. Then she heard the doorbell. When she saw Sejer standing outside, she looked at him in wonder for a long time. Suddenly she decided she simply was not going to let him in. She thought of Tomme and everything that had happened. She had had enough of it all now and wanted things to be normal again. Two people had been arrested and Ruth had read in the papers that the evidence against them was considerable. Ida's funeral had taken place. Helga dragged herself slowly through the days, held together by sedatives. Things were just starting to look up. Perhaps this was merely a courtesy call. Sejer waited patiently all the time it took her to think this.

'I've come to talk to Tomme,' he said. 'It's concerning Willy Oterhals.'

Ruth felt like saying that Tomme was not at home, but remembered that the black Opel was parked in the garage. And as far as Willy was concerned, she felt that he ought to mind his own business and not drag other people down with him. She remained silent and clutched the door frame with one hand.

'He's still missing,' Sejer said, suspecting that she might not be entirely aware of the situation.

'Still?' Ruth said, frightened.

She continued to block the doorway with her body. 'But Tomme's told me everything he knows,' she said in a pathetic attempt at stalling him in the doorway. It was no use.

'I'd like to hear it from Tomme himself,' Sejer said firmly. 'Is he in? Please would you go get him?'

This request was made with such authority that it was impossible for Ruth to object. She stepped away from the door and let him into the hall. Then she went upstairs to get her son. Sejer waited in the living room and noticed that it took quite a while before they both appeared. Tomme looked haunted. Ruth stood next to him, shielding him the way you shield your children from an enemy.

'You already know what it's about,' Sejer began. 'Let me start with the following question. Did you go to Copenhagen to buy drugs?'

'Willy,' Tomme said. 'Willy went there to do some sort of deal.' He spoke to the floor, to his socks. 'I just went along to keep him company.'

'Did you see the drugs?'

'No,' Tomme claimed. He was unable to look Sejer in the eye. Instead he muttered to the floor once more: 'You've probably spoken to his mum, so I guess you already know what happened.'

'I know nothing at all,' Sejer said. 'I've only heard some allegations.'

Tomme felt a sting inside his head and the ticking began again at a brisk, constant pace. It was not unbearable, not even painful. But when he thought that it might go on like this for ever, he felt sick. If he told them everything, the ticking would grow louder and culminate in an inferno of noise. But it was the only way he would regain silence. That was how he thought about what was going on inside him.

Sejer waited. He could see the war being waged; he had seen it many times before and it was so easy to recognise.

'You've stated that the last time you saw Willy Oterhals was when he disappeared down the steps to the underground at Egertorg,' he said. 'Is that correct?'

Tomme could not hold it together any longer. He had been pretending for so long, holding on to so many lies, his stomach was aching, his intestines were contracting and tightening as if held in a vice. He thought, I can't handle this pain, I just want to rest. He started to talk. Instantly the cramps began to ease up. It was like they were draining into an overflow.

'That's not entirely true,' he whispered, and for the first time he looked up at Sejer. His admission made Ruth pale.

'When was the last time?' Sejer said. He was not menacing, just firm and clear.

'On the ferry,' Tomme said in a subdued voice.

He was quiet and took a moment to think. He could sense the outline of his mother from the corner of his eye, she was blurred, but he recognised her fear.

'The return trip,' Sejer said. 'The last evening. Tell me about it.'

'We just hung out in the bar,' Tomme said.

'How drunk would you say you were?'

Tomme thought for a while. 'Willy was quite drunk. I was fairly sober. Three beers,' he explained. 'And I drank them slowly.'

'What might the time have been when you left the bar?'

'Not sure. Midnight perhaps.'

'Did you go straight down to your cabin?'

Tomme was in trouble now. Had anyone seen them? He knew that the ferry had CCTV cameras mounted everywhere. How much of the truth was it possible for him to tell without landing himself in hot water? He looked shiftily at Sejer.

'Well, we did go for a walk on deck,' he said feebly. He tried to come across as desperate, which was easy given that this was exactly how he was feeling. Deeply desperate. And scared, obviously, at everything that can happen without you even wanting it to. Ruth did not dare move. Something dreadful occurred to her. It was a remarkable coincidence that Willy had gone missing, she realised. The fact that he was an adult and should be able to take care of himself did not make it any better. He was missing. His mother had called the police. And Tomme was white as a sheet.

'Was it your suggestion?'

'No. Willy wanted some fresh air,' Tomme said. 'And I suppose I did too.'

Sejer nodded. 'There was a strong gale during the crossing,' he said. 'Being out there at night must have been spectacular.'

'It was. I had to cling to anything I could find. The deck was wet and slippery. And it was bloody freezing. We were freezing our arses off.' He spoke in a firmer voice now because he was telling the truth and he remembered it so vividly.

'Did you fall out over something?'

He hesitated and considered this. 'In a way. Yes.'

'What was it?'

'Willy wanted me to do him a favour. But I said no.'

'What kind of favour are we talking about?'

Tomme felt his mother's eyes on him. 'Well, you know. He wanted us to swap bags. So that I would be carrying the drugs through customs.'

Ruth let the air out of her lungs. Her eyes were glued to her son.

'You're saying that you knew Willy was dealing drugs, but that you were never a part of it? What made Willy ask you after all this time?'

'He felt I owed him a favour,' Tomme said.

'Did you?'

'He fixed the Opel. For free.'

'He was asking a lot in return in my view. What do you think?'

'Same as you. So I said no. And he didn't like it.'

'Go on,' Sejer said.

Tomme did not dare look at his mother. He thought of all the pills they had flushed down the toilet. She was scared that he was about to reveal this, but he did not want to implicate his mother. Instead he focused on the different sounds and images whirling around in his mind. It had to be possible to shape them into a plausible story.

'Willy had brought a pint with him,' he said. 'Up on deck. He started messing about with the glass in his hand. Even though it was bloody windy and he slipped several times and kept having to find something to hold on to, to stop himself from falling over. I was sitting on a crate watching him. I was freezing. All I wanted to do was go downstairs to get some sleep, but he carried on, climbing up ropes, balancing on stuff. He was making an idiot of himself. Finally he started climbing up on to the railings. He went up so high that his knees were resting against the top bar. He dropped his glass,' Tomme recollected. He recalled the gawping expression on Willy's face as the glass slipped out of his hand and disappeared into the depths. Ruth bit her lip. It was as if she had guessed what was coming next.

'And what about you?' Sejer said.

'I was just watching him,' Tomme said. 'Several times I called out to him that he ought to come down, that it was dangerous. He just laughed. I was cold and wet and I just wanted to go inside, but I couldn't leave without Willy. But when he's drunk, he only does what he wants to, it's no use talking to him. I huddled up on the crate and tried to keep warm. And I was regretting going on the trip,' he admitted. 'It was nothing but getting drunk and getting into trouble. I should have stayed at home. So I got up and said, I'm off to bed now. Please yourself, Willy hollered,' Tomme said, exhausted now. 'So I gave up and went down to the cabin.'

Sejer listened attentively to Tomme's explanation. At the same time he noticed that a dark shadow had crept into the living room. Marion, he thought. Tomme's sister. It did not seem as if Ruth had noticed her. Is anyone looking after her? he thought, trying to catch her eye. She avoided his look.

'So what did you do?' he asked, urging Tomme on.

'Went to bed,' he replied. 'We had just the one keycard, so I lay awake waiting for the knock on the door. But it never came. I must have fallen asleep after a while. When I woke up in the morning he wasn't there. I just freaked out completely, I couldn't think. I didn't know what else to do, so I went ashore on my own,' he whispered.

'What you're saying,' Sejer spoke clearly, 'is that you woke up alone in the cabin and could not find your friend Willy. But you never told the crew?'

'No.' Tomme winced.

'This you have to explain to me,' Sejer said brusquely.

'That's what's so complicated,' Tomme said miserably. 'I got so confused. I looked for him everywhere. Thought that perhaps he was playing a trick on me, that he'd found somewhere else to sleep

285

on the ferry, with a woman or something, but I never saw him. And then the crowd just swept me along to the gangway. I kept expecting him to turn up and call out for me. But I heard nothing. He'd just vanished. Later it became so hard to explain,' he stuttered, 'so I made up the story about the underground. That we said goodbye there. But it was only because I didn't understand any of it. And because I thought it was really bad not to have an explanation at all.'

Ruth, who had been standing up until that point, now had to support herself against a chair.

'Grow up, Tomme,' Sejer commanded. 'If the last time you saw Willy was when he was raving around the deck in a gale-force wind, heavily intoxicated, then that's serious. Now look at me and answer my question. Do you think he fell overboard?'

Tomme clapped his hand over his mouth. His eyes nearly jumped out of their sockets. The ticking continued, but it was fainter now.

'That's what I'm so afraid of!' he whimpered.

'It is hard for me to understand why you didn't call for help,' Sejer admitted. 'I'm trying to understand it, but it's hard.'

'I'm not really myself at the moment,' Tomme said, 'with everything that's happened in my family, with Ida and all that. It just all got too much.'

'So Willy's mother called here asking where he was. And still you said nothing?'

'But it was already too late,' Tomme groaned. 'And I haven't done anything wrong. I just didn't want to get involved. I do feel a kind of guilt,' he went on. 'I shouldn't have left him. I can understand it if his mum wants to blame me. But I couldn't make him go back down to the cabin with me.'

'Mmm,' Sejer said gravely. 'I'm thinking something quite different myself.'

Tomme looked up quickly. Something in Sejer's voice disturbed him.

'Willy was travelling with a bag,' Sejer stated. 'A black nylon bag with a white Puma logo on the side. The one he wanted you to take through customs for him. What did you do with it?'

Tomme blinked in terror. 'Nothing,' he said, flustered.

'If Willy had fallen overboard while drunk, his bag would still be in the cabin. You left nothing behind. I've just now telephoned the ferry company to check. All lost property is carefully logged, and no black nylon bag was found in the cabin that Willy booked. So my question is: did someone throw the bag the same way as Willy went? And why?'

Tomme no longer wanted to answer. Privately he thought he had been cooperative. There was a greater degree of calm inside him. Not total calm, but it did feel like he was being allowed a break.

'Version one,' Sejer said firmly. 'You go ashore together. Willy disappears by the underground at Egertorg. Version two. You leave him on the deck. He is completely drunk and stumbling around; you can't make him come downstairs with you, so you

287

give up and go to bed. Next morning he's not there. I'll be coming back to talk to you later,' Sejer said. 'In the meantime, you can prepare the third and final version.'

CHAPTER 26

The days passed. Oterhals did not turn up and was listed in the newspapers as missing. In contrast to Ida, he received very little coverage. A young man missing following a ferry trip to Denmark did not arouse anyone's curiosity. Readers would make up their own minds as to what might have happened to him and turn to the next page. Sejer continued questioning Elsa Mork. As usual she sat with her knees together and her hands folded in her lap.

'We've asked for a professional assessment of your son,' Sejer said. 'It will probably be a while. However, in the meantime I need to ask you. You're the one who knows Emil best. How much education has he had?'

Elsa thought about this for a long time. She could not object to Sejer's methods. He was most professional. She had not expected it and it made her more defensive. Still, it was good to talk to someone who wanted to listen. Talking about Emil was a new experience for her. She had hidden him away and hardly ever mentioned him to anyone. She offered only monosyllabic replies to the sewing circle whenever someone asked after him. She almost pretended he did not exist. But he did. And now she was finally talking about him. And because she had to talk about him, she also saw him clearly.

'He was in primary school well into Year Two. Then they moved him to a special needs class. There he just sat on his own doing nothing. He did talk, but only a little. As time went by the words got fewer and fewer. He was able to write some hopeless-looking letters, or he would draw, but very clumsily. Usually he would just sit there chewing his pencil. Often when he came home from school his mouth was all black. It seemed as if he was scared of letters and numbers. But he liked playing,' she recalled. 'With toy figures. Or cars and building bricks. Then he'd cheer up.'

'Did he ever sit an IQ test?'

'They tried several times. But he pushed everything away, paper, pictures, whatever they put in front of him.'

'So when it comes to his intellectual capacity, we can only guess? No one really knows for sure?' he asked.

'He always refused to cooperate. We have never had an accurate diagnosis of his condition. One doctor used the expression "extremely introverted". That doesn't help us. Once Emil had grown up, I limited myself to taking care of his house. Besides, he was never going to let me get close to him. And now I don't have the strength to try any more,' she said in a tired voice. 'He's fifty-two years old. If I haven't managed it by now, I never will.'

'What about his birth?' Sejer wanted to know. 'Was it a normal delivery?'

'Yes,' she said. 'Nothing to be learned from that. But God knows it took a long time. He was a big baby,' she said, looking down at the table, her cheeks slightly flushed because she was discussing this with a strange man.

'If I ask you what would make Emil genuinely happy, or truly interested, or for that matter really angry, what would you say?'

She squirmed in her chair. It was a good chair, but she knew she would be sitting in it for a long time. 'I'm not really sure,' she said. 'He's always the same. On the rare occasion he shows feelings, it's irritation. Or defiance. I don't suppose he's ever happy,' she confessed. 'After all, is there anything to be happy about?' She looked up at Sejer, hoping for a bit of sympathy.

Sejer got up from his chair and started wandering around the room. Partly because he felt the need to and partly out of consideration for Elsa, who needed some space. An opportunity to lose herself a little in her own thoughts. He knew she was watching him as he walked around, that right now she was furtively studying his back. Perhaps she was assessing his clothes, a charcoal-grey shirt with a black tie, and trousers in a lighter shade of grey with knife-edge creases.

'What about women?' he asked after a pause. 'Is Emil interested in women?'

The thought of it nearly made her laugh, but she controlled herself. 'We never discuss such things,' she said. 'I don't know what he gets up to when I'm not there, but I have never found magazines or any other things that might suggest it. How would he ever get a woman? I've told him over and over that he can forget about that, and he knows it too.' She shook her head in resignation. 'Not even the most desperate creature in the world would take on Emil.'

What an incredibly merciless verdict, Sejer thought, but did not say so. 'Have you ever considered the possibility that he might be talking when he's on his own?' he asked. 'That he can do more than he reveals?'

She shrugged. Pondered his question. 'Yes, I've thought about it. In my most desperate hours. But I don't think he can.'

'Perhaps he talks to the bird?' Sejer said. 'To Henry the Eighth?'

She smiled briefly. 'The bird says no,' she said. 'It says no like Emil Johannes.'

'How about children?' he asked. 'Does he get on with them?'

'They're scared of him,' she said quickly. 'Goes without saying. Given the way he looks. They laugh at him or they're scared of him. No, he definitely does not get on with kids.'

'So a child would never go with him of their own accord? Is that what you're saying?'

She nodded firmly. 'No child has ever been inside Emil's house,' she said confidently.

'Yes,' he said quietly. 'Someone was there. Ida Joner was in his house several times.'

'You don't know that!' she said in despair.

'We do. We have found evidence to suggest it.'

She no longer dared to look at him. Instead she made her hands the focus of her attention.

'Did you buy the nightie, Elsa?' he said quietly.

He was leaning carefully across the table and succeeded in catching her eye. She hesitated because he was addressing her by her first name. It was unexpected and almost overwhelmingly intimate, and it made her soften in a strange way. Then she reminded herself that this was likely to be part of his strategy and pressed her lips together.

'Why would I buy a nightie?'

'Perhaps you needed to save Emil from a dreadful situation?' he said. 'You wanted her to look pretty. She was just a child and you did what little you could for her. In fact it was no small thing,' he added.

No reply.

'Any mother would help their child out of a difficult situation. Not to mention a disaster,' he said. 'Is it not the case that you were only trying to help?'

'I do his cleaning, that's all. And by the way, that's a full-time job in itself. He makes an awful mess.' These words were said mechanically; they were words she had repeated so many times that she spoke them without feeling.

'And the bird moults,' Sejer said. 'There were feathers stuck to the white duvet.'

293

Elsa Mork went completely silent.

'Let's call it a day,' Sejer said eventually. 'I think we need a break.'

'No, no!' Elsa said loudly. Suddenly she could not bear the thought of returning to her cell. She would rather stay here and talk, know that she was seen and heard by the inspector in the grey shirt. She wanted it to last. So she leaned across the table and said the opposite of what she felt. She needed to protect herself; she was about to weaken and she could feel that her body was going to betray her.

'We'll keep on until you've finished,' she insisted. 'I can't stay here for ever, I've got tons of things to do at home!'

He looked straight at her face. 'This is a serious matter and I strongly suggest that you start treating it as such,' he said. 'We believe that your son, Emil Johannes, caused Ida Joner's death. And we believe that you helped him hide her body and later place it by the roadside. Given that your son doesn't talk, this will take time. We need outside help in order to interrogate him, and you must accept that you will be spending some time in custody.'

If this information surprised her, she did not show it. She got up, pushed her chair back in place. Straightened her back and gritted her teeth. Then she collapsed quietly on the floor.

It was a modest fall. First her knees buckled. Her body did a half-turn, and then her torso and her head flopped backwards, causing her to lose her balance. As she hit the floor there was a brief, low thud. She came to almost instantly, perplexed, pale and terribly embarrassed. Later on, when Sejer was sitting in his living room with a glass of whisky in his hand, he thought about it. Falling like that had been a profound humiliation for her. And then to be lifted up by unfamiliar hands . . . She had remained baffled for a long time. She was still dazed when she was back in her cell, lying on the narrow bunk with a rug covering her.

Sejer sipped his lukewarm whisky slowly. Kollberg nudged his shin with his nose. Sejer bent down and stroked his back. The dog no longer displayed the familiar excitement when they were about to go out for a walk in the evening. Sejer thought, you'd rather not go. From now on you just want to lie like this by my feet. Your life's simple, old boy. The dog panted for a long time and then gingerly lowered his head back on to his paws. Sejer kept thinking. If he believed that Emil Johannes was responsible for Ida's death, just what exactly had taken place between them? Why would he harm the one person who came to visit him?

CHAPTER 27

There was an air of high spirits at the morning briefing meeting the next day. Sejer had made it clear that he would attempt to interrogate Emil Johannes Mork.

If nothing else it'll be a fine monologue, Skarre thought. Holthemann stayed silent. He never made inappropriate jokes and he had ceased to underestimate the inspector a long time ago. Sejer ignored them all. If the only thing he would accomplish by sitting in the interrogation room with Emil was staring at him, then he was prepared to sit and stare. Or rather, he wanted to understand. If all he was required to do was arrest people and help them make a confession, the job would be pointless as far as he was concerned. Ideally he wanted to know precisely what led to the deed; he wanted to walk in another person's footsteps and see it from their point of view. If he was able to do that, he could put the case behind him. Admittedly, there were cases where he never reached such an understanding, and they continued to haunt him. But they were rare. Most of the time a crime could be understood.

However, he did not understand the case of Ida Joner. Everyone had described her as a confident girl, well brought up and friendly. Of course there could be sides to her character of which others knew nothing. Or they might not want to mention them. Not wanting to speak ill of the dead. Kids could be merciless. Sejer was aware of that.

Emil Johannes waited in his cell. Everything inside him was mixed up. He was sitting at the desk by the window with his heavy fists resting in his lap. The view from his cell was not interesting, but he studied carefully the little he was able to see. The roofs. The tip of a spruce, the rear wheel of a bicycle. A fence and the street outside without much traffic. A woman walking. Emil watched her carefully. She was probably going shopping. That was why people went outside; they needed something for their homes. His mother, for example, went to the shops every single day to get something. She hardly ate anything; she scrimped and saved every penny. And yet she had to go shopping; it was like a ritual, a daily event. So it was with Emil. He pursed his lips at the pane.

'No,' he said. He turned around quickly and looked at the door. There was a hatch in it. Perhaps there was someone on the other side watching him. Then he thought of his bird. Its water and food supply would last three days perhaps. From then on the bird would remain on its perch waiting for the sound of footsteps. As long as it had water it would be all right. But Emil knew that Henry sometimes grabbed the water supply with its beak. Occasionally it had managed to dislodge the cup from its tiny hook on the bars. Every time it happened it had managed to splash its legs, and then it would rock on one claw while waving the other one energetically to air-dry it.

Emil was restless. It was unusual for him to sit like this, completely inactive. The room was so small, so bare and unfamiliar. He started to walk around and touch everything. He ran his fingers over the desk. There were many marks and scratches in the wood. He traced its four legs down to the floor. The lino was worn and damaged, but clean. He went over to the cupboard and looked inside. There was his jacket hanging on a peg. His boots, looking strangely naked because the laces had been removed, stood at the bottom. He knelt by his bunk and patted the blanket, which was a kind of quilt with a patterned cover. He touched the lamp, but burned his fingers on the shade. He ran his fingers over the shelf and they came away dusty. He clasped the curtain, feeling the fabric, smelling it. It was thick and stiff. He looked under the bed. There was no one there. Finally he sat down by the desk again. He had been everywhere. He breathed on the window. He could draw on the steamed-up bit. He could rub his drawing with his shirtsleeve and do another one. It was like a magic pad. But he was bad at drawing. He wanted to explain. He knew they would turn up with a pen and paper, wondering if he might be able to write. He knew they would ask a million questions hoping he might want to answer them. But he was not very good at writing and he did not want to sit there grunting while they could hear him.

Emil was not used to shaking people's hands either. He had not learned the sequence of movements that constituted a handshake. Sejer gestured towards the vacant chair and the huge man tried to make himself comfortable. He had to ease himself into it to find an acceptable position. Sejer began to talk; he chose his words with care. Emil listened. Nothing in his broad face indicated that he did not understand Sejer, but it took time. First the sentence needed to sink in, then it had to be interpreted and comprehended, and eventually he reacted by blinking his grey eyes or twitching a corner of his mouth. His eyes often sought out Sejer's, but dodged them the moment his glance was returned. He is secretly watching me, Sejer thought.

'This may not be easy,' he began. 'But nothing is impossible. That's my way of looking at it.'

Emil listened and understood. He sat up straight, waiting for Sejer to continue.

'A girl called Ida Joner went missing from her home in Glassverket,' Sejer said. 'It happened on the first of September. She was later found by the road-side out at Lysejordet. And by then she was dead,' he said earnestly, and looked up at Emil at that moment.

Emil nodded.

Oh, Sejer thought, you can nod. Well, that's a start.

Emil Johannes continued to listen, his hands resting on the table.

'When something like that happens, we need to find out a lot of information. It's often the case that we can discover from the body what has happened. But with Ida we can't. There are many of us working on this case and we can't work it out. It is very important to me to find out why. Because that is my job,' Sejer said, 'but also because I want to know.'

He paused here. Because he was speaking slowly and clearly, Emil had understood what he was saying. Sejer helped himself to a Fisherman's Friend and pushed the bag towards Emil, who gave the grey-brown pastilles a dubious look. Then he put one in his mouth. His face took on a surprised expression.

'I know,' Sejer said. 'They're strong. They almost take your breath away, don't they?'

Emil moved the pastille to the other side of his mouth.

'Humans can cope with a great many things,' Sejer went on, 'if we only know why. Ida's mother doesn't know why her daughter died. It's difficult, you understand, losing a little girl. And later having to bury her without knowing why.'

Tears welled up in Emil Johannes' eyes, but they could have been triggered by the icy pastille melting on his tongue.

300

'There are many things I can't tell you about; the law won't allow me. You just have to accept that's the way it is. But we have found a number of items in relation to this case that link you to Ida. We think you knew her. Perhaps your mother did too,' he continued. 'These are indisputable facts. Facts that absolutely cannot be explained away.'

He placed his hands on the table. They were long and slender compared to Emil's coarse fists. He looked at Emil expecting a nod, but it did not come.

'You know something about this, Emil. So do I. I want to start by telling you some of what I know. I know that Ida was in your house, not just the once, but perhaps several times this past year.' He looked at Emil. It was a question of phrasing it correctly. 'Do you deny this?'

Emil battled with the throat pastille. 'No,' he said. The answer was loud and clear.

Sejer felt a rush of relief wash over him. 'That's good,' he said. Perhaps this silent man wanted to tell his side of the story. If he could do it on his own terms.

'Ida was a lovely girl,' Sejer went on. 'I mean, all girls are different. But Ida was particularly lovely. What do you think, Emil? Wasn't she lovely?'

He nodded eagerly in agreement.

'There are people who would like to get their hands on a girl like that if they could. And use her. For their own purposes. Do you understand what I'm talking about now?'

He studied Emil closely and registered that his glance evaded him a little.

'Do you understand what I'm talking about?' Sejer repeated.

Emil nodded once more.

'But she visited you on several occasions. She kept coming back to you. That must mean that you were nice to her. Still I have to ask you this question, which I know you'll find difficult. Did you ever hurt Ida?'

'No!' Emil Johannes said. Suddenly his body became restless. His hands began fidgeting, touched his throat, fiddled with his shirt collar before disappearing back under the table and ending up on his knees. He started rubbing the fabric of his trousers with his palms. 'No!' he repeated. With a kind of righteous indignation, Sejer thought.

He reminded himself that the man was a giant compared to Ida, who was tiny; that he might not always be in control, not always know his own strength. He reminded himself that this man, who appeared to be simple, might not be all that stupid and might even possess a certain talent for acting. He could have become an expert at keeping people at a distance by behaving like an enigma. Sejer leaned forward on a sudden impulse.

'Were you and Ida able to talk to each other?' he asked.

'No, no,' came the reply. This was followed by a violent shaking of the head.

No, I didn't think so, Sejer thought, scratching his neck.

'And if I ask you,' he continued, 'if there is anything at all that took place between you and Ida that you feel bad about?'

Emil considered this for a long time. An awfully long time. Sejer waited patiently. This man did not want to rush. This man took everything that had happened very seriously. He wanted to give an accurate reply. However, now he hesitated. All this time his thoughts were scanning his memories. Sejer could tell from the rapid movement of his eyes that they were roaming an inner landscape.

'No,' he said finally. This time, however, the 'no' was less forceful.

But she was dead when we found her, Sejer thought. Her abdominal cavity was filled with blood. Her body had been frozen. Why don't you feel bad? He reclined in his chair for a moment. Glanced at Emil. Allowed his huge shape to fill his entire field of vision; he was genuinely perplexed.

'You really are a riddle, Emil.'

Emil nodded; he agreed completely.

'And you like being one!' Sejer declared.

Finally Emil gave him a broad, contented smile.

He had few ways to communicate his thoughts. He did not know sign language and he stared nervously at the pen and notepad placed in front of him on the table. Eventually he picked up the pen and started playing with the cap. Then he put it down again. He sat waiting, quietly, but he did not cooperate. He was defensive, but at the same time he did have rights. A solicitor had been appointed, but was unable to assist him much. My client is incapable of expressing himself, he stated, knowing no more than anyone else about who Emil was and what he might or might not have done. Sejer was convinced that Emil was guilty. However, he could not work out what his motive might have been. Was being different reason enough?

Experts declared that Emil clearly belonged to the autistic spectrum to such an extent that it had held back his development. Did Sejer have the right to rush through the interrogation stage of the case purely because Emil was an oddball and might not need a motive at all? Deep down he was scared that he might be missing something. He wondered if there was something he had misunderstood.

'Your mother bought the nightie, Emil. I'm not wrong, am I?'

Emil looked away and clammed up like an oyster. He's protecting his mother, Sejer thought. This is impossible: he wants to explain himself, but he's afraid he'll cause problems for her. He has too many considerations. And too few words. Sejer rested his head in his hand. This was a unique situation. They sat like this, in silence, during most of the interrogations, Sejer hoping that a miracle would happen if only he sat there long enough. Sooner or later Emil would talk. Though he had no reason for thinking so. Did he not long for freedom? Did he not want to go home to Henry the Eighth? He seemed very determined, just like his mother. Of course, she was the most expedient route to under-standing his story. But he was not prepared to let her go on talking day after day without knowing her son's version. It might differ from hers. The most likely scenario was that Emil had killed Ida and later called his mother so she could help him hide the body. Together they had panicked and put her in the freezer while they worked out their next move. But why hide her so well to begin with, only to place her by the roadside later where she was bound to be discovered quickly? It seemed messy. The bicycle in one place and Ida in another. Where were her clothes and the red helmet?

He reminded himself that human beings did not always act in ways that were easy to understand or even rational. People often acted on impulse and justified their actions retrospectively.

'Did you drive out to Lysejordet to leave Ida by the roadside?'

No, Emil had not driven out to Lysejordet.

Every time he had given an answer, he awaited Sejer's next question. At times his eyes were relatively sharp. He was observing Sejer secretly; he took in the room; he listened, tilted his head when-ever something happened out in the corridor. From time to time he nodded briefly to himself as if he was making a mental note. Sejer believed that Emil wanted to tell his side of the story, but without losing the dignity he had acquired by rejecting speech.

'I think you're protecting your mother,' Sejer

305

said. 'You're scared she'll get into trouble because of what's happened. I can understand that. She has always helped you. At the same time I do believe that you want to tell me what happened.' He looked into Emil's grey eyes. 'Am I wrong?'

'No,' Emil said. The corner of his mouth quivered slightly and his fingers wriggled in the air in front of him. He became aware of it and composed himself. Now his hands formed a knot on the table.

Sejer had an idea. 'If your mother told me everything that happened, would I have a true picture of the situation?'

Emil looked up quickly. 'No, no,' he said hurriedly.

'So there's something she has misunderstood?'

He nodded.

'That's very interesting,' Sejer said. 'Great that you're nodding, by the way. You don't like admitting to anything. Don't like saying yes. But sometimes it's really important. I'm scared that I'll make a mistake, you see. I'm a fairly good police officer,' he added immodestly, and this made Emil burst into a spontaneous smile. 'But even though I'm good at my job, there are times when I need help.'

He looked at Emil closely. 'Like you needed help. When you realised that Ida was dead.'

Later on, the bird crossed his mind once more. Henry the Eighth might be sitting all on its own chatting away to itself in Emil's living room, hidden away under a towel. Perhaps it had run out of food and water. It was his responsibility to make sure that the bird was cared for. Perhaps they could keep it at the station. Astrid Brenningen, the receptionist, could look after it. It was supposed to be very easy, according to Elsa; after all, even Emil had managed it.

It was just coming up to 11 p.m. when he let himself into his flat. Kollberg raised his head and looked at him. The lamplight reflected in his dark eyes, but he did not get up. Sejer took the leash down from its peg on the wall. Kollberg was torn, keen to go with him and keen to stay in.

'You've got to,' Sejer muttered. 'You need to relieve yourself. It's about the only thing you're able to do these days.'

They pottered around quietly in front of the apartment block, long enough for Kollberg to flex his stiffening joints and work up a limited amount of body heat. Sejer thought, you can't speak either. Nevertheless, we've understood each other perfectly all these years without any problems. We communicate without words, because I don't expect you to use any. I understand you through other means. I have to access different parts of myself to read your signals. I sit directly opposite Emil and try to work out what he is saying. His body is huge and mighty, it sits so still, but it speaks volumes all the same. I can tell from the healthy colour of his skin that he spends much time outside; his face is weatherworn, his eyes are grey, like mine, a little paler perhaps.

He's quite well groomed; he washes and combs his hair. His clothes are clean because his mother washes them. He's proud, he has self-esteem. He's healthy and his body is strong, presumably. He's in a difficult situation, but he's not making a fuss. He doesn't complain. He sits still and waits. Waits for me to guide him through the story. I can see in his eyes that there are times when he's scared, excited or on his guard. He doesn't look particularly guilty. Doesn't look like a man who would assault anyone. I can't ignore the fact that Ida was an attractive child. Can't ignore that Emil is strong. There's rage inside all of us, and there's desire too.

Had Emil assaulted Ida? Had she started to scream and he had panicked? What had he done to her fragile body that caused her such severe internal injuries that she died? Sejer stopped because Kollberg had stopped. He was sniffing something on the hillside. It looked like a sparrow and it appeared to have been dead for some time. On the surface it looked undamaged; however, when Kollberg flipped it over with his nose, Sejer saw that it was badly decomposed. Instinctively he flicked the bird into the ditch with the tip of his shoe. He yanked the leash, wanting to move on. It was close to midnight. He thought of the quiet time ahead of him by the window in his flat, in his favourite chair, with the dog at his feet. And a generous measure of whisky. A moment he always made time for. A ritual established years back. A single cigarette, which he rolled himself. A carefully selected CD from the shelf.

Sipping his whisky quietly while he daydreamed. Let his eyes wander over to the photo of Elise. Think about her, think good thoughts about her. What am I going to do, it suddenly dawned on him, when the dog's gone and I'm sitting in the empty living room on my own? I'm too old to get a puppy. Sara, he remembered. Please come home soon. It's so quiet here. He looked at Kollberg and felt ashamed. Here I am imagining that you're dead already. The dog had acquired that gauntness often associated with old age; his coat was too big for him.

Quietly Sejer walked back. Stood immobile on the living room floor watching the dog try to settle in his usual spot by his chair. It was a wretched sight. A sinking feeling of despair started in the pit of Sejer's stomach. The dog moved in slow, rigid circles around his own body. Then he started to lower himself to the floor, shaking a little, somewhat unsteady. His hind legs first, then his front paws. It was clearly painful for him to move from standing to lying down. After a protracted and clumsy manoeuvre he was finally lying down. His large head was the last part to be lowered. An infinitely deep sigh then followed; as though he was taking his final breath.

I can't allow this to go on, Sejer thought. He instantly looked the other way. He could not bear to look his dog in the eye.

CHAPTER 28

Elsa Mork used her strength to maintain a feeling of control. She had slept, eaten and given herself a good talking to. She held her head high and for her age she was a fit woman, but she was reaching the end of her life nonetheless. She knew this. Besides, she possessed a strong inner sense of decency. Yet still she fought against the inevitable. Losing her reputation would cause her great pain. She stared closely at Sejer in order to convince herself that he really would believe her if she told him the truth. Or be able to understand it. And the extent to which he would judge her. He was a kind man. This baffled her. When he had arrived on her doorstep with the nightie in the carrier bag, she had felt such fear. In here it was different. She had not felt threatened by him, not for one second.

'Are you just as kind to Emil as you are to me?' she asked on impulse. The next moment she blushed.

'It's easy to be kind to Emil,' Sejer said. 'He's a very charming man.'

He was being completely sincere as he said this.

Elsa felt that she believed him. She suppressed a sob. Gulped as if she was swallowing something too big too quickly. She could cry later when no one was looking. She controlled herself.

'Tell me about Emil,' Sejer said. 'What makes him angry?'

She watched him for a long time.

'Well,' she said bitterly, 'I do when I turn up with my mop. Though he doesn't really get angry. He sulks. Thinks there is no need for cleaning.' She thought about her son and felt powerless. Because he was out of her reach in a way he never had been before. She was used to entering his house whenever she pleased. Now she could neither take care of him nor control him.

'No,' she said, 'I don't think he ever gets angry, to be honest, but then he never sees anyone. If his three-wheeler refuses to start, he just gives it a puzzled look. Then he starts to fix it with great patience. Everything practical such as nuts and bolts he handles really well.'

'But if you think back. His whole life. Since he was a child. Do you recall anything that made him angry?'

She bit her lip. Thought of the nightmare that haunted her. Imagined the condemnation that would follow; she was convinced that telling Sejer about the incident was handing him on a plate precisely what he was looking for. Evidence of frenzied, destructive rage. Nevertheless she started talking to him. In the midst of everything, Elsa had to acknowledge that she was receiving a level of attention she had not experienced for years. And she was getting it from a man. It was the first time she had tried to put the incident into words, and she stuttered slightly.

'He was eight years old,' she recalled, 'and he was playing outside in the yard. We lived in a small house out at Gullhaug. Emil was quite stubborn even when he was little. Getting him to do as he was told wasn't easy. But he was also very fearful. He was scared of the chickens, can you believe it?' She smiled as she said this, and Sejer smiled back at her.

'Our neighbour had a puppy,' she said, 'a beagle I think it was. It had escaped from their house and strayed into our yard. I saw it from the window. Emil just froze when the puppy suddenly came running up to him. It jumped straight up at him, wanting to play. He tried to shake it off, but it was no use. He twisted and turned, but not a sound came out of his mouth. I was standing by the window ironing shirts and soon realised that I would have to go outside and rescue him, but I was feeling annoyed too, I admit it. Most kids would welcome a puppy with open arms. But not Emil. He started kicking it.' She groaned. 'He was wearing heavy boots, that was all he ever wanted to wear, you'd think he was worried something would happen to his toes . . . well, anyway, he started kicking it. He kicked it quite hard.'

She slumped as she recalled the scene. The images made her feel nauseous. 'The puppy ran off and lay trembling on the ground,' she said. 'Suddenly I couldn't move and I began to feel terribly scared. But he didn't stop kicking it. It was like he was having a fit of madness and I was trying to snap myself out of my trance, but I kept holding on to the iron and could hardly believe my own eyes. The puppy flew off all over the place and Emil ran after it, kicking it and jumping on it with all his might. I felt so cold,' she said, her voice quivering. 'Never in all my life have I seen anything like it. When I finally went outside, there was practically nothing left of it. I got a plastic bag from the kitchen and shovelled the puppy into it. Then I buried it in the garden. I said nothing to Emil, I didn't know what to say, I couldn't even look at him.'

She rubbed her face in despair. 'Our neighbour never knew what happened to his puppy. I raked dry sand over the blood on the ground and took Emil inside. I pretended it had never happened. But ever since then,' she said, and finally she had the courage to look him in the eye, 'ever since then I have had a kind of power over Emil. Because I had seen him. Since that day he has done everything I've told him to.'

Sejer digested this story in silence for a while. He did not like what he had just heard.

'In other words, he gets angry when he feels threatened or scared,' he said eventually. 'And he's scared of many things. He defends himself with great rage.'

'We're talking about a puppy,' she said weakly.

'Maybe that's not important,' he said, consoling

313

her. 'People are scared of all sorts of things. Haven't you ever seen normally sensible adults lose it completely if a wasp flies into the room?'

Elsa had to smile.

'But surely Ida was no threat to him?' Sejer said, mainly to himself. Elsa was startled. Shook her head in disbelief, tried to follow where he was going. Everything was happening so quickly now. She wanted to pull back, but it was too late, so she just wailed: 'I don't know! I wasn't there when it happened. And he couldn't tell me!'

The room fell utterly silent. Slowly she realised what she had just said, and it surprised her that she felt less anguish than she had been anticipating. This is where we were heading all the time, she thought. I must have known it from the beginning; I just pretended not to understand.

'Tell me what you saw,' Sejer asked.

Slowly she gave up. She surrendered to the truth. Her story followed, stumbling and faltering, but he did not for one moment doubt that she was telling him the truth.

'Sometimes I visit Emil unannounced,' she confessed. 'I admit I do it on purpose. To check up on him. And now you know why. So that's what I do. It was a long time ago. Several months, I think. He got very agitated when I suddenly pulled up in front of his house. There was a girl standing outside. She was feeding the bird. When the weather's mild Emil sometimes takes the cage outside so Henry the Eighth can get some fresh air and some sunshine. I was very concerned. I thought of how rumours would fly if anyone saw Emil with a little girl. I asked her who she was and where she lived. She said she lived in Glassverket. She told me she had been out on her bicycle and had heard the bird sing. I don't even know if Emil really took any notice of her; it was like they were each doing their own thing. She was busy feeding the bird, he was tinkering with his three-wheeler. I told her to go away and not come back. She did not reply. Finally she gave me a defiant look and then she smiled. But she left on her bicycle and I never saw her again.' Elsa shifted in the chair. 'Not until that awful day,' she whispered.

'So you don't know if that was the first time Ida was there?' Sejer asked.

'I didn't ask. And you know he can't speak. It was the only time I surprised them like that. It troubled me, but I pushed it out of my mind. Then one evening I was watching the news. The second of September. The photo of the missing girl. I recognised her at once. It was the girl who had visited Emil. That's just a coincidence, I told myself, but I was worried. So worried that I didn't even dare drive over to check. Not until the following day. Then I went over to wash his clothes. That's why I go there,' she added, 'and to make sure that everything's all right. But that day, the third of September, I was going there to do some washing. I called him first. He was impossible on the phone. He often says "no" when I ring him to tell him I'm

315

coming over, but I just ignore it. However, on that day he was different. Scared. Desperate almost,' she recalled. 'I became suspicious. And then nervous,' she admitted, 'because you never know with Emil. And I was so worried about the missing girl. So I left the house to do my chores at Emil's and to find out if anything was wrong.'

She gave Sejer a look of anguish across the table. 'He had locked his front door. And put something gooey in the keyhole. I don't know what, chewing gum perhaps. I tried unlocking the door with my own key, but it was no good. I drove back to get some tools I could use to force the door. I was so scared,' she said, 'that everything I'd always feared had finally happened. So I simply broke down the door; I didn't care about anything any more. Not the door, which was badly damaged, or the neighbours who might be watching me. When I finally got into the kitchen, he was behaving strangely. He was so defiant and sullen. I noticed that his duvet was on the sofa and thought, why on earth doesn't he sleep in his bed? And there was such an odd smell everywhere, an absolutely awful stench. I wanted to go into his bedroom, but he wouldn't let me. I tried to open the door, but that too was locked.'

Now she was pressing one hand to her chest and her body slumped in the chair. 'I was so frightened,' she said. 'I couldn't understand what he was hiding from me. I demanded that he unlock the door. I said, I know you, I know when you're in trouble and you are right now! I had to force the door with

316

a crowbar. And when the door sprang open and I saw what was on his bed, I nearly fainted.'

She pressed her lips together and clapped her hand over her mouth as if to prevent any more words from escaping. Sejer sat completely still, waiting. She carried on.

'I recognised her straight away. But I could not understand how she had ended up on Emil's bed. She looked untouched; there were no injuries, no blood, and yet she was dead and I started screaming. I couldn't control myself. Emil Johannes put his hands over his ears and screamed too; he was screaming "no, no" like he always does. I feel dizzy,' she said suddenly. She flopped against the table.

'Have a rest,' Sejer said. 'Take a deep breath and rest for a while.'

And she did. Sejer waited. He imagined the terror she must have felt. It was obvious that a shock like that would make someone act irrationally. He understood her panic and despair. However, he decided that she must also be a very strong-minded woman to have gone ahead with her plan. She had acted despite her fear, panic and distress. Cool, calm and collected.

'I took off her clothes,' Elsa went on. 'Her chest was completely destroyed, as if someone had kicked her, and I looked at Emil because I realised that he must have kicked her, but he denied it. He said "no, no" and I couldn't understand why he would have done it either. She was a lovely little girl. Just like

317

the one I always wanted,' she sobbed, 'when I was younger. And never got. I just got a big, sullen boy who wouldn't talk. Who never wanted to be with anyone. And now he had dragged this girl into his house and kicked her to death just like he kicked that puppy, and I just did not understand why!'

She was silent once more. Sejer tried to picture what Elsa had just told him.

'I knew I'd never get an answer from Emil, so I decided to act quickly and not even try to understand why; all I knew was that I had a son who was different. And that something dreadful had happened. He had disgraced himself and me and I couldn't bear that. Not now when I'm old and my days are numbered. All I've ever wanted is to go to my grave without a stain on my character,' she cried. 'I've kept an eye on him and looked after him all these years so that this would not happen. And now it has.'

'Tell me what you did,' Sejer said.

'I needed time to work out what to do,' she said. 'I shouted at Emil; I said, now you'll do as you're told and no moaning, because if anyone finds out about this it'll be the end for both of us. You'll go to prison, I screamed, and so will I. So now you'll help me, even though you never have before. He was acting so strangely,' she recalled. 'He was standing so straight, like a statue, and I just couldn't understand why he wasn't more distraught than he was. Oh, he was upset all right, but it wasn't like the incident with the puppy. He looked confused. As if everything that had happened made no more sense to him than it did to me. He just shut himself off and I didn't have the strength to probe him for an explanation. Her clothes had to go. They weren't all that clean any more,' she said, looking up at him, 'and the smell was really bad now. I found Emil's summer duvet and wrapped her in it. I asked him to clear out the freezer in the basement. There was hardly anything in it, so that didn't take long. The only thing that mattered was that no one must know. I had to get everything right, had to hide every clue that would lead you to Emil. He carried her downstairs to the basement and placed her in the freezer. Then he disappeared up the stairs,' she recollected, 'while I shut the lid. When I came back up he was rocking himself backwards and forwards in a chair and the bird was making a racket and most of all I wanted to hurl it out of the window to shut it up. Stop its constant piercing screams. It was like the end of the world,' she wailed. 'Emil, silently rocking in his chair, the stench in the house and the screaming bird. I wanted to shut it all out,' she admitted, 'but I couldn't.'

She reached for the bottle of Farris mineral water and began turning it on the table. Perhaps she was thirsty. However, she did not have the strength to lift it and fill her glass, which was next to her. The information from her brain failed to reach her hand; she just kept on turning the bottle. Carefully Sejer took it from her and poured. Finally she drank the cold mineral water.

'I realised that we had to get her dressed again. Something new, with no traces of us. I didn't want you to find her naked. I was thinking of her mother, how awful it would be for her. Eventually I went back home. I decided to buy her a nightie. It's silly when I think about it now,' she said with a bitter smile. 'If I'd gone to Lindex or H&M you never would have found me. Those shops are always packed and the staff are young girls. They hardly notice the customers. But I went to Olav G. Hanssen,' she said, 'because that's where I usually go. Later I went back to Emil's, even though it was late. I just didn't trust him not to do something. But he was still sitting there in his chair. I said, we'll arrange it so they'll find her, but we have to wait. It must be planned carefully. Then I remembered her bicycle. They said on the television that she was riding a yellow bicycle. Emil had hidden it at the back of his house. A red bicycle helmet hung over the handlebars. We carried it downstairs to the basement. The next evening after dark I simply took the bicycle and left it somewhere. It had to be found a long way from our house. I dumped it behind a substation where I knew it would be found quickly. Then we waited some days. I buried the helmet at the back of the house, in a flowerbed. That's where you'll find it,' she said, looking up, 'below a broken basement window.'

Sejer made a few notes and it seemed as if she was pleased that everything was written down exactly the way she told it. She waited politely while he finished, then she carried on just as doggedly as before.

'I kept putting it off. It was just impossible for me to open that lid again. As long as she was in the freezer, everything was all right. We couldn't see her or smell her. I could almost make myself believe it was nothing but a bad dream. And all the time you were waiting and waiting. I kept thinking about her poor mother and I realised that we would all feel better once Ida was found. So she could be buried. Opening the freezer was a shock. She was completely stiff underneath the duvet. Emil came over and wanted to stroke her cheek; he got very upset when he realised she was ice cold. I couldn't get her into the nightie,' she said. 'I hadn't considered that. So we had to wait until she had . . . well, you know, loosened up a little. It took a long time. Several times I was close to breaking down. Then we dressed her. It was terribly hard work. I thought of all the things you would discover, all the clues we might leave behind. I kept hoovering. Then we wrapped her in the duvet once again and taped it up. Emil carried her out to my car late at night. He waited at home in his living room while I drove out to Lysejordet. It was midnight. I placed her by the side of the road.'

She was silent. Her face had a vacant expression as though all emotions had left her. 'But I remember one thing,' she added. 'I thought she looked very nice in that nightie.'

She had nothing more to say. She lowered her head,

321

the way people do when they are awaiting sentencing. She was done with it all. Drained of emotions and pain. But Sejer knew that it would all come back to her again. Every night, perhaps, as a terrifying nightmare. Right now, though, she was empty. And he said nothing of what lay in store for her.

'Was it good to get it off your chest?' he said softly.

'Yes,' she admitted. It was barely a whisper. She leaned across the table and groaned. He let her sit. He had all the time in the world.

'I know that I'm guilty of something terrible,' she said after a long pause. 'But she was already dead when I arrived and could not be brought back to life. And as for Emil, well you can't put him in prison, can you? I was just trying to save him.'

The nightmare, Sejer thought, had already got hold of her. He made a few more notes. She had provided him with a truthful explanation and Sejer believed her completely. Yet he recalled Emil and his claim that his mother's version might not be correct.

'Am I right in thinking that you, like me, don't understand what made him do it?' he asked.

She turned back again and looked at him miserably. 'I don't know for sure.'

'Why would Emil harm Ida?'

'I don't know,' she repeated.

'Haven't you looked for explanations yourself?'

She ran a dry hand across her cheek. 'I suppose I don't want to know,' she said wearily.

322

'I do,' Sejer said. 'He must have had a reason.'

'He's not normal,' she stated, as if that would explain everything.

'Would you describe your son as impulsive?' he wanted to know.

'Not really. No.'

'Or do you think that you know him; do you regard him as predictable and feel that in spite of everything you do understand him?'

'Yes.'

'Has he often surprised you with inexplicable actions or reactions?'

'Never,' she whispered, 'apart from that time with the puppy.'

'So just the one episode?'

'Yes.'

'So why would we regard him as impulsive?'

She shrugged. She was waiting for further information about what would happen to her. He looked at her earnestly.

'You will be charged with a criminal offence. I'm sure you've realised that,' he said.

'Yes,' she said, looking down.

'Your defence counsel will help you in every possible way. She will explain to the court what you've just explained to me: that you were helping your son conceal a crime. The court will assess your guilt and the appropriate punishment. Do you understand?'

'Yes,' she said.

He nodded to himself. 'Would you feel better if

you knew exactly what had gone on between Emil and Ida?'

'Don't know.' She hesitated. 'Perhaps she teased him about something or other.'

Sejer looked at her and immediately picked up on what she had just said. 'He wouldn't have liked that?' he asked.

'Emil is very proud,' she said.

She was taken back to her cell. Sejer went over to the window. He remained standing there shaking his head. He ought to be feeling a sense of relief or a kind of satisfaction. He ought to be feeling that everything had finally fallen into place, that he had reached the end of his journey, that he had done his job. But he felt no satisfaction. Something was bothering him. He dismissed his unease. Forced himself to leave the office. Closed his door with exaggerated care. There were still many things to be dealt with. He had to write a detailed report. And Willy Oterhals was still missing.

The news of Elsa's confession spread rapidly across the town. People could breathe a sigh of relief once more. They expected nothing from the son and they needed nothing either. His mother had told them everything. They considered the case closed. Sejer did not.

The next morning, as he passed through the glass door to the police station, he had an idea. A young mother and her chubby toddler were sitting on one of the sofas in the reception area. The child had curls and round cheeks and Sejer could not determine whether it was a boy or a girl. But he noticed that the coffee table was strewn with colourful toys. Astrid Brenningen, the receptionist, kept a box of old toys that used to belong to her grandchildren. From time to time children would come to the police station and wait while their parents reported damage to cars or other such incidents. Sejer looked at the table in passing. There were plastic figures and animals and cars, and something that looked like a digger. Boats and buildings and a range of machinery and tools. Playmobil, he realised instantly. His own grandchild used to play with that. It was still very popular. That was when he got the idea. It came to him the very moment the toddler reached for two dogs, one black, the other brown, and pushed them towards each other on the table. The child made them jump up and down for a while and turned the game into a wild dogfight. The pouting red lips made eager yapping sounds. The toddler played the part of both dogs, high barks and low growls. Sejer spun around, practically pirouetting on the polished floor, and left the building immediately.

Thirty minutes later he entered the interrogation room. Emil spotted the carrier bag he was holding.

'Sorry, no fizzy drinks or cakes.' Sejer smiled. 'But there should have been.'

Emil nodded. He was still staring at the bag.

'I've had a long chat to your mother,' Sejer said.

'She told me many things. I know you don't want to talk. But I thought you might like to show me.'

He gave Emil an excited look. Then he emptied the contents of the bag out on to the table. Emil's eyes widened. Then suddenly he became anxious. Frightened that he would have to master a new skill with its inherent risk of failure.

'Only if you want to,' Sejer said encouragingly. 'Playmobil,' he said by way of explanation. 'Nice, aren't they?'

The figures lay in a pile on the table, in a ray of sunlight slanting through the window. A little girl with dark curly hair wearing a yellow dress. A man and a woman. A red motorbike. A television, some furniture, including a bed. A potted plant and finally a little white hen.

'Henry the Eighth,' Sejer explained, tripping the hen along the table.

Emil blinked sceptically.

Sejer started separating and sorting the objects. He was working very slowly and quietly, watching Emil all the time. Emil had become alert and his face was showing signs of interest.

Sejer picked up the little girl with two fingers. Her dress was the colour of egg yolk and had thin shoulder straps. 'Ida,' he said, looking at Emil. 'Look. You can change her hair,' he said. He removed the hair from the figure the way you remove a lid, then snapped it back into place. 'Like people trying on wigs.' He smiled. 'But we won't change this. Ida had dark hair, didn't she?'

Emil nodded. He looked at the figure for a long time. You could tell that he was processing it, that he was connecting the Ida he once knew with the little plastic figure.

'Emil Johannes,' Sejer said, lifting up the man. A sturdy builder wearing a blue boiler suit with a hard hat on his head.

'Let's take off his hat,' Sejer suggested. He placed the man next to the figure of Ida. Then he arranged the furniture and other items according to his best recollection of Emil's house.

'This is your house,' he said, indicating a square on the table. 'This is your living room with table and chairs. A television. Potted plants. There's your bedroom, your bed. This is your kitchen with a kettle and a fridge. Here are the people you know. Your mother and Ida. And here's Henry. They didn't sell parrot figures,' he said apologetically.

Emil looked at the colourful interior.

Sejer placed the hen on a chair. 'Do you recognise it?' he asked.

Emil nodded reluctantly. He began to move the objects around to get an exact match.

'You know your own house better than I do,' Sejer conceded. 'So I trust you. Now, let's make a start,' he said eagerly. 'I can't remember the last time I got to play with toy figures,' he confessed. 'When we're adults, we don't play any more. That's a great shame, in my opinion. Because when you play you get a chance to talk about things. Here's Ida,' he explained, 'and that's you. You're in your living room perhaps, because Ida has come to visit you. Here's your mother. She has not arrived yet, so we'll put her to one side for now. Over here, perhaps.' He moved the Elsa figure out towards the edge of the table. She was wearing a red dress and her hair resembled a brown pudding bowl. The figure was standing very straight with its arms hanging down. Three small plastic figures staring expectantly at one another. It was clear that something was about to happen. The three silent figures had a story to tell.

'I thought you might want to show me,' Sejer said. 'Show me what happened.'

Emil looked down at the table and then up at Sejer's face. He stared at the figures again. He could understand this. They were tangible, actual objects that could be moved around. However, something was missing. Something that meant he could not begin. Sejer watched him intently, looking for an explanation.

'I didn't find a girl's bicycle,' he said. 'But she came to your house on her bicycle, didn't she? Or maybe you met her somewhere?'

Emil said nothing. He just kept staring at the figures.

'And I couldn't find a three-wheeler like the one you've got either. Only a red motorbike. Are you able to show me anyway?'

Emil leaned across the table. Held out one hand. His hand was like a huge bowl, a heavy, warm hollow, and he moved it across the table, above all the figures. It reminded Sejer of a crane, guided almost mechanically by Emil's arm, and it stopped right above the tiny Ida figure in the yellow dress. At times Emil's tongue darted in and out of the corner of his mouth, his forehead frowning in various formations. Then he lifted the other hand and picked up the Ida figure with a pincer grip. She dangled by one arm. Carefully he placed her in the palm of his hand. He remained sitting like this, staring. Nothing else happened. Sejer concentrated deeply. It was obvious that Emil wanted to show him something.

'You lifted Ida up?' he stated. Emil nodded. The Ida figure rested on her back in the huge palm of his hand.

'Up. Where from?' Sejer said.

Emil jerked his body without dropping the figure. His eyes began to flicker. What have I left out? Sejer thought. He's looking for something.

'Can you put Ida down exactly where you picked her up?' he asked.

Emil's hand started to move again. Right to the edge of the table, as far away as it was possible to get from the replica of his own house. There he put the Ida figure down with great care. Sejer stared at what was happening on the smooth tabletop, mesmerised.

'You're a long way from home,' he said. 'You found Ida somewhere else? You found her outside?'

Emil nodded. He took hold of the motorbike that was supposed to represent his own splendid vehicle.

He moved it forward with two fingers and did not stop until he reached the edge where Ida was. He picked up the figure, stood her up and nudged her forward. Then he let her fall. A faint clattering sound was heard when the figure toppled. He tried to put her on the motorbike. This should not have been difficult. He could have bent the small figure's legs, but this was not what he was trying to do. He insisted on placing her on the motorbike in a lying-down position. It was tricky; she kept sliding off. His face grew red, but he persisted. He tried again and again.

'You picked Ida up,' Sejer said, 'and laid her down in the body of your three-wheeler?'

Finally Emil nodded.

'Why was she lying down?'

Emil flung out his hands and grew anxious.

'She was injured, wasn't she?' Sejer said. 'Did you run her over? Is that how it was?'

'No. No!' Emil waved his arms violently in the air. With one finger he supported Ida so she rested on the motorbike and with the other hand he moved the motorbike quietly across the table. All the way to his house. There he lifted Ida up and placed her on his bed.

'I think I'm beginning to understand,' Sejer said. He got up abruptly and went over to the wall. Stared at a large map of the area.

'Emil,' he said, 'come over here. Show me exactly where you found Ida!'

Emil stayed in his chair, staring at the map. His face took on a frightened expression.

'I'll help you,' Sejer encouraged him. 'Look. This is where we are now. In the centre of town. The yellow area is the town,' he explained, 'and the broad blue ribbon is the river. You live over there. This is your road, Brenneriveien. Your house is about . . .' he leaned forward towards the map and pointed, 'there!' he said firmly. 'And when you drive into town, you go this way.' He traced the route with his finger to show him. 'And Ida,' he said, still looking at the map, 'she came from over there. Her house was in Glassverket and she came cycling along this road. This black line. All the way along Holthe Common. She was going to Laila's Kiosk. Do you follow?'

Emil stared shamefaced at the table. He picked up the white hen, clutched it in his fist and soon the figure was drenched in sweat. He could not recognise the landscape he knew so well in this pale two-dimensional version.

'Ida was hit by a car, wasn't she? Did you see what happened to her?'

Emil nodded.

Sejer was so agitated, he had to make a huge effort to appear calm. 'I didn't bring you a car. That was my mistake. Did you see the car? Did you pass it?'

More nods.

Sejer went back to the table. 'But her bicycle,' he wondered, looking at Emil. 'The yellow bicycle. It was intact when we found it. So she was not riding it when the car hit her?'

Emil looked around among the plastic objects. He found a potted plant and placed it next to Ida.

'She had got off her bicycle to pick flowers?' Sejer said.

Emil nodded again.

She managed to walk a few steps, Sejer thought. Then she collapsed. And you saw it. You could not drive past and pretend that nothing had happened. So you lifted her up and placed her and the yellow bicycle in the body of your three-wheeler. But you don't talk. And you didn't know where she lived. There you were sitting on your three-wheeler with a little girl in the back. The best solution you could think of was to drive her home to your house. And put her to bed.

'Was she alive when you put her on your bed?'

Again Emil made his fingers into a pincer grip. There was a tiny gap between his thumb and his index finger.

'She was still alive? Did she die while you were watching her, Emil?'

Emil nodded sombrely.

'So what did you do?'

Emil grabbed the red motorbike and drove off.

'And later, when you came home again, your mother phoned,' Sejer said. 'But she got it all wrong.'

He got up and went round to Emil's side of the table. Now all he needed was one further thing, a single answer to reach his goal. He hardly dared open his mouth.

'The car, Emil. What kind of car was it? Perhaps you can tell me what colour it was?'

Emil nodded eagerly. He searched among the figures. Finally he picked up the Ida figure with the yellow dress. Yellow, Sejer thought. Well, it's a start. But Emil removed her hair. It lay on the table rocking. A black, shiny shell.

CHAPTER 29

The interrogation room looked like an ordinary office with pale, neutral furniture. It was neither inviting nor daunting. However, when the door closed, Tomme felt the walls around him tighten like a net. Slowly they started to close in on him. He had been held for several hours. What if he simply refused to talk? Would he be able to keep it up? However, if he kept silent, he would be unable to tell them about his mitigating circumstances.

'I know what happened now,' Sejer said. 'But I'm missing some details.'

'Well, I'm impressed,' Tomme said in a strained voice, 'given that you weren't even there.'

'Perhaps I understand more than you give me credit for,' Sejer said. 'If I'm wrong, you can correct me.'

Tomme turned his head away, showing Sejer a pale cheek.

'You can't run away from this,' Sejer said. 'Don't kid yourself.'

Tomme felt in his heart of hearts that he was no criminal. Was that how they all felt? Everyone on remand, upstairs. In custody. The thought was so scary it made him gasp for air.

'What are you thinking about?' Sejer asked.

'Nothing,' Tomme said quietly. But his head was ticking. Perhaps it would be best to let the bomb explode. He imagined that the silence that would follow would feel similar to the relief you experience when you have been fighting nausea for a long time and you finally give in and throw up.

'I feel sick,' he said.

'Then I'll take you to the bathroom,' Sejer said. 'If you want me to.'

'No,' he said.

'You don't feel sick?'

'I do. But it'll pass in a moment.' Tomme moved away from the table where they were sitting. Shoved the chair with the back of his knees. Then he leaned forward.

'I hit Ida with my car,' he said.

'I know,' Sejer said gravely.

Tomme was still slumped forward. 'Her bike was parked by the side of the road,' he said. 'Right in the middle of Holthe Common. I could see it from far away. An abandoned bike. Yellow. I thought it was weird that it had been left like that, on its stand. I didn't see anyone. No cars,' he said quietly. 'And I wasn't speeding either, I never drive too fast!' His voice broke and was reduced to a feeble squeak. 'I was changing a CD,' he admitted. 'I had to bend down to look, it only took a second or two. I inserted the CD into the player and turned up the volume. Then I sat up again. I noticed someone was climbing the verge, holding flowers or something. I had veered a little off the road. There was a bumping sound and she was flung aside. I slammed on the brakes and looked in the mirror. Saw that she was lying on her back on the verge.'

Tomme paused. He was recalling these moments now; it was like standing by a void. His fear felt like a thousand fluttering insect wings inside his body. They started in his feet, swarmed up his legs, rushed through his stomach and heart before brushing against his face. Afterwards he felt numb.

'I was going to reverse,' he said, 'but I was shaking so badly. I had to sit still for a while to calm down. Then I saw in my mirror that she had stood up. She was standing on her own two feet. She was swaying a little, but she was standing!' he shouted. 'Then someone came towards me on the road, on a three-wheeler.'

Tomme lost his train of thought for a moment and tried to decide if the ticking in his head had ceased. He was certain it was fainter now.

'The man on the three-wheeler,' Sejer said, 'Emil Johannes, he doesn't talk. You knew that, didn't you?'

'That was the worst of it,' Tomme said. 'Because some people say he talks and others that he's mute.' He gave Sejer a guilty look. 'Given that I'm sitting here, he must have managed to say something.'

'Yes,' Sejer said. 'He did. Was it Willy's idea to cover up the dent by making it worse? Did you confide in him?'

Tomme nodded. 'He said it would be easier should anyone ask questions. That it was easier to talk about something that had really happened. In case you decided to check up on the car. In fact, I only damaged the right front light.'

'No one forced you off the roundabout?'

'No.'

'Why did you go to Denmark with Willy?'

'As long as we were together, I thought I would be able to control him in some way. And I owed him a favour. It was hard to say no.'

'I want the truth about the crossing,' Sejer said.

Tomme listened to the sound inside his head. The ticking grew stronger once again. 'We argued on the deck,' he said. 'He wanted me to carry his bag through customs and I didn't want to. He got mad. I went downstairs to the cabin to sleep. When I woke up he was gone. I don't care where he is; I've had enough of Willy to last me a lifetime!' He clenched his fists in defiance of his cruel fate, and red patches flared up on his gaunt cheeks. 'I hit Ida with my car, but it was an accident. She came climbing up the verge and she stepped right out in front of me! I know I should have stopped, but as far as I could see, she was all right. You can't blame me for whatever that other guy did to her afterwards!'

Sejer copied Tomme. He too pushed his chair away from the table. The extra space allowed him to cross his legs.

'Is that what you thought? That Emil Johannes had abducted her and killed her?'

337

'I could think of no other explanation,' Tomme said.

'Ida died from the injuries she sustained when she was hit by your car,' Sejer told him. 'You hit her in the chest. The fact that her bicycle was undamaged had me puzzled for a long time, but now I understand. Emil wanted to help her. He lifted her up from the road and put her in his own bed. And there she died.'

Tomme managed to shake his head faintly, as if he was refusing to believe what he had just heard.

'You both made mistakes,' Sejer said. 'However, in contrast to Emil Johannes, you had more options. You are responsible for Ida's death.'

An awful stillness followed. The silence Tomme had longed for filled his whole head. It overflowed and poured out of his mouth like cotton wool. His tongue stuck to the roof of his mouth and felt dry like paper. In desperation he started to claw with his fingers at the seat of his chair. The seat was covered with a stiff fabric; it looked like he was trying to dig his way into the stuffing.

'Tomme,' Sejer said. 'Put your hands in your pockets.'

Tomme did as he was told. The silence returned.

'As far as Willy Oterhals is concerned,' Sejer said, 'he's bound to turn up. Sooner or later. In some form or other.'

Tomme tried to swallow the cotton wool rather than spit it out. He felt sick again.

'It might take time,' Sejer continued. 'But I know

that he'll turn up. When you were standing on deck, watching him stagger around drunk, did you consider the fact that he was the only one who knew your terrible secret?'

'I wasn't thinking. I was freezing,' Tomme said.

'Let's try again,' Sejer said. 'Was it the case that he fell overboard and you saw it as a convenient way of finally ridding yourself of him?'

'I don't know what happened,' Tomme said. 'I'd gone down to the cabin to sleep.'

'And his bag, Tomme. What did you do with that?'

'The crew probably nicked it,' he muttered. 'Also, it was full of pills. They're worth a fortune on the street.'

'Not the pills Willy bought at Spunk,' Sejer declared. 'Because your mother flushed those down the toilet.'

Tomme tried to bury himself deeper in his chair. He thought everything was unreal, that it was only a computer game. He was the little white mouse in the labyrinth. And Sejer was the big cat approaching him softly.

'What happened to Willy?' Sejer asked once more.

Willy, Willy, Willy . . . Tomme heard his name as a distant, fading echo.

Finally he slipped into silence. It was like falling down a pit. This is better, he thought, feeling elated. All I can hear is the sound of my own breathing and the distant traffic outside.

I will never speak again.

CHAPTER 30

Many people passed through the door of the police station every day. They spotted the beautiful bird in its grand cage immediately. It whistled prettily to everyone who walked past it. Henry had been collected in a riot van, the only vehicle tall enough to contain its huge cage. The bird was a fast learner. Skarre had taught it to whistle the theme tune from *The X Files*, and also the five famous notes from *Close Encounters of the Third Kind*. Astrid Brenningen looked after the bird. She topped up the seed and water dispensers and replaced the newspaper in the tray. For a long time the newspaper carried photos of Ida. Henry could look down at her from its perch. Skarre had attached a cardboard sign for the benefit of curious passers-by: Mind your fingers! Despite this, there were many who learned this lesson the hard way. People were forever coming to the staff room in search of plasters. Holthemann, the head of the department, who possessed most of the qualities required of a good boss, such as intelligence, diligence, authority and meticulousness, but who was also entirely without a sense of humour, muttered regularly that the bird ought to be taken to a pet shop and kept there till the case was over. He always threw Henry an angry glance whenever he passed the cage. The bird might be small. It might not even be very bright, but in common with many other animals, it instantly sensed the disgust exuding from the grey, bespectacled man. So every time Holthemann was nearby Henry whistled 'You Are My Sunshine'.

Two men and one woman were busy preparing the case for the defence in the forthcoming Ida Joner trial. The list of mitigating circumstances was endless. Tomme was an immature teenager who had acted in good faith. After all, Ida had stood up after the collision. Elsa was a dutiful mother who wanted to protect her reputation and that of her disabled son, who in turn could not be held responsible for anything at all. As far as the still-missing Willy Oterhals was concerned, it was a mystery that would in all likelihood remain unsolved until they found him, dead or alive.

Tomme was held on remand. He lay curled up on his bed with his hands covering his face like a shield. He felt he was in the wrong place. What am I doing here? he thought. In an institution with thieves and murderers? His head was still ticking. He got through his day one second at a time. He often tried to daydream, tried to nibble his way through this mountain of time that lay before him. It's getting smaller, he told himself. It's getting smaller very slowly, and that's why I can't see it, but it is getting smaller.

It was a merciless winter. Lengthy periods of extremely cold weather. Helga Joner continued to live in a world of her own. She did not see her sister Ruth any more. Tomme had killed Ida with his car and now he was awaiting sentencing. It had been Tomme all along. She believed that Ruth had known this from the beginning. She thought so many dreadful thoughts.

One day Sejer turned up. Helga was pleased to see him. He represented a link to Ida that she did not have the strength to sever. Sejer noticed a chubby puppy bouncing around between Helga's feet. She invited him in and made him coffee and for a while they sat in silence. His presence was enough for Helga, and deep down she hoped that they would always stay in touch. She wanted to say it out loud, but did not dare. Instead she looked at him secretly and it struck her that he was thinking of very serious matters.

'What are you thinking about?' she asked cautiously. She instantly felt surprised at herself. It was like emerging from a hiding place where she had spent a very long time. For the first time since Ida's death, she felt concern for another person.

Sejer returned her gaze. 'I'm thinking of Marion Rix,' he said. 'Your niece. It's very hard for her.'

Helga bowed her head. Deep inside she felt ashamed. She had thought about Tomme so much,

342

and later about Ruth and Sverre. She had blamed them. Shunned them. She had forgotten all about Marion.

'She's being bullied at school,' Sejer said.

'Have you talked to her?' Helga said anxiously.

'I've spoken to one of her teachers. He told me.'

Helga buried her face in her hands. The puppy rushed around, snapping at her slippers. 'Well, I certainly don't blame Marion,' she said in a tired voice.

'No. And perhaps she needs to hear that. But the words have to come from you. Could you manage that?'

'Yes,' said Helga, looking up. 'I can manage that.'

The puppy let go of her slipper and crept underneath the coffee table towards Sejer. It started to snap at his trouser leg with great enthusiasm.

'I have a dog too,' he said quietly. 'But he's very old now. He can hardly walk. I've got to have him put down soon,' he confessed. 'I've made an appointment with the vet for tomorrow afternoon. And I've got to go home and tell him.' He nudged the puppy gently.

Helga was flustered. 'So will you be alone then?' she asked.

'No,' he said. 'No, it's not as bad as that.'

'You should get yourself a new dog!' she urged him.

'I'm not sure,' he said reluctantly. 'After all, I can never replace him.'

*

Helga wandered around deep in thought for a long time after Sejer had left. And when she woke up the following morning, she was still thinking of him. When the evening came and the twilight bathed her house in a blue light, she knew that his dog was dead. She lifted her own puppy up on to her lap. It dangled soft and warm in her hands. She buried her face in its chubby body and inhaled its smell. No, it was no substitute. Just something to cuddle. She liked to smooth its tiny ears against its head, only for them to spring back when she let go. She liked its tiny paws with the tender pads. She liked twirling the smooth tail with her fingers. She spent many hours in front of the fire staring into the flames.

March came, and April. Then everything burst like a dam and the rapid thaw set in. Water rushed down from the hills and melted snow dripped from the roofs. Slowly Helga's garden woke up. There were new shoots in the flowerbeds, tender and pale green. Marion came to visit every now and again. She liked taking the puppy for walks.

People rushed out of their overheated houses; they flung open windows and doors. They went outside and turned their faces towards the sun. It was a miracle every single time. The more adventurous ones headed for the sea, where the air still had a chill about it. But they liked the roar of the waves and the way they lapped against the shore. Kids were out looking for smooth pebbles. Mothers dipped their hands in the cold water as they shivered and laughed. A fresh wind was coming. Every now and again a wave would show off and raise itself above the others before breaking against the shoreline. A woman and a child were looking towards the horizon.

'Look, there's a boat!' the woman called out. 'A tanker. It's enormous!'

The boy followed the boat with his eyes. He was too far away to see how the bow broke the waves. It felt like for ever before the first wave came rolling in. A violent force parting the water; the swell grew and rolled towards the mainland, gaining in strength.

'Watch out,' his mother called, 'we need to run away from it!'

The boy squealed with excitement. Giggling, they ran back, exhilarated by this show of force. From where they were standing, they could not see the body rotating slowly just beneath the surface of the water. It was heading their way. The waves crashed against the shore and an ice-cold spray of water hit their faces. The woman laughed out loud, a silvery, infectious sound.